Julie wasn't sure she could deal with the mounting wall of revelations. And she didn't care for Brett's commanding tone. He sounded just like he must while negotiating a contract.

"My plans can't wait," she told him.

"They must." There was urgency in his voice. He leaned forward, his voice growing deeper. "I've taken a couple of days off, and I'm taking you back with me so you can meet these people and learn for yourself what's going on. Learn about the true character of this guy you're planning to marry."

For a moment, Julie stared at Brett. Her heart beat wildly.

"You're kidnapping me?"

"No. I'm borrowing you."

Borrowing the Bride

by

Roni Denholtz

Borrowing the Bride

COPYRIGHT © 2011 by Roni Paitchel Denholtz

Cover Art by *Angela Anderson*

The Wild Rose Press
PO Box 708
Adams Basin, NY 14410-0706
Visit us at www.thewildrosepress.com

Publishing History
First Champagne Rose Edition, 2011
Print ISBN 1-60154-933-4

Published in the United States of America

Dedication

For Janet Lee Burns
Best Friends Forever!

Chapter 1

Footsteps sounded behind her, and Julie Merritt knew the moment she was being followed on the city street.

She gripped the bridal headpiece tightly, the beads and sequins digging into her gloveless hand. No one walked in front of her or on her side in the cold sunshine of the November afternoon.

Her best bet, she decided, was to turn and hurry back to the bridal shop she'd left a minute ago, instead of trying to run away. The person behind her would be startled.

She took a breath of frosty fresh air and whirled around.

Brett Ryerson collided with her.

Julie gasped. Brett's hands grabbed at her to keep her from toppling. Her already rapidly beating heart accelerated. In the clear air, she could smell the spicy aftershave he'd always worn. She tilted her head up to look at him.

Although she'd been thinking of Brett recently, her first love was the last person she'd expected to see in Morristown on this late Wednesday afternoon.

Brett was as handsome as he'd always been. At just over six feet two inches, he towered over Julie by a foot. His handsome features usually wore a boyish, enthusiastic expression, but now he was scowling. Eyes that changed from hazel to almost green regarded her. His hair, a shade between light brown and dark blond, looked slightly windblown.

Julie put out a hand to steady herself as he gripped her and her fingers met the softness of his thick blue sweatshirt. She could feel surprising warmth through the fleece and quickly withdrew her hand.

"You're following me?" She wanted to sound annoyed, but her voice came out frightened instead.

Or excited.

She was too close. She deliberately stepped back, away from his large, steadying hands.

"Yes." He met her look squarely. "I have to talk to you."

"What—what about?" She wished her voice wasn't giving away her uneasiness. Calling upon her three years of teaching experience, she tried to collect herself. Sometimes she had to present a calm front to her students, though inside she might be feeling turmoil. She consciously relaxed her stiff position, breathed more slowly, and willed herself to sound calmer.

The scowl left his face, and for a moment, she couldn't read Brett's expression.

"About your brother Jonathan."

"Is he all right?" Concern edged her voice. Although she got along well with both her half-brothers, Julie had always been closer with Jonathan, the youngest.

"Yes...that is, he's okay...but I'm worried." Brett hesitated, seemed to be weighing something. "Look, Julie, it's a long story. Let's go somewhere where we can talk."

Now she was worried too. Was something wrong with Jonathan? "All right." She shifted her position.

"There's a coffee shop around the corner." Brett inclined his head to the right. "We can sit down there and have a cup of coffee."

Coffee was the last thing Julie needed. Her nerves were already jangled from the last two nights, when she'd tossed and turned, thinking about the future.

But she turned and walked briskly up the street. Brett easily fell into step with her.

And now, it sounded like she had something else to worry about. What was going on with Jonathan? And how was Brett, whom she hadn't seen for several years, involved?

Julie glanced up at him. He was watching her carefully as they walked. She swallowed, turning the corner.

In a minute they were inside the coffee shop. At four fifteen in the afternoon, it was quiet, with only two teenage girls sitting in one booth near the front.

"Let's get a booth," Brett said. He took Julie's hand and led the way toward one in the back.

Vibrations flowed through Julie at his touch. As soon as they reached the booth, she pulled her hand away. She started to slide in, then stopped. She'd almost sat on the layers of gauze from the veil attached to her headpiece. She'd forgotten she was holding it.

Carefully, she smoothed out the white folds of the veil and wrapped them around the beaded headpiece. Placing it in the corner of the booth, she looked up to find Brett watching her. He was frowning again.

A waitress approached with menus.

"Just coffee," Brett said. "Julie?"

"Decaf for me."

The waitress left, and for an uncomfortable moment, they regarded each other solemnly. A shiver crept up Julie's spine. It seemed only yesterday she had sat in booths like this with Brett, smiling, sharing stories, and holding hands.

She shook off that thought.

"What about Jonathan?" Julie asked. "You said you were worried about him?"

Brett leaned forward. His eyes looked more green than hazel today; but she pushed the observation aside and concentrated on her brother.

The waitress brought their coffees and milk. Brett dumped sugar in his and stirred it briskly, adding milk from the small pitcher. Julie stirred in a sweetener substitute, watching Brett all the while.

He was uneasy, and it was catching. She took the milk when he placed it by her and added some to her coffee.

"Brett?"

"I said I was worried," Brett repeated. He met her look. "Not exactly about Jonathan."

"What do you mean?" She blew on her coffee, then took a sip of the hot, fresh-tasting liquid.

"Jonathan and I are the ones who are worried," Brett said. He drank some coffee and set it down. The ceramic mug clinked against its saucer.

"What's wrong?" Her voice sharpened.

"We're very worried…about you." He met her look squarely.

"About *me*?" Julie stared at him, astonished.

"That's right. Jonathan and I have been in contact the last few weeks. We're both very concerned."

"Why?" Julie stared at Brett, puzzled. Why her brother would get in touch with Brett—or vice-versa—made no sense. She'd broken up with Brett more than three years ago, and he'd been hurt and angry. They'd had no contact since then, although she'd heard about him through mutual friends. The regrets had come later.

Brett leaned forward and spoke tersely. "We're very worried because you don't know what kind of man you're marrying."

Julie stared at Brett. They were worried because they thought she didn't know Warren?

She asked the question out loud. "You think I don't know Warren?"

"I *know* you don't know Warren." Brett spoke

4

the man's name with distaste. "And Jonathan knows it too. Look, Julie," he went on before she could protest, "there are things you should know about your fiancé"—there again, he hesitated as if Warren's name were spoiled milk—"things that I'm certain would make you think twice about marriage."

For just one second, a current of amusement zipped through Julie. "You honestly think I don't know Warren Wesley?"

"Yes. Look, Jonathan isn't fond of him either."

She nodded. "I know." Jonathan had never cared for Warren. Adam, her other half-brother, had been more neutral in his opinions. Only her mom and stepdad appeared enthusiastic that Julie was engaged to a rising political star.

She drank more coffee before responding, and when she did, she tried not to sound smug. "I believe I know Warren pretty well." She said it slowly, carefully, as if speaking to a student.

"I bet you didn't know he has a child."

Julie almost choked on her coffee. Coughing, she sputtered, "Wh-what?" She must have heard Brett wrong.

"I said I bet you didn't know that Warren Wesley has a child. A daughter." He leaned his elbows on the table and bent toward her. "I know this must be a shock. I'm sorry." His voice gentled as he regarded her.

It *was* a shock. But Julie wasn't about to tell him that. "That's—that's ridiculous," she said, still coughing. "You must be—" She wanted to say he was making it up, but Brett's serious expression made her hesitate. He obviously believed it to be true. "You must be mistaken."

"I wish I were, for your sake."

Even as Julie protested, her mind rapidly rewound to times Warren had seemed evasive about the women in his past. She found herself believing the accusation *could* be true.

The waitress approached with a glass of water. Julie sent her a grateful smile and grasped it. "Thanks." She drank some, then set it down.

"Do you have any proof?" she asked. This time, as she reached for her coffee, she noticed her hand was unsteady.

"No—but I know someone who does." Brett hesitated again. "I think it's very important that you meet her. And—some other people."

"Go on," Julie urged when he stopped.

Brett leaned back against the booth. "I want you to meet some people who *do* know Warren Wesley well," Brett continued. "I—look, Julie, you really need to learn some things about him. It's imperative. Then, if you do decide to go ahead with this— marriage—at least you'll be going in with your eyes open."

She noticed how he stumbled over the word *marriage*. What had gotten into Brett? Even if he knew something about Warren, why should he care? Had Jonathan put him up to this?

She rejected that thought. Jonathan might give advice when asked, but he believed in letting others solve their own problems with a minimum of guidance. At the age of twelve he'd announced he wanted to be a psychiatrist when he grew up, and now that he was almost eighteen he was following his plans, applying to colleges to study pre-med.

"Who do you want me to meet?" Her voice shook slightly. Julie sipped her coffee. She hoped Brett hadn't noticed how unnerved she was. Could part of her agitation be because she was sitting across from Brett?

"The mother of his daughter, for one," Brett replied. "And a couple of other people who can tell you firsthand about their dealings with Warren." He shifted his position. "You need to speak with them right away."

"Well, tomorrow I'm going to the New Jersey Teachers' Convention in Atlantic City," Julie said.

"I know what your plans were. I discussed this with Jonathan," Brett said. "Your plans will just have to wait. This is very important, Julie, and Jonathan is in complete agreement. He's going to meet us here in a few minutes."

"He is?" One surprise was building on top of another. Julie wasn't sure she could deal with the mounting wall of revelations. And she didn't care for Brett's commanding tone. He sounded just like he must while negotiating a contract.

"My plans can't wait," she told him.

"They must." There was urgency in his voice. He leaned forward, his voice growing deeper. "I've taken a couple of days off, and I'm taking you back with me so you can meet these people and learn for yourself what's going on. Learn about the true character of this guy you're planning to marry."

For a moment, Julie stared at Brett. Her heart beat wildly.

"You're kidnapping me?"

"No. I'm borrowing you."

Chapter 2

Julie felt her heart stall, then skitter. She couldn't suppress her gasp.

"*Borrowing*?" Her voice squeaked.

"Yes." Brett sat back, and the booth's leather seat hissed slightly. His eyes glittered a bright golden green, his face calm but determined. "It's only for a few days, Julie. Just so you can be exposed to what's going on. And make an informed decision."

"Why don't you just tell me everything?" Julie demanded.

"I'd rather show you. You might not believe everything if I told you." He shifted in his seat again. "I wouldn't do this if it wasn't important. Besides, I have Jonathan's approval."

Julie swallowed hard. Every nerve in her body had leaped up at Brett's suggestion; she wasn't sure if it was in protest or something else. Something she couldn't quite label. Excitement?

She rejected the thought immediately.

She also pushed aside the topic of her brother. She'd deal with that when he met them. She reached for her coffee again, but when she banged the mug against the saucer, she withdrew her hands and gripped them in her lap. She must try to remain as calm as Brett.

"Why should I go with you? If you give me the names of these people, I can contact them myself." She was proud that her voice held only a tinge of scratchiness.

"I'm going along for your sake." When she stared at Brett, he added, "So you have someone to look after you. For your protection."

"That's ridiculous," Julie snapped. She wished her heart wasn't beating so hard. "I don't need—"

The door to the restaurant opened as a bell jangled. Julie's eyes went to the door.

Her brother Jonathan strode into the coffee shop. He wore a varsity sports jacket over jeans and a T-shirt, and a cap that held the insignia of the New Jersey Nets basketball team. His coloring was as dark as hers, like their mother's, but unlike Julie and their mom, he was tall—as tall as Brett. Both he and Adam got their height from their dad, Ted.

Until Jonathan moved forward and sat down beside Brett, Julie had held a slim hope that perhaps this was some kind of bizarre joke. But one look at Jonathan's serious expression, the way he aligned himself on Brett's side of the booth, had her heart accelerating and her mouth going dry. This was serious. Brett meant every word.

"Hi, Julie." Jonathan smiled briefly, but it didn't reach his eyes. "I guess Brett's been talking to you about Warren?"

"He certainly has." With an effort, Julie kept her voice even, though it still sounded raspy. "He says you agree with this—this scheme."

Jonathan sighed as the waitress approached.

"Coffee?" she asked, smiling widely at Jonathan.

"No. Just a coke. And a large pretzel."

Jonathan was silent until the waitress returned, setting down a soda loaded with ice plus a thick pretzel. He took a few gulps of soda, then broke off a chunk of the pretzel.

A typical teen, Julie thought with affection, always eating and drinking. Then she caught Brett's eyes. He smiled briefly, and she knew he was thinking the same thing she was.

For one moment, she felt an electric connection between them.

"A month ago I ran into Brett," Jonathan began after swallowing a piece of the pretzel. "I was at the electronics store with my friend Tim. Brett was there with his friend Jeremy. We went to shoot some hoops. Later we got to talking."

Julie remembered how good a basketball player Brett always was, and how he'd practiced with Adam and Jonathan when he was dating Julie.

Jonathan took another swig of soda. Placing the glass down, he met Julie's look. "We thought there were some things about Warren that should be checked out. I know you must think this is crazy," he continued. "But, listen. You need to know stuff about Warren. Serious stuff. Brett can show you things about him that—well, that you really need to know."

She'd bet Brett was the one who'd thought things should be checked out. "You're right, this plan is crazy," Julie said aloud. "Why should I—go with Brett—to find out things about Warren? Things I already might know?"

"You don't know a lot." Jonathan's mouth turned into a grim line. "And trust me, what you don't know could hurt you."

"But Brett could just tell me," Julie said. "He doesn't have to take me—drag me around who knows where—to prove something. And"—she sent Brett a glance—"I don't need protection."

"You have to hear these things firsthand," Jonathan stated. "And—"

"And you may want some moral support when you do," Brett said firmly.

"Moral support? Oh, really." At her scathing tone, Brett raised his eyebrows. Julie knew didn't usually speak so sarcastically, but Brett's incredible suggestion had elicited an extreme reaction on her part. She met his look with what she hoped was a challenging one.

"He's right." Jonathan's forceful tone had her

turning to gaze at him. "Look, Julie," he continued, leaning forward, "I wouldn't be going along with Brett's suggestion if I didn't think it was really important. Go with him. Listen to what these people have to say about Warren."

"But I have plans!" Julie didn't like the way her voice shrilled. "I can't just put my life on hold for a few days."

"Tomorrow's the New Jersey Teachers' Convention," Brett said. "I know you don't have to work Thursday and Friday, and then there's the weekend."

"Yes, but I was going to go down to the convention, meet Kendra, and go to a couple of workshops. There's one I really need to attend!"

The coffee shop's bell jangled again, and a silver-haired man and woman entered, laughing.

"What time is the workshop?" Brett asked.

"Two o'clock. And the convention's in Atlantic City."

"No problem. I set up our first appointment for the morning. Shannon lives near Toms River. That's on the way to Atlantic City. We can see her, then get back on the road and you'll be on time for your workshop." Brett's voice held a note of finality.

Had he planned it like that on purpose? She wasn't about to give in so easily. "That might take care of one problem. But Sunday I'm supposed to go to an afternoon cocktail party in Warren's honor. He won the mayoral race. The party's being given by some political big shots. I can't miss that."

"You'll be there." Brett's voice hardened. "Although you may not want to be. We'll be finished with everyone we have to see by then." He paused, then added, "Warren won't even know you're gone."

"How do you—" Julie began.

"I told Brett this weekend would work best," Jonathan said. "That Warren had to fly to Boston

11

this morning to see his grandfather and tell him about his successful bid for mayor."

"You—Jonathan!" Julie could scarcely believe her brother was cooperating in Brett's wild plan. She sat back in the booth and stared at her brother. "Why?"

"Because it's important, Julie. Because I don't want to see you end up with—with someone who's going to use you or mistreat you," Jonathan said earnestly. "Honestly, Julie, I think Warren's using you."

Julie could hardly contain her astonishment as he continued.

"I never liked Warren. Neither does Adam, even though he hasn't spent as much time with him as I have, being at college and all. Look, you're a beautiful, smart, sweet person. You'd be an asset to Warren's political ambitions. Adam and I think he's using you. And Brett thinks so too."

"I think I can handle things myself," Julie protested. "You don't have to get involved, Jon."

"Have I ever asked you to do anything that was bad?"

He hadn't. And that was why, as Julie looked at her brother, she suddenly knew she was going to go along with this insane plan.

"No, you haven't." She looked down at her mug, the aroma of the coffee faintly floating up to her. She hastily took a gulp. It had cooled, but it felt good as it slid down her throat. When she looked up again, Jonathan was nodding.

"Then go. I'm positive you'll be glad you did."

"I doubt it." She turned her head to focus on Brett. For a split second, she could have sworn she saw a look of satisfaction flash across his face. Then it was gone.

She drew in a sharp breath and opened her mouth for one more protest. And then she caught

Jonathan's expression.

His earnest face was frowning, and the eyes that were as dark as hers looked concerned. More than concerned. He looked worried.

She swallowed. Jonathan was *not* a worrier. If he wanted her to do this, he must know something. Something he thought was crucial.

"It's important." Jonathan's words echoed her thoughts.

"It's more than important." As Brett spoke, Julie switched her gaze to look at him. "It's your life we're talking about, Julie." Brett's eyes now reflected as much worry as Jonathan's. "We don't want to see your life ruined."

"Aren't you being a bit melodramatic?" she asked, her voice sharp.

"No."

Julie drank the last of her coffee. As she replaced the mug, it clinked loudly in its saucer. She moved her hand to rest on the napkin, staring at the blue and white advertisements on the paper placemat in front of her.

Another woman would probably get up and walk out of the coffee shop, either laughing or indignant. But there was a reason for her to go along with this plan, a reason she hardly dared admit to herself. Certainly not to Brett. Or Jonathan.

"You need to know about Warren's true nature." Brett spoke matter-of-factly, quietly.

Julie was still staring down when he covered her hand with his large one. His hand was warm as it rested on hers, surrounding her fingers. Tingling sensations shot along her nerves at his touch.

For a moment, Julie experienced a rush of déjà vu, flashing back to the first time Brett had ever taken her hand, when they'd walked into the movies on their first date. As if it were yesterday, she recalled the warmth that had seeped through her at his touch.

The same exact heat was pummeling through her now, just as fast.

Julie snatched her hand away.

Shoving both her hands under the table, she reached for her bridal veil. She fingered the netting, trying to erase the feel of Brett's masculine, warm fingers with the brisk texture of the veil.

She wasn't succeeding. Her hand remained hot.

She met Brett's eyes. Green sparks seemed to leap from them, and she wondered if holding her hand had caused any reaction in him.

"All right." She gave him a challenging look. "I'll go along with your plan."

"I'm glad." Brett said the words simply. And yet, he looked tense.

Was she crazy? Julie looked at Jonathan. Her brother was finishing his soda. He caught her eye and smiled.

"Good choice. You'll be glad you found out the truth about Warren," he reiterated.

"Maybe I know some of this already," Julie muttered.

But she hadn't known that Warren Wesley had a child. What else had he kept hidden from her? What else had she simply overlooked, or ignored? Her friend Kendra had remarked a couple of times that Julie was too trusting. Julie had never taken the remark seriously.

Until now.

She found her gaze returning to Brett. Was she wrong to trust *him*?

But Brett had always been honest and kind. She had been the one to end their relationship, not Brett.

Still, she wondered why Brett was going to such lengths to "protect" her, as he put it. Wouldn't it be simpler for him to just give her the information and let her contact these people herself?

And how had he learned all this info anyway?

"How do you know all these things about Warren?" Julie asked.

"I did a little research." Brett's words came out clipped. He began to slide out of the booth. "Let's go."

"Go? You mean—now?" Julie's thoughts whirled, like autumn leaves tossed by the wind. She'd thought she would have time to go home, reconsider the idea.

"Yes." As Julie started to protest, he continued. "We'll pick up clothes and stuff you need from your apartment. Then we'll get on our way."

"My car is here," Julie interrupted. She was beginning to feel the little control she had quickly slipping through her fingers.

"Jonathan can drive it to your place and we'll leave it there. We'll give him a lift back and go on to my condo."

"I don't have basketball practice today," Jonathan anticipated Julie's next question. "I have the time. And there's no school tomorrow. Mom's not expecting me home till after she leaves for the hospital Women's Club meeting."

Julie opened her mouth, then shut it abruptly. She had already agreed to this zany plan. And she wanted to know the worst about Warren. Whatever it was. And— She shifted her position, recalling the warmth of Brett's hand on hers.

"Let's get going," Brett repeated. "If we leave now, we'll avoid the worst of the traffic."

Jonathan slid out of the booth and extended his hand. "Your keys?" Seeing the question in Julie's eyes, he said, "Brett drove me here. My car's at home." Since he'd gotten his license, Jonathan drove Ted's old Mercedes.

Julie bent her head and fished her keys from her purse. "Here." She looked back at Jonathan.

He gave her a grin that she was sure he meant

to be reassuring, as Brett also left the booth. Julie followed.

They exited the coffee shop. The cold air felt good against her warm cheeks. Julie folded the veil carefully around her arm, the sequins on the headpiece glinting against the orange ball of the late-afternoon sun.

"Where's your car?" Jonathan asked.

Julie pointed to it in a parking lot down the street, and Jonathan strode off.

She was left alone with Brett.

"My car's right there." Brett indicated a dark blue Jeep.

He opened the door and Julie stepped up into the car. She was enveloped by that invigorating new car smell. Glancing around, she noticed that the back held a black laptop computer case. There were a couple of issues of *Sports Illustrated* and a newspaper folded against the laptop.

All part of his career reading, Julie assumed. Brett was a lawyer in a firm specializing in contracts for athletes and sports teams.

Without looking at her, Brett entered the car on the other side and started the engine. Their seat belts snapped into place and he backed out of the parking space. In moments he was headed out on the road leading from Morristown, with Jonathan ahead in her smaller silver car.

Julie studied Brett as he watched the road. His usually boyish, cute face wore a serious expression, and in profile his mouth appeared set in a determined, grim line. His large hands gripped the wheel, and for a moment she recalled their warmth as he had grasped hers.

And more. She remembered his hands stroking her gently, long ago.

She shifted in her seat, and Brett glanced at her.

"Don't worry."

"I'm not worrying." She turned to look out the window.

But she was. *Was she crazy?* she wondered again. Brett, usually easygoing, seemed tense and brooding. Not as she remembered him.

Maybe he had changed. Maybe he wasn't the same guy she used to date, and had once loved.

She swallowed. What if he was different? This whole scheme was weird. Maybe he had become weird too.

Was he really "borrowing" her? She fiddled with a zipper on her purse. Or was he actually kidnapping her?

She looked at him again. He was concentrating on the twists of the road that led from Morristown to the suburbs. The car climbed the hills easily. They wound through clusters of houses and condos, the sky darkening as they drove.

This didn't exactly qualify as a kidnapping, Julie reminded herself. She was going along with the idea. Because she wanted to learn more about Warren, of course. Even though—

She watched as Jonathan slowed at a yellow light, and Brett halted behind him.

Besides, Jonathan was here. If she changed her mind when she got home, she'd simply tell Brett to forget it.

She eased down in the seat and tried to appreciate the late autumn scenery as the car climbed the county road. Once the road ended and they were on a highway, they navigated traffic through western Morris County and finally into the town of Hackettstown. She felt better as they approached the side street where she rented part of a two-family house, only minutes from the middle school in the next town where she taught Earth Science. She actually sighed as Jonathan parked in the driveway.

Perhaps she'd pretend to go along with things for Jonathan's sake. At least for now. Once they'd dropped him back home, she'd have a long talk with Brett and reassess the situation.

Brett pulled up behind her brother, and Julie hopped out of the car. He quickly followed. Jonathan smiled as he walked toward Julie. He handed Julie her key ring and the canvas bag containing her teaching materials, which she'd left in the car.

They entered her side of the house. "I'll just be a few minutes," she told Brett and Jonathan and went down the hall to her bedroom.

She'd already taken out a small suitcase, thinking that tomorrow, on the way back from the convention, she might stop and visit a friend from college. The suitcase sat on her bed. Julie threw jeans, sweaters and other assorted clothes inside. She grabbed shampoo and makeup, sneakers and a magazine and tumbled them into the bag. She glanced around. Had she forgotten anything? Socks. Short boots. Earrings. She added them.

Her answering machine held no messages. She briefly checked her cell phone. No messages. Another glance around the room, but this time she hesitated.

She walked over to the dresser, and picked up the Waterford crystal ring holder her mother had given her for her birthday a few years ago.

Running late for work this morning, Julie had rushed around and forgotten to put on any jewelry. Her college class ring and her engagement ring gleamed on the holder, and she studied them for a moment.

The college ring brought back warm memories of four good years. Most of them were spent dating Brett, sharing love and dreams. She'd chosen the ring, picking the school colors and the insignia of the honor society she belonged to.

The diamond ring, though stunning, had not been her own choice. Warren had selected it and surprised her with it when he'd proposed. A carat and a half, the large, pear-shaped diamond flanked by two baguettes was what he deemed appropriate for the fiancée of a rising political star who hailed from a wealthy family.

But she had always wanted a ring with a marquis diamond.

Julie took both rings off the holder and slid them on. Thoughtfully, she flexed her fingers.

She sighed and picked up her suitcase.

Jonathan was sprawled in the big old easy chair in her living room. Brett was staring at some photos on the wall unit which contained her TV, iPod dock and a collection of music CDs and DVDs.

"I'm ready." Julie purposefully made her voice strong.

The ride to the Randolph area was quiet. Jonathan listened to his iPod. Brett tuned in to a news station, leaving Julie with thoughts which ping-ponged across her brain. Kidnapped? Borrowed? Should she go along and find out the worst about Warren? What if Brett was wrong?

But a sinking feeling had warned her at his first words that there were truths here, truths she could not ignore. Added to what she already knew...

And how much should she reveal to Brett about what she already suspected?

The sky had been dark for a while by the time they turned onto the road in Randolph that approached her section of town. A couple more turns on smaller streets, and then Brett turned into the circular driveway. He pulled up to the large brick colonial where Julie had lived since the age of eleven when her widowed mother had married Ted Shaw, a wealthy businessman. The house was meticulously kept and a little imposing, looking down the hill at neighbors' homes across the street, which were almost but not quite as big.

Jonathan hopped out of the car. "See you soon." Julie opened her mouth, but even as she did he was slamming the door and waving. Brett drove the car around the driveway.

She glanced back to watch Jonathan enter the house. She felt the same way she had on her first day of teaching, leaving the security of the faculty room for the vast unknown of her first class.

Brett turned the car, and they drove down the street.

"How about Chinese food for dinner?" It was the first time he'd spoken for several minutes. His voice was almost cordial.

"Okay." Her stomach was beginning to complain about its emptiness, and she realized that she hadn't eaten since lunch. Here it was after six o'clock, and she hadn't even had a snack, only the cup of coffee. She'd left school and driven directly to Morristown that afternoon.

Brett turned onto a main road.

"I wish you hadn't involved my brother," Julie said, trying to be low-key.

"I had to. Besides"—he glanced at her sideways—"he was as concerned as me. Adam is too. It seems like only your mom, and maybe Ted, are in favor of your marrying Warren Wesley."

"I know." Julie's tone was dry, and Brett shot her another look. He probably suspected her mother was impressed by Warren's money.

Brett handed her a cell phone, dictating a number to call. "Order whatever you'd like. I'll have pepper steak and fried rice."

Typical single male, with the number to his favorite Chinese takeout place memorized. Julie added her own order, for sweet and sour chicken, and disconnected. Within a few minutes they were pulling up to a small Chinese restaurant.

"I'll be right back," Brett told her.

She recognized the area, although not the restaurant. Julie had heard that Brett had purchased a condo within the last year.

He was back in moments with the package, which he handed to Julie. Delectable aromas jumped through the brown bag and made her stomach churn with hunger.

Within a few minutes they reached a development of attractive condos. In the streetlights, Julie noticed they appeared fairly new. A garage door opened ahead of them, and Brett pulled in.

"Let's eat." He turned off the engine and reached for the bag of food. "I'll get your stuff out of the car later."

Julie followed Brett into a hallway and up a flight of stairs. They passed a living and dining room, and went into a kitchen that opened up into a family room containing a large TV, a couch and some exercise equipment.

Julie glanced around the gleaming kitchen. The table occupied an alcove in the family room. She busily unpacked the food while Brett took out paper plates, forks and spoons, and cans of soda.

"You still like diet Pepsi?" he asked, passing her a can.

"Yes." Had he really remembered and bought it for her? Julie shrugged out of her jacket, then scooped rice onto her plate.

Brett placed a can of regular coke beside his plate and sat down at the table across from her.

The taste of spicy pineapple in a hot, sweet sauce burst on her tongue. Julie savored the food, wondering how she should approach the topic of possibly leaving. She knew she'd think more clearly after having dinner. She was starved.

They spoke little while devouring the food, which was excellent. Julie noted that Brett kept his place fairly tidy.

Was there a woman in his life now? She might as well ask. "Are you going with anyone right now?"

"No." His answer was short, his expression unreadable.

She tried a different tactic. "How are your folks, and your sister?"

"My parents are fine. Jodi's finishing law school."

"Good for her." Julie smiled. She'd always liked Brett's kid sister.

Once they'd eaten and put leftovers in the refrigerator, Brett started to get Julie's things.

"Wait." Julie put up her hand. "I need to talk to you, now that Jonathan's not here."

"Okay. Let's go into the living room."

Brett led the way to the living room, a good-sized room that held a large brown leather couch, loveseat and a couple of chairs, plus a wall unit containing another flat-screen TV and CD player.

This room looked like it belonged to Brett. A couple of family photos, one of him with his high school basketball team, sports books and music CDs made the room surprisingly cozy. Julie sank into a corner of the couch.

Brett moved to the CD player, selected a CD and popped it in. Within moments, bright and lilting jazz flowed from the speakers. The music slid down Julie's spine in soothing waves.

"Have you heard the new one by The Rippingtons?" Brett asked, seating himself at the other end of the couch.

"Just a few songs, on the radio." Brett had gotten her interested in jazz originally, and even after they'd broken up, Julie had continued listening to the jazz station on the radio and buying CDs. The

Rippingtons had been one of their favorites, and Julie and Brett had gone to one of their live concerts together.

It had been so romantic, listening to the music, her head nestled on Brett's shoulder, his arm around her—

Julie pushed the mental image away and concentrated on the here and now.

"I don't think this is such a good idea," she stated. "I think it would be better if you just gave me the names of the people you want me to meet, and I went home."

"No."

Julie sat straight up. Her heart, which had been beating at its regular pace during dinner, accelerated. "What do you mean, no?"

Had he once been an easygoing, caring, happy person? Now Brett's face seemed shadowed, his tone unemotional, almost hard.

"I mean, no. I'm still borrowing you. You've got to see this through."

"What if I've changed my mind?" she demanded.

"No way. Besides," he added, a mischievous grin appearing on his face, "you can't go anywhere without me. Your car's at home, and I have the keys."

Chapter 3

The muscles in Brett's chest tightened as Julie stared at him, and he wondered what she was going to do. Cry? Scream? Normally, she was a calm person, not the kind to become hysterical or overreact.

But he recognized that this was hardly a normal situation.

From the first, the idea of "borrowing" Julie had been both logical and absurd. Logical because he thought it would work. Absurd because it was just that—absurd. Insane.

And yet, he couldn't think of any other way to convince Julie that Warren Wesley was a first-class creep. Borrowing her was the perfect way to prove a marriage to Warren would be a horrific mistake.

Julie opened her mouth, then snapped it shut. The spark in her beautiful dark brown eyes spelled mutiny. Despite her expression, she waited a few seconds, then spoke, her tone surprisingly even.

"You have my car keys...I should have guessed. I didn't even look at my key ring when Jon gave it back to me. He gave the keys to you?"

"Yes. I want you to see this through," Brett repeated.

"I could call Jonathan, or my parents."

"You could," he matched her smooth tone. "You're hardly a prisoner here. But then," he added, leaning forward so their faces were only a foot away, "wouldn't you wonder what information you were missing? Wouldn't you regret not knowing the whole truth?" The scent of her floral perfume reached out

24

toward him.

"I might be able to find out in some other way." There was uncertainty in her tone as she leaned back.

"Maybe. Maybe not." He deliberately made himself sound nonchalant, as if it didn't matter to him personally. As if sitting so close to Julie, being near her again after three years, hadn't affected him in ways he'd never expected. "Think of this," he continued, "as an adventure."

She started, and he knew she'd caught the trace of sarcasm in his voice, and recognized what he referred to.

The day she'd broken up with him, she'd told him she still cared, but she didn't think she was ready for a big step like marriage.

"I need some space," she'd said that day. "Some time to be on my own, maybe have some adventures."

As he studied her now, Brett thought, for just a second, that he saw tears in her eyes. Then Julie blinked.

"This is an adventure?"

"You could call it that." It was certainly an adventure for him. An adventure in keeping his emotions in check. Not to mention his libido.

Ever since he'd first taken hold of Julie, his senses had been bombarded by dangerous stimuli— her nearness, her beauty, her charm—and most of all, her unconscious sensuality. All that had burnt him over and over like invisible sparks flying from her and singeing his skin. And her smile—when she forgot their situation and smiled at him, her warm smile was enough to melt the iceberg he'd carefully built around his heart.

He swallowed. *Damn.* He'd known being near Julie again might be dangerous. But he'd had no idea how potently she would affect him, even after three years.

Could he handle it?

He had better, he told himself grimly.

Which wasn't going to be easy. Julie was still slim, with beautiful wavy dark hair, big eyes, and a smile that lit up the universe. She was, in a word, gorgeous.

She settled farther back into the couch and regarded him warily. "An adventure. Well..." She looked away, in the direction of the stereo. The smooth music curled around them, mellowing the tension in the air. Her hand stroked the material of the couch, and he noticed she still wore her class ring. And a pretty big diamond on the other hand.

"Okay." She turned back to him. "We'll try this—adventure. Maybe I'll—learn something." There was a definite catch in her voice.

She was going along with his scheme. Brett regarded her.

It was almost too good to be true.

In fact, he'd been edgy all along because she hadn't objected as much as he'd expected. His plan was going almost too smoothly.

"I'm glad. I know you'll learn a lot." He stood up. "I'll bring your things up to the guest room."

He went back to the car and got her pink suitcase. When he returned to the main level, she followed him upstairs.

He gave her a quick tour, watching as she looked into the master bedroom and luxurious bathroom and exclaimed over the size of the two closets. She glanced around the second-largest bedroom, which he'd turned into his home office, complete with computer and bookcases, and then followed him into the guest bedroom.

He'd put his old dresser, desk and night table into this room, which, though smaller than the others, still had space for a double bed. Decorated with a blue comforter and blue and white curtains, his sister had assured him it was comfortable when she'd last visited. A small TV sat on one corner of the dresser.

"This TV has cable, but you can watch one of the TVs downstairs or in my bedroom if you prefer a bigger screen," he said, putting her suitcase down. "You should leave your suitcase packed; we'll probably be staying in south Jersey tomorrow night."

She raised her eyebrows in response but said nothing.

"Do you need anything?" he asked.

She looked around the room. "I'm fine. This is very nice. In fact, your condo is gorgeous. I wish I had this much room in my apartment."

That had surprised him, too, that Julie lived in a small apartment in an older, two-family house. With all Ted Shaw's money, he wondered why she hadn't bought a house or a condo of her own. Despite the fact that she was Ted's stepdaughter, Ted had always been fond of Julie and treated her well. And he lavished money on his beautiful wife, Elise. Elise had never been cheap with her daughter, either.

"I'm surprised you don't own something yourself," he probed.

Julie laughed. "Teachers' salaries have improved a lot in the last few years; I could probably buy something small, but I couldn't afford anything like this." She shrugged. "But I do like my job despite the pay."

That didn't explain her small apartment, but she said no more. Brett watched as she bent and zipped open her suitcase. Her feminine curves in her red sweater and black pants set his pulse racing.

"I'd like to take a shower. Then I'll check out the Weather Channel on one of the other TVs." She straightened up, catching his stare.

"Are you still watching that? You mean you

don't know yet what the weather will be for the next few days?" He teased her without thinking. She had always been fascinated by the weather; she had taken many meteorology courses in college, along with astronomy and geology, when she'd majored in Earth Science Education.

Julie shot him a piercing look. "Yes, I still watch that. And yes, I can predict the weather. I do that with my classes. But I like to see if our predictions match the Weather Channel's."

Brett leaned against the wall, folding his arms across his chest. "So, Ms. Merritt, what is the weather forecast for the next four days?" he challenged.

"Tomorrow will start out sunny and cool." She folded her arms to match Brett's. "It will get colder as the day goes on, then cloudy. By evening we should have rain, maybe even sleet."

"And then?"

"And then, Friday will be overcast, maybe with some more showers. Saturday will clear up, but remain cold for November. Sunday there's a chance of rain, I'm not sure how much of a chance."

"You don't know?"

Her chin moved up. "You can't always predict accurately for more than five days; predicting the next three is the most accurate," Julie said. "You hung around me enough in college to know that."

"Yes, I did." He made the statement without emotion.

But emotions were tumbling inside of him. He had a strong urge to go over to Julie and sift her silky dark hair through his fingers; he had to rein in the impulse.

"You'd better pack some sweaters," she told him. "The next few days will be cold."

Not cold enough. Since he'd been with Julie, he'd been constantly warm.

He straightened up.

"Let me know if you need anything. The guest bathroom's there." He pointed to the beige bathroom down the hall.

"Thank you." Was there a trace of sarcasm in her voice, or did he imagine it?

Brett left the room and she shut the door. Entering his study, he went over to his computer. Might as well check his e-mail. Maybe there was a message from his friend Don. He should have that additional info on Warren Wesley by now.

Brett had removed the phone from the guestroom this morning, but if Julie really wanted to, he knew she'd find a way to call Warren. She probably had a cell phone in her purse. He'd have to watch her carefully.

That was the hard part.

For a moment, he pictured her getting ready for her shower, stripping the clothes off her slim but curvy body. His mouth went dry and he could feel his temperature rise.

Damn. This was going to be a lot harder than he'd imagined.

He sat down abruptly. He had to take his mind off Julie.

Checking his e-mail, he saw no messages from Don, only a note from a college buddy who now lived in Texas.

A door down the hall opened. Brett gritted his teeth, unable to stop himself from picturing Julie in a long robe with nothing underneath.

Stop it, he told himself harshly. Stop concentrating on every little move she makes.

"Brett?"

He turned in his chair. She was still dressed and standing by the door to his study. She looked flustered.

"I, uh, I forgot to pack pajamas." Her cheeks

were pink. She pushed back a lock of her wavy dark hair.

"You forgot to pack your pajamas?" He mentally kicked himself when he heard his own words. He sounded like an idiot.

"Yes." She leaned against the doorway. "Do you have something I could borrow?"

"I don't usually keep women's clothing in my home. Not even for my sister," he added, seeing Julie's cheeks grow rosier.

"I didn't mean—oh, for goodness' sake, you must have something I can borrow. A pajama top or an old sweatshirt or something?"

"Yeah. But everything would be too big." He stood up, surveying Julie. He topped her height by a foot. He was struck by a rush of familiarity. He'd always seen her as kind of soft and fragile. Though he knew she was emotionally strong, he felt the familiar need to protect her.

At the same time, the need to protect was at war with his inner core, which remembered his other needs. And Julie's.

After they'd been dating exclusively for months, they'd finally made love. Julie had been a virgin, but their lovemaking had been tender and sweet. And as time went on, their sexual relationship had grown, so that she was as passionate as he.

Dwelling on those nights now could cause a fuse to blow in his brain. He'd better pull back mentally.

But the words seemed to fall from his mouth. "You could sleep nude." He grinned at her.

Her cheeks reddened even more. "I'd get cold."

"I could keep you warm." The words tumbled out, accompanied by an ache deep inside. Even as he spoke, he wanted to kick himself.

"Have you forgotten I'm engaged?" she asked tartly. She waved the fingers of her left hand. The diamond flashed.

Julie's words spilled on him like cold water dousing hot memories.

"I'll get you something," he said dryly.

Julie moved aside as he passed, then followed him into his bedroom.

He opened a drawer and grabbed the first pajama shirt he saw. He turned. Julie was close behind him, and he shoved the blue-and-white striped top at her.

"Here."

She took it and held it up, giving it a quick onceover. "This will be fine. Thank you."

Her eyes met his, and for a long, drawn-out moment, neither one spoke. The air around them smoldered. He could almost taste the smoke. He felt heat, and his heart pounded.

He stepped back. "Need anything else?"

"No." Her voice was small. He wondered what she was thinking at that exact moment.

He went back to his computer and heard Julie go into the bathroom and start running the water. Deliberately, he pushed away tantalizing thoughts of her and tried to concentrate on replying to his e-mail.

He didn't quite succeed. Images of Julie kept cropping up in his mind.

He'd never get anything done like this. He went downstairs and dialed Don, but Don didn't answer his cell phone. He left a brief message. "Let me know if you've found out anything new."

He turned on the TV and flipped between a basketball game and a sports talk show discussing football. One team was clobbering the other by twenty points. The talk show was dull.

He had to do something to get his mind off Julie. Something, anything to keep the hot images at bay.

Exercise. It usually helped when he was upset.

He'd tire himself out so he wouldn't think of that

beautiful, sexy woman wearing his nightshirt, right under his roof.

****

By ten o'clock Julie crawled into bed, exhausted. What a day.

The warm shower had been refreshing, and the scent of her vanilla body lotion soothed her. The TV in the guestroom was tiny, so she had tried to watch the Weather Channel in Brett's room, since she knew he was downstairs with the TV on. But even though she'd curled up on a large, old navy blue armchair, her eyes kept moving toward the king-sized bed.

Brett slept there.

How many other women had slept there with him?

She knew it wasn't the same bed he'd had in his first apartment. That bed, where she'd finally lost her innocence, where Brett had tenderly initiated her into the delights of lovemaking with the man she adored, had been smaller. In that bed she'd learned to let go of her inhibitions and they'd both become true lovers, bringing each other to ecstatic heights, the kind she'd only dreamed about before she met Brett.

The kind she'd never felt with anyone else.

Definitely not with Warren.

She squirmed in the chair. She'd never be able to relax if she kept flashing back to those passionate hours she'd spent in Brett's arms.

Sighing, Julie returned to her room. She just couldn't keep her mind on the weather when she was in such close proximity to Brett's bed.

She tried watching a situation comedy on the thirteen-inch TV; she flipped through the magazine she'd brought. Finally, she switched out the light, leaving only the small desk lamp on as a nightlight.

Now she pulled her comforter up to her chin,

burrowing in the bed.

She wondered when Brett had last worn the pajama top. She turned her face into the collar. It was rumpled and soft, as if it was older. A trace of Brett's spicy aftershave clung to it. She inhaled once, twice. Yes, the scent of the aftershave was there. She felt a pang deep within.

And she wondered if this guestroom bed was the one Brett had had in his first apartment...

She lay quietly for a few minutes. It was cold in here, she realized. She tugged the cover closer. Her feet and legs were bare, and within minutes she began to shiver. The light comforter was not enough.

She sat up. She'd have to ask Brett for another blanket.

The thick carpeting felt good against her bare feet. What an idiot, she chastised herself as she headed downstairs. Here she remembered to pack body lotion and shampoo, but forgot essentials like pajamas and a robe!

Lights were on in the living room, but it was empty. Raucous whistles and cheers followed by an announcer's voice indicated Brett was watching TV in the family room.

As Julie approached, she heard heavy breathing.

She stepped into the room. Brett was sitting on some kind of exercise machine, his arms pulling at weights. He wore black sweatpants but his chest was bare; his muscled shoulders and dark blond chest hair glistened with sweat as he exercised.

Julie stopped. Brett looked so sexy, so *male*, that for a minute she couldn't breathe. What would it feel like if those arms encircled her and pulled her taut against his hard, damp chest?

He was staring at her as if he'd seen a ghost.

"Julie?" His voice was strained, his breathing labored. "Are you okay?"

She took a deep breath, pulling herself together.

"I-I'm cold. Do you have an extra blanket I could have?"

"I'm sorry." He stood up, reached for a towel and threw it over his shoulders. "I should have raised the heat upstairs. And the last time Jodi slept over it was August, so she didn't need the heavier blanket. I'll get it."

Brett approached, and Julie stepped back. She didn't want to get too close. She felt like a candle that would melt if it got too close to the heat source.

Brett hesitated as he neared her. "I'm sorry," he repeated.

"It's—okay." Julie's voice trembled. In fact, her cold shivers had turned into another kind of trembling. She hugged herself, suddenly conscious that the pajama top, though long sleeved, was made of thin material and revealed a lot of her legs.

Brett brushed by her. Heat seemed to radiate from him, and she had to control her impulse to put out her hands and warm them against his superb male physique. Tall, broad shouldered and well muscled, Brett appeared to be in better shape than ever.

She followed him upstairs and down the hall to a linen closet. He reached in and pulled out a thick blue blanket.

"Thanks." Julie grabbed the blanket. The velour felt soft and she wrapped it around her, both for warmth and concealment.

"I'll turn the heat up too. Do you need anything else?" Brett's voice sounded strained. It must be because he'd been exercising hard.

"No. Thanks," she said again, then turned and went back to the guestroom, shutting the door firmly.

She crawled into bed, snuggled into the soft blanket and pulled the comforter over it. Now she should feel warmer.

She heard Brett moving around, then a clinking noise as the heat came on.

She wasn't going to think about Brett Ryerson or his warm, hard body. She wasn't going to imagine being pulled close to him.

She would think instead about Warren Wesley. She pictured Warren, with his aristocratic face, wearing crisp tennis whites and swinging a racquet. Sophisticated and clever, that was Warren.

But the image left her cold.

****

Brett didn't sleep well that night.

He couldn't erase the image of Julie wearing only his pajama top. The short top had clung to her large breasts and revealed her shapely legs all too vividly.

He'd finished his workout after he'd seen her, pushing himself to the limit. Then he'd forced himself to take a colder-than-usual shower.

But it hadn't helped. Pictures of Julie, looking both innocent and sexy, still flashed across the TV in his mind.

Besides those images, his usually peaceful sleep was punctuated by fears that Julie would somehow sneak out, and he got up twice, walked over to the guestroom, and listened to make sure he heard her breathing. Then, in the middle of the night he woke up, hard as a rock, with wisps of an erotic dream surrounding him. It took a while to return to sleep, and then he woke again. This time, he heard Julie go into the bathroom and come out a few minutes later. Apparently she wasn't sleeping well either.

He'd set the alarm for seven, and woke up the minute it buzzed. Throwing on clothes, he checked the suitcase he'd packed the day before, then knocked on Julie's door.

"Julie. Time to get up," he said.

"Huh? Oh…oh," she rambled. She'd never been a

morning person. "All right…I'm getting up…"

He went downstairs and took out the muffins he'd bought yesterday, checking the coffee which was on an automatic timer. He poured himself a large mug, then poured an equally large one for Julie. They'd need it today.

He'd deliberately chosen to start Julie's enlightenment with Shannon. He thought that her story was the most heart wrenching, and would elicit the greatest reaction from Julie. Certainly the circumstances were the kind soft-hearted Julie would sympathize with.

After that, he was convinced she'd want to know the rest about Warren. And between Shannon's story, Arnold's and Felicia's, Brett was sure Julie would finally face the fact that her fiancé was a number-one jerk and not fit to even hold her hand.

He was about to go upstairs and call her again when he heard her walking around. Within a few minutes she stepped into the kitchen.

"I need coffee," she said.

There were shadows under her eyes, and Brett knew she hadn't slept any better than he had. And she'd always needed a good night's sleep. Despite this, in her long denim skirt and long-sleeved, pale green T-shirt, her legs encased in dark blue pantyhose, she looked more delectable than any of the muffins on the plate.

He reached for his coffee and swallowed. The rich, roasted aroma and taste should have been more comforting.

It was going to be a long day.

"Did you sleep okay?" he asked.

"All right," she replied slowly. Her dark eyes met his. He couldn't read their expression. "Being practically kidnapped isn't the best way to get a good night's rest."

"Borrowed," he corrected.

"Borrowed," she repeated. She reached for the mug he handed her, adding the artificial sweetener he'd left on the table. "I had to leave that little desk light on." She poured in milk and stirred her coffee rapidly.

Desk light? With a start he remembered. Julie didn't like sleeping in the dark. Even as a college student, she'd had a nightlight.

She'd explained to him years ago that after the car accident that killed her father on a dark, rainy night when she was three, she'd become afraid of the dark and had had frequent nightmares. Her mother let her sleep with a small light on, and later she switched to a nightlight. Since it was a drunk driver who had crashed into her father's car when he was returning from working late, she'd also been careful about drinking.

He should have remembered. "I'm sorry I forgot about the nightlight."

She reached for a muffin. "It's all right. I should have given it up long ago, but I still use it. I—" She stopped.

And then he remembered the rest.

Only when he'd held her in his arms at night had she felt safe enough to sleep in the dark. She'd told him so, more than once, as they'd snuggled together.

At the thought, warmth unfurled in him.

And then another thought intruded. She still used a nightlight? What about when she lay next to Warren?

Didn't she feel safe then?

The idea of Julie lying next to Warren was extremely distasteful. He took a gulp of coffee to erase the bitterness.

She was staring at the muffin she'd picked up. At least he had remembered her favorite. "I know you like carrot," he said, picking up a blueberry one for himself.

She looked at him, surprise on her face. "You remembered?"

"I remember a lot of things."

She hastily turned her head, not meeting his eyes, and bit into her muffin.

She didn't talk much during breakfast, and Brett wondered just what was going on in her head. Regrets? Probably.

Still, he was amazed at how smoothly his plan was proceeding, and how she was going along without too much fuss. It made him uneasy. He glanced at her as she stirred her coffee again. Would she suddenly try to get away? Would she attempt to call Warren?

Once she met Shannon, he was sure she'd want to go ahead with the rest of his plan. He didn't want to delay their trip and hurried through his breakfast.

"You said you took off from work?" Julie asked as they cleaned up.

"Yes," he answered tersely.

By eight thirty they were on their way south. He turned the radio to his favorite jazz station, and the combination of light banter from the disc jockey and smooth music soothed him. His muscles and nervous system were keyed up like a wire flowing with electricity. He hoped the music would help them both relax.

"Where are we going?" Julie asked.

"A small town near Toms River. Shannon Kolinski Dwight lives there."

With schools closed and no school buses to impede their way, traffic was lighter than normal on the back roads, and they were soon driving down Interstate 287, then the Parkway.

"I told you it would be sunny this morning." Julie's sudden statement interrupted his thoughts regarding a lawsuit being brought by a hockey player he represented.

"Yes. You did." The sun was glaring, and he'd put on sunglasses.

"By this afternoon it will be getting cloudy. Y-you'll see," she said.

Brett detected the slightest catch in her voice. Was Julie nervous?

For the first time, he wondered if she had previously suspected that Warren had another life. Maybe that was why she was so amenable to this plan. Maybe she already had her own suspicions about Warren Wesley.

He settled back, hope smoothing away his worries like a massaging hand.

****

They arrived at the house before eleven.

Julie stared at the large, gold, older Cape Cod home, and a rush of nervousness filled her like bubbling soda. Who was Shannon Kolinski Dwight? Was she really the mother of Warren's child?

Why hadn't Warren told her?

She was still stunned over the revelation that Warren had a child. It was something she'd never suspected, though she knew Warren had lots of former girlfriends. Warren was good-looking and sophisticated and wealthy. He was thirty-three, older than her by seven years.

She'd been sure he hadn't cheated on her since they'd gotten involved, but could she have been wrong?

And what about her other feelings regarding Warren? Were they right? What other secrets had Warren hidden from her?

Slowly, she got out of the car.

"Shannon's door is on the other side." Brett pointed. "This is a two-family."

On the left side of the house, wooden stairs led

up to a small deck. Julie paused, looking up. The house was neat from the outside. How had Brett found Shannon? She'd have to ask him later. Taking a deep breath of the frosty air, she walked to the stairway and went up, Brett at her heels.

Brett leaned over and rapped on the door.

"Just a minute!" called a voice from inside.

They waited silently in the cold. Julie stuck her hands in her coat pockets.

In a minute the door opened.

"Come in."

They entered, and Julie got her first look at Shannon Kolinski Dwight as Brett introduced them.

She was younger than Julie expected—she couldn't have been much more than twenty or twenty-one. As short as Julie but painfully thin, Shannon had chin-length, whitish-blonde hair that looked bleached, straight and worn with bangs. Her pretty eyes were a gray-blue color. She wore a lot of makeup, and her small mouth was a ripe coral.

As Shannon waved them in, Julie felt as if she were walking into a wall of smoke. The air was laden with it, thick and warm and bitter. Sunlight streaming in the window only accentuated the smoke. Julie wanted to repel herself away from it. She coughed.

Shannon was lighting a cigarette she held in her thin hand, and Julie noticed her hand shook. "Want one?" she asked, dragging on it.

"No thanks," Julie said. She hated cigarettes.

Shannon was pretty and fashionably dressed. She wore a blue-and-black striped sweater, short black skirt, black tights and black shoes with chunky heels. Inexpensive jewelry of a matching blue necklace and earrings completed her outfit.

Very together. Except that Shannon seemed anything but together.

Her hand was still shaking as she blew out

smoke. She indicated a plush, off-white leather sofa in the small living room. "Sit down."

The sofa seemed out of place, both dwarfing the room and incongruous with the rest of the furnishings. Two gold chairs and a Mediterranean-style, dark wood end table blended with the avocado shag-style carpeting. The furniture reminded Julie of furnishings she'd seen at friends' homes—hand-me-down pieces from the seventies. Except for the large black TV, the sofa was the only modern piece.

The room was neat, with only a large glass ashtray on the side table to mar the tidiness. The ashtray was full of cigarette butts and ashes. Beside it was a small picture of a blond baby in a gold-toned frame.

Julie breathed shallowly, trying not to cough again. Theme music from a popular educational children's TV show drifted into the room.

Shannon glanced toward the sound. "Victoria's playing in the bedroom. We can talk." She sat down in the corner of the couch and dropped ashes in the ashtray.

Julie sat down on the opposite corner of the couch, trying to move out of range of Shannon's smoke. Brett took a seat on one of the chairs as Julie studied Shannon. Even with the bright sunlight coming in the window and the large lamp turned on, her face was shadowed by smoke, like a woman from the East wearing a thin veil.

"Well." Shannon looked at her.

"Tell Julie everything you told me." Brett's voice was soft and kind. Julie glanced at him. His face wore a sympathetic expression.

"Well..." Shannon repeated. She stared at Julie uncertainly. "I know Warren's your—your fiancé. He'll have an absolute fit if he finds out we talked, but you should know...what kind of guy he is." Her eyes darkened and her voice hardened as she spoke.

She took another drag from her cigarette.

"Go ahead," Julie said, matching Brett's soft tone.

"I met him over three years ago when I was working at Danny's Ice Cream Parlor. Near the beach. I was eighteen and had just graduated from high school. It was my summer job. I was going to go to fashion school in the fall." Her voice sharpened. "Warren was—well, you know, good-looking and dashing and older and sophisticated—you know! And you could see he had loads of money, that fancy sports car and his friends and all throwing down twenties and fifties for an ice cream cone."

She paused, reflecting. "He came on to me, and he came back every Saturday for a few weeks in a row and flirted more. My boyfriend—Ray Dwight— and I weren't getting along too well. We'd been fighting a lot. I flirted right back." Another pause, another drag on the cigarette. Julie tried to press farther back into the sofa, away from the spouting smoke.

"He asked me out, and I said yes. The next Saturday after work he took me out to dinner, and afterward we started kissing and...well, you know...we ended up screwing right there in his car. In the driveway. We never even made it inside his vacation home, that first time. We just couldn't wait." She stopped and looked for Julie's reaction.

A glacier slithered around Julie, surrounding her. She swallowed, then coughed again. "Go on."

Shannon ground out the cigarette stub without looking at the ashtray. "That's how our hot affair got started."

Hot? With Warren?
Julie flinched.

Before she could contemplate Shannon's words further, Shannon continued. "I—I'm sorry. But you should know."

Her apologetic words barely registered. A hot affair? Cool, calculating Warren, who measured his moves by their political correctness?

"Go on," Julie repeated, her tone scratchy. Her throat felt tight.

"We...well, things continued for several weeks. I was seeing Ray also," Shannon said candidly. "But I really fell for Warren. Ray and I had taken chances and...I never got pregnant..." She drew a sharp breath. "I didn't even *think* about birth control the first few times Warren and I—well, anyway, I took chances with him too." She stopped.

Julie pressed her hands together, glancing at Brett. His expression was serious as his eyes met hers. In all the time they'd made love years ago, they'd always used protection.

How could Warren have been so careless to have sex with Shannon without considering the consequences?

Shannon's hands began to shake badly, and she reached down and pulled a pack of cigarettes from the black purse lying by the couch where she sat. She flicked a match, lit one, and inhaled before continuing.

"I got pregnant."

Julie found she had been holding her breath, and she exhaled noisily.

"I was—pretty sure—it was Warren's baby." Shannon's mouth twisted briefly. "I went to talk to him. He was furious. He'd assumed I was on the pill, and well—we fought. He wanted to know how I could let this happen." Her voice held more bitterness than the smoke drifting through the room. "It was like—like he'd had nothing to do with it, like he wasn't even there!" She pulled at the cigarette again.

"I was scared. My mother—you see, she told me her older sister got pregnant and had a boyfriend who wouldn't marry her, and when she had the baby everyone made fun of her. How awful it was. Her sister had to move away. So my mom always told me and my sister if we ever got pregnant, we better get married, or she'd throw us out of the house. She meant it, too." Shannon stood up abruptly and began pacing, the cigarette clutched tightly between her fingers. "I knew my family would be no help. I was on my own!" Her voice, agitated before, became distraught.

Julie's heart went out to Shannon. Young—only eighteen—she must have felt she had no one at all to turn to. Not even the father of her baby.

"It must have been so difficult for you," Julie said softly.

Shannon's words echoed Julie's thoughts. "It *was* hard. I asked Warren to marry me—I actually asked him! But he refused, saying he liked me, but I wasn't the type he would m-marry." Her voice broke. She stopped and dragged at the cigarette. "I guess I wasn't rich and upper class like him."

Julie almost jumped in her seat. On several occasions, she'd thought that Warren was too impressed by her stepfather's money, and she hadn't liked it. It looked like she'd been correct.

"I talked to my friends," Shannon continued. "I thought about an abortion but—it's against my religion, I just couldn't." Another drag on the cigarette. "Warren offered to pay, even tried to arrange the whole thing, but I told him no." She stopped, staring out the window at clouds drifting across the sky. "I finally decided...the best thing was to...pretend the baby was Ray's and marry him."

Julie couldn't see Shannon's face, shrouded by smoke and turned toward the window. But her voice sounded close to tears.

Julie bit her lip as a piece of her heart broke off at Shannon's pain.

Sudden music burst from another room, and

Shannon shook herself.

"I even told myself it *could* be Ray's baby. So we got married. Ray wasn't too happy either." She stopped. The pause went on so long that Julie was about to say something. She regarded Brett.

Brett's face was dark. He must have heard all this before, and yet he seemed angry.

Angry at Warren, Julie thought.

Shannon sighed loudly. "Warren agreed to help me out, financially, as long as I signed some papers his fancy lawyer friends wrote up. Basically, it said he'd send me money if I refused to claim that my baby was any relation of his. So I signed. I didn't want to—to go through trying to prove the baby was his." She sat down. "I just wanted to marry Ray, have my baby, and get on with my life. Get on *without* Warren Wesley."

The knife-sharp edge of her voice sliced through the thick atmosphere of smoke and tears.

"And then Victoria was born, and I looked at those dark blue eyes…and I knew she was Warren's kid." Shannon stood again and paced to the hall, then back. Dropping once more onto the couch, she crushed out the second cigarette. Her whole body trembled.

"I'm so sorry." Julie spoke before she even thought about the words. What was she sorry about? "Warren should have treated you better. It was— horrible of him to be so—so callous."

"It's not your fault. You probably didn't even know him then."

"She didn't," Brett interjected.

"No, I didn't." Julie shot him a glance, shaking her head. She felt close to tears herself. Was it just the smoke, or Shannon's story? The burnt smell of cigarettes was overwhelming. She reached out and grasped Shannon's hand. Her thin hand was cold and smooth.

"Victoria—" Shannon began, when a childish voice said, "Ma?"

A chubby little girl toddled in. At least, she looked like a little girl, but as Julie focused on her, she looked more like a baby. The round face smiled, but she walked with a peculiar gait.

Dressed in a pink corduroy pants outfit, she had hair as straight as Shannon's, but of a light brown color. It was pulled back with a frilly pink hair bow. The eyes shining behind her glasses were the same bright blue that was the trademark of Warren's family. He, his mother and sister had those same color eyes.

Victoria was definitely Warren's child.

This child, who seemed much younger than her age, had something wrong with her, Julie realized. If she had time to study her, she might be able to pin it down. For now, it was enough to see she had a problem.

"This is Victoria." Shannon turned to the child. "Want some crackers?"

"Cwac-kes," the child said, then dropped down and crawled over to look at Julie.

"Hi," Julie said softly.

The little girl stared at her.

Shannon left the room, coming back a minute later with a plastic bowl filled with crackers and a small bottle. "And juice." She handed them over.

As the child reached for them, Shannon looked at Julie. "She has some birth defects. And she's retard—I mean, developmentally disabled. That's the term they told me to use. Mildly."

It was as if a hand was squeezing Julie's heart.

Chapter 4

Brett studied Julie as she listened to Shannon's sad story. Julie's expression revealed that she was still the kind-hearted girl he'd known before. Empathy, caring, horror—all were apparent on Julie's face as Shannon spoke. And when Shannon announced that Victoria was developmentally disabled, he saw Julie blink back tears.

Only when Shannon had talked about her steamy affair with Warren Wesley had he been unable to read Julie's reaction. He'd seen Julie flinch, but he couldn't be sure whether her expression was one of shock, hurt or anger. Maybe it had been a combination. As Shannon went on, he observed Julie closely and thought she'd looked surprised. Had Julie thought Warren had no secrets? That he lived a clean, untarnished life?

He felt much worse than he'd expected about smashing Julie's mental picture of Warren and hurting her like this. But he would have been sorrier *not* to educate her. It had to be done. For her own good. He shifted his position on the chair, trying to push away the guilt.

Shannon had agreed completely with him that Julie should know the truth. He'd talked to Shannon only a few weeks ago, after Don, his private eye buddy, had tracked her down.

Now Julie was asking about how Shannon was managing, and the difficulties of raising a developmentally disabled child. Her tone was full of sympathy, and Shannon responded, her body relaxing slightly from its tense pose.

"Does—does Ray help?" Julie asked hesitantly.

"We're separated." Shannon shook her head, her bleached-blond hair swinging. "He doesn't even see her," she added bitterly. She glanced at Victoria. "See, after Ray and I got married, we lived with his parents for a while, then we got our own apartment…we were doing okay. Except that Ray and I still fought a lot. And we were real upset about Victoria…but Warren was sending me a nice check every month, and I didn't have to work. I bought clothes for Victoria and me, and this couch…I even put some money in the bank…" For the first time, she looked at Brett.

He'd heard the whole story before, although with Julie, Shannon had described details she hadn't mentioned to him. Like the fact that she had slept with Warren on their first date.

Maybe that was why Julie was so upset?

Brett shifted his position again, leaning away from the puffs of smoke which were irritating. He could even taste the acrid cigarettes.

All this smoke couldn't be good for her daughter. As he had the thought, Julie turned her head and caught his eye.

And he knew she was thinking the exact same thing.

It was uncanny, he'd often thought, how sometimes they were on the same wavelength, sharing the same thoughts.

"Ray was getting suspicious about the extra money I had," Shannon continued. "We were fighting more and more…one day he got the mail before I did, and opened the envelope from Warren's secretary, and found the check. He accused me of cheating on him, but I never did once we got married." Sudden tears clouded Shannon's eyes. She looked down at Victoria, who calmly drank from the small bottle and stared at Shannon's shoes.

"What happened then?" Julie's voice was low.

"We—we had a fight. I yelled out the truth. I probably should have kept my mouth shut, but we'd been fighting so much lately, and he was accusing me of—he called me…" Shannon's voice trailed off. She reached for her purse again. "He called me—a slut." She withdrew a pack of cigarettes.

The poor kid. That's what Shannon was, barely a kid. With all the problems of an adult. Brett knew she hadn't even turned twenty-two yet.

He glanced at Julie and leaned toward her. He wanted to catch a faint whiff of the vanilla scent that had been surrounding Julie since last night. But the stale, smoke-filled room prevented that.

Julie seemed all sympathy. But what about her feelings toward Warren? Wasn't she angered by his callousness?

"That was the end for Ray and me," Shannon was saying. "He walked out that day and went back to his parents. We filed for divorce, and he—he refused to help me. He said I'd tricked him all along." She struck a match. "I guess he was right."

"Did you get in touch with Warren then?" Julie asked.

Shannon shook her head. "No. I—I wanted his checks to keep coming. They were a nice amount. Luckily, one of my aunts owned this house, and her mother-in-law used to live up here, in this apartment. But she'd died the year before. So my aunt—she's a widow and her kids are grown—said I could move in, and she charges me almost nothing for rent. But I'll pay more when I can get on my feet," she added hastily.

"How are things going for you?" Julie asked, her voice quiet and still kind.

"Okay. I work at Fashion Parade," Shannon said. "It's a store near here, and they have great clothes, and I get a discount." She blew smoke, seeming undisturbed that Victoria was sitting right in front of her. "The hardest part was getting child care for Victoria. Now she's in a preschool handicapped program part of the day. They have today off because of the teachers' convention. My girlfriend Liz watches her afternoons on the days I work. I have to work Saturdays too—and Liz or my brother and his wife take turns watching her then." She looked down at Victoria, and a smile softened the tumult on Shannon's face. "Victoria's a good kid, but she has a lot of problems."

Shannon turned and focused on Julie again. "I'm still getting the checks from Warren, which I need, because even with hardly any rent to pay I'd never make it on my salary, with food and Victoria's clothes and toys..." She brought the cigarette to her coral lips. "But Victoria and I, we're getting along okay..." She inhaled.

Not to mention the cost of cigarettes. Shannon must spend a huge chunk of her salary on them, judging by the way she continually smoked. Brett wanted to shake his head.

He watched as Julie sagged into the couch, and he felt a wave of sympathy for her. He'd heard the whole thing before, and he wasn't deeply involved like Julie was. It must be overwhelming for her to hear the story like this for the first time, with so many personal details.

He wanted to get up, sit beside her, and clasp Julie's hand—and he almost did. But as he fought the impulse, Julie made her own gesture.

She leaned toward Shannon and covered Shannon's free hand with her own. "Is there anything I can do?" she questioned, her voice low.

Shannon just looked at Julie for a moment. Then she took a sharp breath. "I—no. But thanks for asking." She sniffed, then turned and ground out her cigarette.

Julie was reaching for her own purse. "Look, I'm going to write down my phone number." She took out a small pad and a pen and scribbled. Then she ripped off the piece of paper. The staccato rip seemed to echo in the quiet room. The TV's distant buzz from another room was the only other noise.

"Here."

Shannon turned back and took the piece of paper, smoothing it between fingers that shook. Brett saw her blink rapidly.

Amazing, he thought, and wondered if Shannon was thinking the same thing. Here was Julie, presented with the sordid details of her fiancé's private life that she'd never expected—details about Warren that were unflattering and nasty, details that revealed Warren Wesley's callous nature. And yet Julie's reaction was unlike what he would expect of most women. She was probably hurt and horrified, maybe angry too. But instead of recoiling, or denying, she was looking to help Shannon.

Brett swallowed. He'd always known Julie was a rare gem. And now he'd witnessed the proof of just how exquisite her character was.

A rare jewel, he thought as he watched her writing down the phone number Shannon dictated.

How did someone like Warren Wesley snare a fiancée like Julie Suzanne Merritt? He certainly didn't deserve her!

Brett could only hope Julie would realize that in the next three days.

****

When they returned to the car and headed south, Julie was quiet, her face drawn.

Brett should have felt happier. It was obvious his plan was working and Julie had been exposed to the dark side of Warren Wesley. It looked like this, the saddest of the three stories Julie would hear, had affected her deeply. She stared out the window, looking away from Brett, and he heard her sniffle several times.

But he didn't feel happy, or satisfied. Instead, Julie's distress caused an ache to grow inside him. He hated to see her so upset.

When they stopped for a red light, he put on jazz music again and asked cautiously, "Are you okay?"

"I'll—be—all right." Her voice came out jerkily.

He put a finger under her chin. Her skin was warm and soft and felt too good against his finger. Gently, he turned her face toward his.

Tears were sliding down her cheek.

It was like having a knife in his gut.

"I'm sorry you had to hear this, Julie. More than you know. I wanted you to know the truth," he said, his voice husky. "I'm just sorry it hurt you so much."

She pulled away and blinked. Her eyes went from sad to flashing, their dark brown intense.

"I'm not hurt," she protested. "I'm crying because I'm so sorry for poor Shannon. And I'm so—damned—angry! How could Warren be so cold? How could he desert Shannon and their child? And act like it wasn't his problem?"

The sudden honking behind them startled Brett, and he looked to see the light was green.

Brett drove forward, eyes on the road. "I don't know," he said after a moment.

"How did you find her?"

"My friend helped me. Want to have something to eat?" He didn't want to belabor the point that he'd had Warren investigated by Don.

"Maybe something quick, in a little while. Whenever—whenever it's convenient." She turned and looked out the window again, and Brett found himself thinking about Julie and her kindness to the young woman who'd given birth to her fiancé's child.

Julie had always been a soft-hearted, sweet person.

When he'd first met her, at a college party, he'd been attracted to her because she was so pretty. And then they'd spent the evening talking, and he'd realized she was a warm, caring person.

The longer he'd known her, the more he'd realized just how warm, and caring, and kind Julie was. Whether it was helping her roommate study or cheering up a friend who'd broken up with her boyfriend, Julie was there. Sometimes it surprised him, especially after he'd gotten to know her family, most notably her mother.

Elise Shaw was a very attractive woman who turned heads even though she was middle aged. Taller than Julie by several inches, with coloring and hair that was lighter, she was slim and elegant and had the same gorgeous face as Julie. And yet she didn't exude the kind of warmth Julie did. She was never mean, yet Elise approached life and others with a certain businesslike, matter-of-fact outlook that Brett found hard to warm up to. Ted Shaw, her husband, was more congenial than Elise was.

Brett had asked Julie once about her, and Julie had just shrugged, claiming that was the way her mother was.

"My real father was different," she'd told him with a wistful sigh. "I remember him. He was very warm."

Brett had concluded that Julie took after her deceased dad.

As he pulled into a parking lot by a popular sandwich chain a few minutes later, Brett was convinced that Julie had not changed. Despite being engaged to Warren Wesley, the Snake of the Year, Julie was still a caring person.

What would she do with her new knowledge? It would change the way she viewed Warren. But what action would she take?

Would she call off her wedding?

****

"Remember, I'll be waiting for you right here when you get out."

Julie nodded. Brett's low-pitched warning didn't quell the uneasiness in her middle. In fact, his tone only agitated her further. He obviously wanted her to know he wasn't going to let her bolt.

Not that she hadn't thought about it a few times today.

She followed the other teachers streaming into the room from the crowded hallway. Ever since they'd left Shannon, she'd been filled with a mixture of sadness, anger, and nervousness. Sadness because of Shannon's plight. Fury at Warren. How could he do this to Shannon? How could he shirk his responsibilities, except for the monetary ones? And how come savvy Warren Wesley hadn't bothered to use birth control when he'd fooled around with Shannon? He was no inexperienced boy. He'd been around. Whatever had caused him to throw caution to the wind and take chances? That wasn't like the Warren she knew at all.

And what had made Warren start an affair with a young woman who was so out of his usual social league? He dated women from fine families, or professional women. Julie had long ago recognized that Warren was a snob. He'd told her he was very selective with his dates.

Maybe he'd lied.

She walked silently down the aisle in the middle of the large room, behind the throng of people attending the workshop on helping learning-disabled students deal with academic subjects. She'd looked forward to hearing this speaker for weeks. Gripping her notebook, she followed a heavy woman who was kidding around with a man so tall he looked like a pro basketball player, and scanned the room for

Kendra.

What else was she going to learn about Warren? Her nervousness didn't dissipate as she looked for her friend.

Brett's behavior had grown increasingly tense throughout the day, and it disturbed her. He'd been very quiet after their meeting with Shannon, and she had no idea what he was thinking. Probably about how awful Warren was. And maybe he thought she was an idiot to be engaged to Warren. Whatever his thoughts, Brett had been almost brooding by the time he'd parked the car in Atlantic City and walked her to the meeting room at the convention hall.

He'd told her he would wait right outside the room, so as soon as the lecture was over, they could resume their trip.

"Don't forget," he'd whispered once as they entered the building. "You have to finish seeing this thing through."

Something in his voice had made her shiver. Or was it the fear of what else she would learn? Whatever it was, she knew she had to find Kendra, and at the very least tell her friend about this bizarre situation.

She glanced again around the room, looking for her tall, blonde friend.

"Julie!"

The exclamation made her turn. There was Kendra, all the way on the left, waving. She smiled and indicated the seat she had saved.

With relief, Julie moved toward her.

Kendra Nielson smiled widely as Julie squeezed down the aisle. Tall—over five feet seven inches—and lithe, Kendra had long, naturally pale blonde hair and bright blue eyes. With a Swedish mother and Danish father, Kendra's looks reflected her Scandinavian heritage. The contrast between her fair good looks and Julie's dark ones often made people comment.

Kendra taught math, and the two had been fast friends since the first day they'd met, at the teacher orientation for the new middle school. Both right out of college and newly hired to teach in the same building, something had clicked between them, and Julie knew she'd made a lifelong friend.

Kendra lived not too far from Julie but was staying over in Atlantic City tonight with her former college roommate. She'd invited Julie to join them, but Julie had declined, thinking she was going to call and visit her college friend Lindsay on the way home.

"How are you?" Kendra asked in her usually perky voice as Julie slid into the seat beside her. Then, as she took a look at Julie, she drew in her breath. "Is everything okay?" Her voice sharpened.

The moderator was calling the workshop to order and began introducing the speaker, who had a long list of credentials.

"I can't talk now," Julie whispered to her friend. "Meet me in the ladies' room around the corner as soon as this is over, okay? I—I've got to tell you what's been going on."

Kendra nodded, her expression perplexed.

The speaker was interesting and told some amusing anecdotes. Julie was glad to turn her attention to the subject of learning-disabled students. She took notes as the woman spoke, and for a little while she almost forgot about Warren Wesley, Shannon, and even Brett.

But as time passed, she began to feel fidgety. Would she get much time to speak with Kendra? She wanted someone besides her brother to know about her situation. Would Brett grab her when she left the room and haul her away before she had a chance to talk? She knew he wouldn't object to her visiting the ladies' room, but how much time would she have to talk before he got suspicious?

She'd have to make it a quick conversation.

The minute the workshop was over and people finished applauding, Julie stood up.

She didn't want Brett to see Kendra with her. Though he'd never met Kendra, if he saw them talking, Julie was certain he'd be distrustful.

"Meet me in the ladies' room around the corner to the right," she hissed. "It's important. I've got to speak with you."

Leaving her astonished friend behind, Julie scooted out of the room.

Sure enough, Brett was lounging against the wall opposite the room. The minute he saw her, he strode forward.

"I have to go to the ladies' room," Julie said, doing her best to sound normal. "There's one around the corner."

"Okay." Brett fell into step beside her. "How was your workshop?"

"Excellent. I'm very glad I went. I think I picked up some good info." She shot him a look. He looked no more positive than he had earlier.

"Glad to hear it."

As they approached the restroom, Julie saw people from the workshop next door entering. It was bound to be crowded, but a line would buy her more time.

"Looks like there's a line," she said. "This may take a while."

"Okay."

She joined the line and forced herself not to look back for Kendra. Would she get there quickly?

Once on the inside line, Julie stepped aside and let several women go ahead of her. Two minutes crawled by. She shifted her position, holding tightly to her notebook and purse. *Where are you, Kendra?*

The door opened again, and her friend entered behind a thin red-haired woman who smelled like smoke. Julie moved backward to stand beside Kendra.

"What's going on?" Kendra demanded. Her tone was forceful but her expression was clearly anxious.

"I'm so glad to see you." Julie breathed a sigh of relief. "Listen…" She pitched her voice low, for Kendra's ears alone. Rapidly, she explained to Kendra what was going on, as they moved further up the line.

"But—" Kendra's eyes were wide.

"Move up," someone said impatiently behind Julie. It was her turn next.

"I'll tell you the rest when I get out," Julie said and entered the available stall.

She couldn't take much more time. Brett would be waiting.

Kendra was already standing by the polished countertop when Julie went to wash her hands.

In a low voice, Julie finished telling Kendra about Brett and briefly described the encounter with Shannon, ending with, "And so here we are, because I insisted on not missing the workshop. I really wanted to be here—and I knew I'd see you and I wanted someone to know what was going on and where I was in case—in case something happens."

The words burst from Kendra. "Are you *crazy*?"

"I'm wondering if I am." Julie pulled out a paper towel.

Kendra leaned against the sink, eyes glued to Julie, lines of concern etching her face.

Then she bent toward Julie and spoke in her ear. Her words, though low, cut through the swirling conversations in the room like the school's paper cutter slicing through a thick stack of paper.

"Why didn't you tell Brett you broke your engagement to Warren?"

Chapter 5

Julie swallowed, facing Kendra's accusing expression. Why hadn't she? She couldn't even be one hundred percent sure of her own motivation.

Fortunately, there were so many people talking that Kendra's low-pitched question hadn't reached anyone else's ears. In any case, these strangers couldn't care less.

Julie crumpled the paper towel, and the sound grated harshly. "I—well, you know it's only been a little over a week since I broke it off," she said, pivoting to throw the paper in the garbage. "And I promised Warren I wouldn't say a word until after his celebration party on Sunday," she continued, turning back to Kendra. "He—he wants things to look good until then. I haven't told my family yet, either. No one but you and Jessica—"

"But you could have told Brett!" Kendra stood up straight. "This whole thing—to persuade you to break an engagement that's already ended—it's a sham! Why on earth are you going along with it?"

Julie was silent, searching for an answer, though she was afraid she already knew.

"I want to find out the worst about Warren—"

"Uh-uh." Kendra shook her head vigorously. "Be honest with yourself, girlfriend. That's not it, is it? You wanted to be—to spend time with Brett!"

"Yes." Julie's voice was low, but clear. She'd had a conversation with Kendra about Brett only last weekend. She'd admitted to her friend that she couldn't stop thinking about Brett, that she'd had him on her mind even before she broke her engagement to Warren.

She'd been pretty sure that Warren would be angry when she ended their relationship, and maybe hurt, but after several weeks of soul-searching, she'd decided she couldn't marry someone like him. The caring feelings she'd once thought she'd had turned out to be merely infatuation, and she had no desire to become Mrs. Warren Wesley.

Warren had taken the news fairly well. He must have suspected that her feelings had waned, especially over the last few weeks. Still, he'd persuaded her to keep up the pretense till after Sunday's party with his powerful political friends— the party to celebrate his election. He'd been so certain even ten days ago that he'd win.

And she'd decided to be a good sport and help him out.

"But this—this is no way—" Kendra protested, when another group of women entered the room.

Brett would be growing impatient. Julie stopped her friend. "I have to get going or he'll start getting suspicious. Look, I'll call you in a day or two, okay? And I'll see you at Warren's victory party."

Kendra's expression was anxious, her mouth tense, and this did nothing to ease Julie's own agitation. "Are you sure you know what you're doing?" Kendra demanded.

"Yes." Julie smiled. "Since I broke up with Warren, I'm finally beginning to feel like I *do* know what I'm doing. Even though this whole situation is kind of crazy—yes, I do know." She leaned over and gave her friend a quick hug. "Thanks for your concern. I'll call soon. Love you!" Before Kendra could voice more objections, Julie turned and hurried away.

She was right. Brett was pacing when she returned to the hall.

"What took you so long?"

Julie smiled at him. "There was a line, and I had to fight to get to the mirror to check my hair." Boldly, she took Brett's hand. "Let's go."

He cast her a long, suspicious look, then pulled her down the wide hall, through the throng. His hand was warm and large, and hers felt surprisingly secure in his.

Julie wondered if he felt her engagement ring against his hand, and a feeling of guilt flashed through her, not for the first time. What would he say if he knew she hadn't told him the truth? She hadn't lied, exactly; she'd just omitted the crucial fact that she'd broken her engagement to Warren. Brett hadn't even noticed that she wasn't wearing her ring when he'd first caught up with her, and she'd agreed to his scheme, despite her conflicting thoughts.

Julie was afraid in her heart that Kendra was right. She wanted to have the opportunity to spend time with Brett again. She hadn't been able to get him off her mind lately and had finally come to the conclusion that she wished she could reconnect with him, get to know him all over again. Not for the first time, she'd considered that their break-up had been a mistake on her part.

And then Brett had come along yesterday and presented her with a nice, easy, complete, Brett-inspired opportunity to spend time with him. Maybe it wasn't foolproof, but how could she not take advantage of it? It only required some acting—and the truth was, she did feel conflicting emotions about the whole thing.

She was also curious about Warren. Warren's selfishness and snobbery were reason enough to end their engagement. She didn't need justification for her break-up. But she was beginning to realize her worst fears about Warren were not only being confirmed; her own suspicions had just scratched the surface.

They took the long escalator down. As Brett led her past a group of laughing people and headed for the doors, Julie glanced at his profile. His expression was as tense as his hard grip.

She swallowed, and a sudden lump settled in her stomach. What would Brett do when he found out she hadn't told him the truth? That he'd spent all this time and energy when it wasn't necessary? It had occurred to her earlier that he would be angry. He had always been a great believer in honesty. Now, she wondered if he would be furious.

She'd have to tell him eventually.

Soon.

But not quite yet. She'd wait till he was a little less tense, wait till he saw she was affected by the people he was introducing her to.

And she was affected. Her meeting with Shannon had been heart wrenching, and she knew that, had she still been engaged to Warren when she met Shannon, she would have broken the engagement afterward.

Maybe she'd better allude to that fact. Although she was not yet ready to say Brett's scheme had worked.

They practically burst through the doors out into the November air. The salty sea air was refreshing after the warm, crowded hallways. But it held a chilly bite.

Julie breathed deeply. The sky had turned gray during the last couple of hours and was now overcast.

"I was right. It is going to rain later," she said, hurrying to keep up with Brett's long strides.

Brett glanced at her. "It seems so."

A sudden gust of wind made her shiver. Or was it Brett's cold tone?

Could he know she was tricking him?

She rejected that thought. Only Kendra, Julie's friend Jessica, and Warren knew the engagement was off. And Brett hadn't spoken to any of the three.

They reached the parking lot, paid the attendant, and in a few minutes were on their way out of Atlantic City.

"Where to now?" Julie turned toward Brett.

He clicked on the radio. "We're heading back north."

"Do you want to get a cup of coffee?" she asked, wishing she'd gotten one herself.

"I had one when you were in the workshop." He paused, then added more quietly, "I'm sorry. I should have gotten one for you. I forgot you like to have one in the afternoon."

"It's okay," she said.

But Brett insisted on driving around and looking for a donut shop, and then running in to get her a cup of coffee to go. Once back in the car, Brett suggested an early dinner at a seafood restaurant that was nearby.

"I'm not very hungry," she said, sipping her coffee.

Julie looked at the clock on the dashboard, surprised to see it was nearly four o'clock. The hour workshop and the time she'd spent with Kendra had whizzed by. "Maybe we can eat in an hour?" she asked and settled back.

They fell silent, and Julie stared reflectively out the window as they drove smoothly along the Atlantic City Expressway.

"Sorry we couldn't spend an hour trying the slot machines," Brett said suddenly.

Julie looked at him. A small smile crossed his face.

"I really didn't want to risk your seeing someone you knew there," he continued. "I want you to finish with this plan."

"Oh. Well, that's honest," Julie said quietly. "It's okay. I rarely ever gamble, and I still limit myself to fifty bucks." At Brett's sudden grin, she found herself smiling too. "In fact, I think the last time I went to Atlantic City was with you, when you won fifty dollars on the slot machine—" She stopped suddenly, the memory rushing back so totally she felt like wind had knocked her over.

They'd gone with friends, enjoying the novelty of gambling, the bright lights and intermittent clinking of the coins from the slot machines. They'd dressed to match the glitz of the casinos and shared a late-night drink. Then Julie and Brett had walked barefoot on the beach in the romantic moonlight.

And spent a passionate night together after their moonlit stroll.

Julie shivered involuntarily as the remembered sensations of that night bombarded her. Her pulse leaped and her heart clamored as much as the slot machines in the casino.

Brett turned his head, and the sudden gleam flashing in his hazel eyes told her he remembered too. She felt her cheeks grow warm and looked away. She had to submerge the haunting memory of being wrapped in Brett's arms.

"You don't have to worry." She switched the subject from their trip to Atlantic City. "I'll finish with your plan. I'll meet the other people too and hear their stories."

"Thank you." Brett's voice sounded slightly surprised.

"In fact"—this was as good an opening as she was likely to get—"I'm glad I met Shannon."

"You are?" There was definite surprise in his voice.

"Yes. I—I needed to know about her and little Victoria." Julie looked back at Brett. He was staring at the road. She wished she knew what he was thinking. Should she let him know just how deeply she was affected? "I can see why you—you wanted me to know." She let her voice catch.

He didn't answer right away, just steered the car, eyes straight ahead. After a minute, he said, "You do need to know, Julie. You have to know what Warren is really like." He spoke gently.

I know exactly what he's like. And that's why I decided not to marry him.

But she hadn't known the extent of Warren's coldness. Cautiously, she added, "I—suspected—that he had another side to his character. But I didn't know..." She deliberately let her voice trail off. This was the first hint she'd given Brett so far that all was not well with her engagement to Warren. Planting a few subtle hints would, she hoped, cushion the surprise when Brett found out she had hidden the fact that her engagement was broken. She would tell him the truth soon...but she didn't know when. When the moment seemed right.

In the meantime, she really should try to enjoy the time alone with him.

Afraid he'd sense the conflicting emotions cascading through her, she focused her attention outside the window, watching the thick gray clouds scooting eastward across the sky.

They drove in silence, and after an hour, Brett pulled off the main road onto a local one. "I'm getting hungry," he told her as he followed signs for places to eat. Eventually he pulled up to a simple-looking diner. Leaving the warmth of the Jeep, they were struck by a cold wind.

The diner was bright and warm and not too crowded. They were shown a booth and given a menu. Although Julie's stomach felt empty, she didn't think she could eat much. Glancing at the menu, she saw the soup of the day was chicken and rice. It sounded comforting and ideal for the kind of day she'd just experienced.

Brett ordered a hamburger deluxe, and she ordered the soup and a grilled cheese and tomato sandwich.

While they waited for their food, Julie asked Brett about some of the local New Jersey teams and listened as he spoke about their chances in football, basketball and hockey. He asked about her classes, and Julie found herself telling him some amusing anecdotes.

It was almost as if they were old friends.

Except that she was sitting across from a devastatingly handsome man—a man she still felt irresistibly drawn to.

A man who had once been her lover, who had known her intimately.

The waitress, a young woman, returned with their food. She openly admired Brett as she served them, making Julie more conscious than ever of Brett's masculine appeal.

Julie's soup was warm and delicious and just as comforting as she'd hoped. She felt some of the tension ease out of her as she ate.

They spoke little during the meal, but Julie felt better when she was finished. She was too full to eat dessert, but Brett managed a piece of lemon meringue pie as she sipped coffee and tasted a bite of the pie. They talked sporadically as they finished, and Julie noted that Brett kept to noncontroversial topics like her students, the workshop she'd attended, and his job, which she found as fascinating as he did.

"We just picked up another New Jersey minor league baseball team to represent," he told her.

After a moment, he looked at her. "I've been wondering..."

"Yes?"

"I was kind of surprised to see you living in a

66

small apartment. I thought you'd be in a bigger or fancier place, a condo maybe."

Julie raised her eyebrows, slightly amused. "Because my family has money? My parents actually offered to help me buy something," she told him, seeing the slight flush on his face. "But I—I wanted to be out on my own for a while, make my own way before I did anything like asking for their help. I guess I just want to be independent," she finished.

She saw a look of puzzlement cross Brett's face; then it disappeared.

It seemed that all too soon they were leaving the restaurant. The air outside had grown even colder while they were inside, and damp as well. The chill wind bit through her.

Brett flipped on the radio, and cool jazz surrounded them as they drove back to the parkway in the dark, mostly silent now, and then northward. Julie tried to think of nothing more than the moment as she sat beside Brett. Rain began to splatter the windshield and became steadier. Brett slowed the car's pace when the rain turned to sleet as they drove farther north.

It was just after eight thirty when he turned onto a different highway, then drove for a few minutes before pulling into the parking lot of a large hotel.

"You were right about the weather," he said as he turned off the car. Sleet struck them as they emerged from the car, and they hurried into the hotel, Brett carrying their suitcases.

The lobby was wide and brilliantly lit. A banner proclaimed, "Welcome Northern N J Association of Accountants." Julie lounged on a sofa while Brett checked them in. She caught sight of the hotel's store, which held a large magazine and newspaper stand.

Brett returned, and Julie pointed to the store.

"Can we stop there? I'm all out of reading material."

"Sure. I had our suitcases sent up."

The store was as brightly lit as the lobby, with soothing classical music pouring from hidden speakers.

Julie moved to the magazine stand, Brett following close behind. She began scanning the headlines of some popular women's magazines, and Brett moved several feet away, standing before the sports section.

He quickly began perusing the magazines and, picking up a basketball periodical, he flipped through the pages. Julie studied his face. For the first time all day, he appeared relaxed, no longer tense, just absorbed in looking at the magazine. He closed it, put it back, and took out another.

She supposed if she was inclined to try and escape, this might be the perfect time to sneak out, run to the ladies' room, and hide.

But she didn't move. She was determined to go through with Brett's preposterous plan, despite her mixed emotions and Kendra's warnings.

And now his plan didn't seem as ridiculous as she'd first thought. She was learning, unfortunately, things about Warren that she should have known.

And spending time with Brett…

The young woman standing behind the nearby counter snapped her gum, and the sound pierced the room. Brett looked up and caught Julie staring. She turned away, peering at the magazines in front of her.

She continued to study several magazines while Brett moved to stand slightly to her right. Her heart thumped harder as she felt his closeness. She selected the latest issue of *Cosmo*. She needed something light and fun to read.

And maybe a novel for when she was finished with the magazine. She turned toward the book display, zeroing in on the romance section. A new paperback by Heather Graham caught her eye immediately, and she picked it up eagerly. Just the thing.

She spent a few minutes glancing over other titles, then looked up to find Brett watching her closely. "Find something?" he asked.

"Yes." She held out her choices. "A magazine and a novel."

"Do you want anything else? Candy or something?"

"Just a soda," she said.

She turned toward the counter. Passing a pharmaceutical display, she noted aspirin, antacids, and a large assortment of condoms.

For a moment she couldn't stop looking at the colorful packages.

Would Brett try to seduce her while they were together these next few days?

Would she try to seduce him?

Chapter 6

Brett watched as Julie's cheeks grew rosy, and she hurried to the store's counter.

He moved to stand next to her. She averted her face.

Had she noticed the prominent display of condoms in the aisle they'd just walked through? He suspected from her reaction she had. And she was probably thinking along the same lines he was.

Once, he would have bought a couple of boxes, teasing her afterward about her embarrassed reaction.

"Do you think we're the only ones buying them?" he used to ask.

"No," she would protest, "it's just that everyone will know..."

"So? They'll be jealous, knowing I'm going to make love to my beautiful girlfriend tonight," he would respond in a low voice, and Julie would always blush.

Something tightened inside Brett at the memory, and he could have sworn that Julie was remembering, at this moment, too. Her cheeks were as pink as they used to be.

The gum-chewing clerk unfolded herself from her position propped against the wall. She moved to the register, a bored expression on her face.

"Need anything else?" the young woman asked as Julie plopped down her book, magazine, and soda.

Julie was reaching for her wallet. "No." Her voice was low.

"I'll get it." Brett already had his wallet out and

leaned over Julie to hand the clerk a couple of twenties, adding his three magazines, two granola bars and soda to Julie's choices.

"You don't have to—" Julie began.

"It's no problem." He met her eyes, and for a moment they stared at each other.

He was right. She had noticed the condoms. He was sure of it. And she was probably remembering...

Julie turned her head, looking down at the magazines he was purchasing. The clerk scanned the latest issues of *Time*, *Basketball Digest*, and *Hockey Digest*, a coke, and finally the granola bars. She punched the register, snapping her gum again.

It wasn't the first time today Brett had been pierced by recollections of making love with Julie. On the way out of Atlantic City, when they'd talked lightly of the time they'd visited the city and gambled with friends, he'd been nearly overwhelmed with memories of the passionate night that followed their visit. And he suspected, from Julie's reaction, that she'd been bombarded by memories, too.

He picked up the bag the clerk was handing him, thanked her and slipped his wallet back in his pocket.

As he turned, he couldn't help one last look at the nearby aisle holding the boxes of condoms for sale.

He wished he could buy a box right now. But daring to hope he could get Julie in his bed when she was engaged to someone else—it was futile.

And if he kept thinking about sex with Julie, he was going to go crazy.

This whole adventure was turning out to be a hundred times more difficult than he'd anticipated.

He had known it might be hard to spend all day and night with Julie, to be in close proximity to the woman he'd once loved, the woman who had ended their relationship. What he hadn't expected was the constant barrage of sweet and exciting memories of all the good times.

Especially memories of the times they'd spent in bed.

He steeled himself against the recollections. He had to concentrate on the here and now.

"C'mon," he said, and led the way to the elevators.

They were silent on the way up. Julie looked lost in thought, and Brett wondered if it was memories of him or disturbing thoughts about Warren that occupied her mind. Over dinner, she'd looked tired, and he'd suspected it wasn't only lack of sleep, but the revelations about Warren that were wearing her out.

They reached the sixth floor and Brett led the way to their room. He slid the electronic key into the box, opening the door when the light blinked green. Their suitcases were already inside, and he held the door for Julie.

She hesitated.

"You got us *one* room?" Her voice squeaked as she entered and regarded the two queen-sized beds.

"Yes." He said it in a matter-of-fact voice. "This was the only room left on the non-smoking floors. There's a conference here." Did he imagine the accusing look in her eyes?

"And you wanted to keep an eye on me," she said. "I told you I would see this plan through. I'm not going to run away."

Oddly, he believed her.

Was he being too trusting? "You don't have to worry." His voice came out gruffer than he'd intended. "I won't try anything."

Something flashed across her face—flashed and then was gone.

"I wasn't implying you would." Her tone was clipped. She entered the room, and he shut and latched the door behind her.

"Who will we be seeing tomorrow?" she asked. He saw her hesitate again, then move to place her purse on the bed closest to the door. She sat on it and looked up at him.

Her eyes were wide, and the expression she wore was innocent. Almost trusting.

"Arnold Fredericks." Brett sat on the other bed and faced her.

This was going to be difficult, really difficult. Now they would not be separated by a couple of walls. They were going to spend the night in the same room, in close proximity.

He had said he wouldn't try anything.

But it wasn't going to be easy.

"Arnold was a kind of business partner of Warren's," he continued, deliberately turning his thoughts away from Julie and toward Warren and his shady past.

"What kind?"

Brett leaned back on his elbow. "The kind who ended up in jail."

"*Jail?*"

"Yeah." He didn't want to tell her too much, wanted Arnold to present the dark facts of his partnership with that stupid Warren.

"Is he—is he in jail now?"

"Yes. That's where we're going to see him tomorrow."

"Why?" Her fingers gripped the bedspread, bunching the dark green material.

Brett leaned back. "I'd rather have Arnold explain that."

He wondered if Julie would protest. Or if she would refuse to go. He was fully aware that most women would be reluctant to visit someone in prison.

He heard her suck in her breath, then exhale

slowly.

"Okay," she said. She glanced down at her hand, then released the material and smoothed it with her slender fingers. The diamond flashed. "How did you find Arnold? And Shannon?"

"A little detective work," he said. When she stared at him, he added, "I did some checking on Warren. It wasn't that difficult to unearth these people."

"But you took the time to do it." Her tone was even. She crossed her legs, and for one moment, Brett let himself savor the image of Julie, sitting on the bed. He wondered if she had any idea how appealing she looked.

"Brett?"

He started. She must have said his name more than once.

"Uh...what?" He had to stop thinking about Julie this way.

"I said, you took a lot of time to locate these people." She spoke patiently.

"Uh—yes. A detective buddy of mine helped me find Arnold. I told you, you should know what kind of guy you're engaged to," he finished.

"I'm learning." Her voice was dry.

He stared at her for a moment. Her expression revealed no traces of sarcasm or resentment. She appeared to be simply stating the facts.

"Good." Could she be having second thoughts about her engagement already? Was his plan working even more quickly than he'd hoped?

She stood up, her movement graceful. "I'm going to take a shower." She reached for her suitcase. Unzipping it, she began to go through the contents without looking at Brett.

He glanced away. Better check his messages— maybe there was one from Don with additional info on Warren. He'd check the voice mail on his cell phone, then his e-mail.

The only message on his phone was one from a coworker, updating him on some contract negotiations with a pro baseball player. He plugged in his laptop and checked his e-mail. There was a note from Don.

The note was brief.

"Warren Wesley left Wednesday AM on scheduled flight for Boston. Expected back Sunday.. Nothing unusual happening to date. Don." The message had been sent at 6:12 PM.

Brett saved the message, then exited. Snapping his laptop shut, he was conscious of the sound of water running in the bathroom.

Don't even think about it, pal.

He turned on the room's TV, as much for distraction as anything else. After flipping channels, he found a hockey game and settled on the bed to watch.

A skirmish was breaking out on the ice, and it had his full attention until the door opened and Julie left the bathroom.

Wearing his striped pajama top, her black hair still damp, she looked damned cute. No, more than cute. She looked...delectable.

His pulse rate jumped.

He swallowed. *Don't even think about it.* The phrase repeated in his head.

As if she was self-conscious, she scurried over to the bed, a trail of vanilla scent following her, climbed under the covers, and reached for her magazine. She said nothing. She opened the magazine and began to read, not even glancing at him.

Brett sipped his coke, trying to concentrate on the melee taking place on the ice as a referee attempted to separate the fighting hockey players. After a minute he glanced at Julie.

She was watching him.

As soon as she caught his eyes on her, she bent her head toward the magazine again.

Maybe she was as uncomfortable as he was.

"Is it on too loud?" Brett asked.

"No, it's fine." Her eyes remained fixed on the magazine.

He returned to watching the game, but was acutely conscious that a beautiful woman, clad in his pajama top, lay in bed only a few yards away.

Maybe he'd better take a shower. A cold one.

Should he leave her alone?

He glanced at the bed, where Julie appeared absorbed in her magazine. In pajamas, she was less likely to leave. Besides, she had told him she wouldn't run.

He stood up. "I'm getting into the shower."

She looked up then, her eyes dark. He couldn't read the expression there.

But she must have read his thoughts. "I told you, I'm not going to try to escape." She said it quietly, with dignity.

She might if she could read your thoughts, buddy.

"I didn't say you would." He met her eyes squarely.

"No, but you were thinking it, weren't you?" she asked lightly. She gave him a brief smile. "Even if I didn't want to find out the rest about Warren, I'm too tired to try to get away. In fact, I'll probably go to sleep soon."

He could use a good night's sleep himself. "I'll turn the TV off," he offered.

"It's all right, you can watch when you get out."

He showered, making the water cooler than he usually did, telling himself he was too tired to think about Julie sleeping nearby.

As soon as he got out of the shower, he poked his

head around the door. Julie was still in bed, reading. He toweled off rapidly, and when he walked back into the room, she was looking sleepy.

The hockey game was almost over, and he watched the final minutes, able to lose himself in the game as the team he favored won by a point. He listened to the commentator, then turned off the TV and settled under the covers to read one of the magazines he'd bought.

Without the noise from the TV, he could hear the plink of sleet striking the window, only slightly muffled by the curtains. The wind whistled. Despite the chilly weather outside, inside it was warm. An almost cozy atmosphere settled over them like a thick blanket.

Several minutes passed, and then Julie reached out and snapped off her nightstand lamp. Brett watched as she scooted further beneath the covers, pulling the blankets all the way to her chin.

Was she cold? Or using the blankets as a kind of shield? He remembered the days when she would snuggle next to him, pulling the covers up, and whisper how nice and warm he was.

He *had* to stop thinking along those lines.

"Will my light bother you?" He strove to make his voice neutral.

"No…" Her sleepy voice stirred his senses more than he cared to admit. Damn, this was difficult. Julie lay there looking so cute and sensual, and any normal man would be tempted to slide under the covers beside her. And he was only too normal where Julie was concerned. Slide right under the covers and run his hand—

"I like having the light on." It was barely a whisper. He recalled how she'd told him this morning she still used a nightlight.

"Okay. Should I leave it on all night?" Their cool, calm conversation was almost funny, especially in contrast to the warmth flowing through his veins.

"No. I know…you like to…sleep in the dark." She was almost asleep.

Something else welled up inside him then, something he couldn't quite identify.

"Goodnight, Julie." He whispered the words. "I'll leave the bathroom light on and the door cracked open."

"G'night." Julie's words were so soft he barely caught them. She sighed.

At that moment, he recognized the feeling that tugged at his heart.

Tenderness.

Brett swallowed.

That was the last thing he wanted to feel regarding Julie.

He had once been totally in love with her, and then they'd broken up. She'd wanted some time to figure things out, to test her wings, she'd said. Time to experience a little freedom, a little excitement in her life. Adventures. She'd grown up in a fairly sheltered environment, hadn't dated much before him, and was still young. Even though she loved him, she needed some space, she'd said. Just for awhile, till she could be sure he was what she really wanted.

And he hadn't wanted to give her that time, hadn't wanted to share her with anyone or anything else. He'd forced her to choose between him and complete freedom. No in-betweens.

She'd chosen freedom.

And his heart had split in two.

And now she was engaged to Warren Wesley, a man who wasn't even good enough to hold her hand, let alone marry her, make love to her. Brett gritted his teeth. He'd discovered Julie had known Warren barely three months when they became engaged. Warren must have swept her off her feet, given her the excitement she'd craved three years ago.

And after talking to Jonathan, he'd decided that for Julie's own good—and his own peace of mind—he had to show Julie just what kind of person Warren Wesley was.

Well, now Julie was discovering the truth about Warren. He could allow himself to feel sorry for her, he told himself firmly. Feel sad that this woman was going to be disillusioned. Just as he had been disillusioned with love after Julie broke his heart.

But sympathy was all he was going to feel. He would not allow himself to experience anything else. No way.

He tore his gaze away from his former love and focused on the magazine.

It took a while, but Brett finally became absorbed in a piece about a new basketball coach. When he finished reading, he got ready to go to sleep, glancing at Julie a couple of times. She appeared deep in dreamland.

He got into bed and switched off the light.

He was afraid he would have trouble sleeping again, but he was weary enough to go to sleep almost immediately.

He slept deeply…until a cry broke through his slumber.

He sat up, instantly awake. He heard it again, a cross between a cry and a moan. Julie.

He fumbled for the lamp on the night table, finally clicking it on.

Julie lay in bed, eyes closed tightly, clutching at the cover. She was frowning. Another sound escaped her.

He stood up and crossed over to her bed. As he did, she cried out, "No!"

"Julie! Julie!" He grasped her shoulders. Her eyes flew open.

"It's okay. You were having a bad dream," Brett

said reassuringly, dropping to sit beside her on the bed.

"Oh! I—I—" She stared at him for a moment, as if she was disoriented. "Brett..." Her wide, frightened eyes made her look vulnerable.

"I'm right here." Without thinking, he put an arm firmly around her and pulled her against his chest, sliding down to hold her.

Her breathing was rapid as she shivered next to him. She clutched the baseball T-shirt he wore as a pajama top and burrowed her head into his chest.

"Shh," he soothed, stroking her satiny hair. "It's okay."

They lay like that for a few minutes. Gradually Julie's breathing slowed and became more even, and her trembling ceased.

"I'm sorry I woke you." Her voice was small.

"Don't worry about it." He continued to stroke her hair.

"It was—the same nightmare I used to have."

He knew which nightmare she was talking about. She had had the nightmare several times when she was sleeping with him. She had described it to him the first time he'd witnessed it, how she sometimes dreamed about monsters chasing her down a dark road. She'd had the nightmare since she was a child and her father had been killed in the car accident. She'd told him she had it less frequently as she got older, usually only when she was upset or stressed. But when it occurred, it always seemed vividly real to her.

"It's gone now," he told her, still holding her close. It felt wonderful to feel her clinging to him, and for several minutes, Brett simply enjoyed the embrace.

Then Julie pulled away. "Thank you." She looked up at him. With her eyes dark and wide, her hair tousled and the scent of vanilla still clinging to her, she looked young, innocent and much too appealing.

This was no good. He shouldn't be so close to her. Brett stood up.

"Go back to sleep," he ordered. A glance at the digital clock told him it was just after two AM. He bent and tucked one of the blankets around Julie, then moved back to his bed, switching off the light. He opened the bathroom door further so more light came from there.

"Thank you..." she murmured again.

He listened to her breathing grow slower and deeper. She seemed to fall asleep fairly quickly.

It took him longer this time to return to sleep. He kept reliving the feel of Julie, warm and soft and clinging, held against his heart.

****

Julie felt some apprehension as they drove toward the prison to see Arnold Fredericks.

Over breakfast at the hotel, Brett had assured her that it was a minimum security prison, filled with more white-collar criminals than with hardened types.

"People who were caught embezzling, tax fraud—that sort of thing," he'd said. "This isn't where they incarcerate murderers." He'd dug into his stack of pancakes. "I wouldn't take you to that type of place," he'd finished.

Julie had felt a little better, and managed to eat a decent breakfast and drink surprisingly good coffee.

She'd slept well, except for the nightmare she'd had during the night. She could still recall the feel of Brett's comforting arms around her, his warmth as he held her and soothed her from the frightening dream she'd had since childhood. Part of her, she admitted to herself, had wanted Brett to stay right there for the rest of the night. Being held against his

81

warm body had been not only comforting, but a vivid reminder of the times—too many to count—she'd found heaven in his arms.

When she'd met Brett, she'd been only nineteen, and though she'd had several boyfriends, she'd been inexperienced. When they'd finally made love, Brett had been patient and tender. It hadn't taken long before she was as eager as he was. Their nights together had always been both passionate and loving. Brett was a wonderful and thoughtful lover, and she'd felt ecstasy when she was with him.

And she'd known, last night, that if she succumbed to the temptation to seduce him, she'd feel it again.

But this wasn't the time. She'd known that for sure. Brett thought she was still engaged, and was generally suspicious about her. She had hurt him deeply three years ago. And though she might regret that now, she wasn't sure if she was ready for another relationship with Brett.

Although she'd been thinking about it for weeks.

It was no surprise she'd had the dream last night. She had it periodically when she was upset. And the last two days had certainly left her in turmoil. Besides the soul-searching and the break-up with Warren, she was uneasy about Brett's scheme, torn by feelings of attraction and suspicion toward him—and guilt that she was keeping her engagement's end a secret.

She had to tell him soon.

But she wanted to meet these people he'd lined up, hear what he felt was so important from each person.

And spend time with Brett, a little voice whispered through her mind.

Still, she wasn't thrilled about visiting a jail. To get her mind off of it, she decided to bring up a different topic. "What are we doing this afternoon?"

she asked casually.

"This afternoon? After visiting Arnold?" Brett frowned. "I hadn't thought about it, really. We won't be visiting Felicia till tomorrow."

"Was she another girlfriend of Warren's?"

"Yeah." He briefly glanced her way.

"Oh. Well…" Julie decided to take the plunge. "I need to do some shopping."

"Shopping?" He made it sound like she had just suggested skydiving.

"Yes. I planned to get a dress today—for Warren's party on Sunday. It won't take me long to find one," she added, knowing that Brett, like so many men, didn't like spending a lot of time in malls. "We can just go to the nearest mall—or if we're heading back home, to Rockaway."

He looked dubious.

"Please," she said. "While I'm there, I can get pajamas and—" She was about to add that she planned to start her holiday shopping, but shut her mouth. She'd better just leave it as a quick shopping trip.

"I guess we could," Brett agreed, though without enthusiasm.

"Thank you." Julie gave him a big smile.

They fell silent. After a few minutes, Julie turned to watch the road.

The day was cold again, and gray. Puddles dotted the road and bare-branched trees dripped from last night's rain and sleet, but no precipitation fell from the sky now. Julie didn't mind a gray day. She enjoyed the contrast in the weather, but she knew most people would label today's weather bleak.

That term applied to the prison atmosphere, she decided half an hour later as they walked down a once-white hall. Even before she saw Arnold, the stark walls and chipped gray linoleum floor seemed to echo a feeling of gloom. She caught a faint whiff of disinfectant as they walked. The whole building held an air of something… Julie tilted her head, feeling it seep through her.

Hopelessness, she decided. An atmosphere of hopelessness as thick as today's clouds.

They sat at a battered table, and a security guard brought in Arnold Fredericks.

He was short for a man—no taller than Julie's mom, who was five five. With a slight build, even the fact that he had some weight around his middle didn't hide his weak-looking appearance. He had medium-brown, wavy hair, medium-brown eyes and a small mouth with thin lips.

Arnold sat down opposite Julie.

"This is Julie," Brett said tersely. Evidently they had discussed her before.

"Hi, Julie." Arnold didn't smile, just looked her over carefully. "You look like someone Warren would go for."

"What do you mean?" Julie asked.

"Good looking, well dressed." Arnold shrugged.

Julie glanced down at her simple light blue sweater and black jeans. She had wanted to look attractive but casual while she was with Brett.

"Thank you," she replied.

"And classier than some of the chicks he's gone for," Arnold continued.

Brett interrupted. "Why don't you tell Julie something about yourself, and how you know Warren? And everything you told me when I saw you a couple of weeks ago?"

"Huh. Warren. That—" He mumbled an obscene word. Brett made a movement, and he added, "Sorry. I know she's a lady." He turned his full attention on Julie. "But it's true. Warren is a real jerk. It's his fault I'm here."

Julie had been expecting something like this. Arnold appeared to be a whiner. "It is?"

"It sure is." Arnold grimaced, and his voice became even more petulant. "It's his fault."

"How do you know Warren?" If she didn't steer Arnold back to the reason they were here, she had a feeling he'd spend all his time complaining.

"I grew up two blocks from where he lived," Arnold said. "His mom is like a third cousin of my mom's, so they used to see each other pretty often. I'm six years older. We didn't really hang out together much when we were kids."

He stopped. "When I got—when I dropped out of college, Warren's father helped me get a job with one of his friends who owned an appliance store. It was boring, I couldn't stand it, so I quit." He shrugged. "I had a couple of other jobs—my father was on my case to work if I wasn't going to finish school. He could have supported me, helped me get a better job." He made a face. "I had a couple of different jobs...my dad didn't have as much money as Warren's dad—he was loaded—but I was an only child and he could have done better by me. He was always telling my mother I was lazy. She stuck up for me at least."

"You must have felt resentful," Julie said carefully, wondering what this was leading to.

"Yeah. That's it. Sometimes Warren and I would get together, drink or smoke a few joints and complain about our fathers. Sometimes we'd pick up girls." Another shrug. "We got along good in those days."

This was the first that Julie had ever heard of Warren resenting his father. Warren usually praised John Wesley as a good role model, an outstanding citizen and pillar of the community. It was the first she'd heard of Warren smoking, too. Warren, with the squeaky-clean image?

"Go on," Julie said when Arnold paused.

"Well, I got this idea for a business—boat

accessories. I liked to go out on boats. So did Warren. I talked my father into helping me start a store. It did pretty good at first. Warren sent me some of his rich friends as customers. But then he was away at college, and some of them stopped coming around." The whining note re-entered his voice. "We had a long winter that year, and when Warren finished his semester he wasn't around much. He was so wrapped up in that chick, Kyla."

Julie had heard about Kyla from Warren. His first love, he'd told her, who'd dumped him after a year to move in with a wealthy plastic surgeon.

"A lot of Warren's friends weren't buying from me anymore," Arnold continued. "Finally, the store went under."

Julie wondered if Arnold's personality had anything to do with the failure of the store.

"Then what did you do?" she asked.

"Uh…yeah. That's when I got the great idea to start a magazine," he said. "I had taken a couple of journalism classes when I was in college, so I figured it would be a piece of cake. I got my father to invest in it. I tried to get Warren to be a sales rep—people really liked him, you know, they looked up to him."

"I know what you mean," Julie said. "Warren can be Mr. Personality when he lays on the charm."

"Yeah, yeah, that's it. But he wanted to finish college, and spend time with Kyla, so I had to get someone else." Again, she heard the whining note. "It was a good magazine—great, really. It was all about boating in New Jersey, New York and Connecticut. But we couldn't get enough ads to keep it going." He shook his head, frowning. "We had to fold after a year. My father said he didn't want to pour any more money into it."

Julie sensed that Arnold was leading up to something, so she sat quietly, regarding him.

"I took a couple of jobs, got married, then

convinced my father to try to open a deli. I think he felt sorry for me 'cause my first wife left me after six months. Anyway, we got off to a good start, then went into a slump. My father said we were going under. I knew we could make money if we just went a little longer! But there was no convincing him." Bitterness coated Arnold's voice.

So he was out of work again, and his father was probably out a lot of money. Julie glanced over at Brett. His face was impassive. He must have heard all this before.

"What did you do then?" she asked, leaning forward.

"I tried a couple more different jobs. I got married again. Then my father died, and after two years Mona—my wife—took off." Arnold scowled. "I didn't know what to do. My mom said I should start a restaurant, since I liked the deli business. I asked Warren what he thought." His expression darkened. "He thought it was a great idea, he said. He helped me—invested in the business too. That was four years ago. I started a Continental restaurant, it was real nice, kind of...classy. Warren was—he called himself a silent partner. Said he and his father wanted to invest in it but keep out of the day-to-day business. He thought this was the best business for me, that it was a great idea—" Arnold broke off, twisting his mouth. "Great idea—hah! Even then he was probably making his plans."

"Making his plans—for what?" Julie had a sinking feeling in her middle.

"We started having some problems. Money problems. And then the restaurant burned down."

"It burned?" questioned Julie. "Totally?"

"Yeah." Arnold leaned forward suddenly. His eyes blazed with a fierce light, just like the fire he was describing, as they met Julie's. "And Warren started the fire."

Chapter 7

Brett watched as Julie sat back and exhaled loudly.

"Warren started the fire?" He heard the incredulous note in her voice.

He had no trouble believing Arnold. But maybe Julie did.

"Yeah, he did." Arnold's voice rose. "*And left me to take the blame.*"

Julie blinked, but she didn't recoil or show fear. Once again Brett found himself admiring the woman he'd once cared for so deeply. She was taking this astonishing news well.

"Tell me what happened," she said calmly, looking straight at Arnold.

"Not much to tell." Arnold sat back, his face still wearing a dark scowl. "We were having a few problems, and then late one night, the place went up in smoke. They investigated and said someone started a fire.

"At first I thought it was one of the cooks or waiters," he continued. "I threatened to fire a couple of them for goofing off. I was real upset—this was the business that was sure to make me rich. Then the police started asking me questions—me! As if I would—they found that some money was missing, and started pointing fingers at me. They thought I was embezzling!" He leaned forward again, and Brett could see the rage overtaking Arnold's face. "They arrested me for arson. I ended up here, and Wonder Boy goes free." The resentment in his voice was as thick as the smoke in the fire must have been.

"How do you know—" Julie began.

"I know," he interrupted. "I *know* Warren started that fire."

"But—"

"They had proof someone started it!" he declared. "And proof someone was taking money from the business. I—I used to take a little here and there, to pay my bills, but not that much! And I was going to pay it back, I swear! As soon as we started to do better!"

Brett watched as Julie gazed at Arnold, a mixture of sympathy and—could it be horror?—on her face. He hoped she was horrified by Warren's behavior.

The interview with Arnold was also confirming what he'd observed when Julie met Shannon. Julie still had a soft heart.

He sure hoped she would harden it when it came to Warren.

Arnold looked away, toward the blank wall, and seemed to attempt to calm down as Julie spoke soothingly.

"It's okay, Arnold. I believe you," she said softly.

He looked back at her.

"So…you were found guilty…although you didn't set the fire," she continued in a matter-of-fact voice.

"Yeah. Your boyfriend took the stand and testified against me," Arnold said. The extreme bitterness in his tone sliced through the air. Arnold seemed to grow more resentful with every word.

"He told them—" He stopped.

"Yes?"

"He told them…that I had a gambling habit." Arnold almost hissed as he said it. "It wasn't true. I gambled sometimes, it wasn't a habit, and I was going to pay back the business, I swear!"

Julie sat back, and Brett observed the concern

on her face. He suspected she shared his own pity for Arnold. It was obvious that Arnold was irresponsible, constantly blaming others for his own problems. But it was equally obvious, to him at least, that Warren had taken advantage of his weak cousin's character traits to manipulate him, and to try to recoup some of the losses in the business venture.

"I believe you." Julie's voice was breathless, strained. Brett turned and studied her. Yes, there was sympathy in her expression. "That was— terrible of Warren. Even if he didn't set the fire, to watch you go to jail—"

"He did set it." Arnold's words were firm. He propped his arms on the table, leaning forward again.

"And one of these days he's going to pay. He's going to pay for what he did. I'll get even."

Julie flinched visibly. She glanced over at Brett, then turned back to Arnold.

"What goes around comes around," she said, her tone surprisingly gentle. "I'm sure Warren will get what's coming to him, eventually."

A feeling of relief bubbled up in Brett. She did believe Warren was guilty.

She looked at Brett again. He could feel her uncertainty.

"Julie's right," he added. Standing, he moved behind her and placed a reassuring hand on her shoulder. That vanilla cologne she wore floated up to him, a welcome scent in the stale room. He felt a tremor go through her. She was hiding her tension from Arnold, but her uneasiness was there, beneath the surface.

He kneaded her shoulder reassuringly. "Warren will get what's due him eventually." *Like losing his fiancée*, he hoped. Between Arnold's pitiful story and Shannon's tragic situation, Julie must be having second thoughts by now. She had to be.

Julie's hand came up and touched his where it rested on her shoulder. Her hand was ice cold, and he covered it with his warm one.

He could feel another tremor go through her.

Arnold's expression was dark and grim. "Yeah, he will," he said. "He'll get what's coming." He bent forward and dropped his voice.

"Sooner than you think."

****

They stopped for lunch at a chain restaurant. While Julie went to the ladies' room, Brett called his friend Don from his cell phone.

It occurred to him as he listened to the ringing that he hadn't seen Julie use a cell phone. Was she communicating with Warren right now? How come Warren hadn't called her a hundred times in the last few days? Or had her phone been off?

If Julie was his fiancée, he'd want to know where she was.

Julie had said almost nothing during their twenty-minute ride here, except that she felt very sorry for Arnold. To Brett, she looked shaken, though not as sad as when she'd met Shannon.

Don wasn't in his office, but he got him on his cell phone.

"How's it going, buddy?" Don's cheerful tone greeted him.

"Actually, well," Brett admitted. "Better than I expected at first. She's really sticking with the plan."

"Good," Don said.

"Any new developments?"

"Just one," Don answered. "One of Warren's pals went to Julie's place last night, got out and knocked on the door, and walked around the house for a couple of minutes. When the neighbor looked out, he left. I think he was checking to see if Julie was there or not. I had one of my new guys tailing him—I wanted to give him some practice—and he saw the whole thing."

"Hmm." An uneasy feeling assailed Brett. "What do you think it means?"

"It could mean anything. He wanted to check on her, see if she might really be there, or he had a message for her. Maybe he wasn't sure she was really going to Atlantic City like she planned, or he thought she might be back early. I had it confirmed this morning that Warren's still in Boston. Maybe he didn't get—"

"Here she comes," Brett interrupted. "I've got to go. I'll call you later."

"Later."

Julie returned to the booth and slid in opposite Brett. Her eyes were bright, but he saw no traces of tears like he had after their conversation with Shannon.

He wanted very badly to ask her how she felt about their meeting with Arnold, how she was viewing Warren Wesley now. He searched for the right words.

"That was certainly enlightening." She reached for her soda and took a sip.

"Had you ever heard about Arnold before?" Brett asked.

She shook her head. "No. Not a word. I had no idea that Warren even had a cousin named Arnold. And he never said anything about being in the restaurant business."

"What do you think of Arnold?" That sounded safe enough. Maybe she would volunteer on her own what she was thinking about Warren if they kept talking.

Julie sighed, placing her drink down carefully. The glass clinked against the polished table. "I think Arnold is kind of pathetic. You know, one of those guys who never grew up. He kind of drifts through life, dependent on his parents—and other family members. Not taking charge of his own life, and blaming everyone else for his troubles. Never realizing that a lot of his problems are his own fault."

Brett felt his heart sinking. Was she going to believe this was all Arnold's fault? That Warren had no hand in causing the fire or in Arnold's arrest?

"He's the kind who would be easy to manipulate," Julie continued, eyes focused on her fingers as she played with a spoon. "He's weak. And Warren's sharp." She turned her face up to regard Brett. "I think it's very likely Warren used Arnold, set him up to take the blame. Even if the fire was accidental, he might have decided to take advantage of the situation. And…it's probable that it wasn't accidental, that Arnold was right. Maybe Warren arranged for the fire."

Brett exhaled, surprised to realize he'd been holding his breath. "So you do believe Arnold." *And me*, he added silently.

The waitress approached their table, placing the steak and shrimp special in front of Brett. He watched as Julie began to pick at her chicken Caesar salad. The food smelled good, and suddenly he was ravenous. He pierced a shrimp and began eating.

"Yes, I do," Julie said. She chewed thoughtfully. After a moment, she added, "Knowing Warren, he would have hired someone else to do his dirty work, not actually set the fire himself. He would want to keep his hands clean, so to speak."

Brett tried not to show outwardly that he was relieved, and very glad, that Julie was taking Arnold's side against her fiancé.

"I know Warren took quite a few accounting classes when he was in college," she continued. "He would probably know how to doctor those books without Arnold finding out."

This was news to Brett. "I didn't know that. I thought he studied political science."

"He did. But he took a lot of business and accounting courses too. He runs the family business, you know—they manage some apartment buildings and commercial properties. And he told me once that he didn't want to depend totally on politics. That he wanted to keep the family investments—they have plenty—as a cushion, and needed to know enough to maintain them properly." She took another bite of her food. "Mmm...this is pretty good."

This was looking better and better. "So you think he embezzled money, then hired someone to start the fire?"

"Yes, and let poor Arnold take the blame." She sighed loudly, and her shoulders sloped. "I wish..."

"Yeah?"

"I wish there was some way we could prove Arnold was innocent. But Warren..." She shook her head. "Warren would never admit to having anything to do with an incident like that."

"Even to you?"

"Even to me." She met Brett's eyes. "Warren never did talk about his past that much."

"Maybe because he didn't want you to know some of these things?"

"Maybe."

It was on the tip of his tongue to ask what she thought of Warren now. He opened his mouth.

"I think..." Julie set down her fork and looked squarely at him. "I think there are a lot of things about Warren that are...disturbing."

Satisfaction burst through Brett. *She's changing her thinking.* She's seeing Warren's true character. She's seeing all the evil Warren managed to hide from her.

Just as he had hoped she would!

Julie was watching him, and he wondered if any

of these glad feelings showed on his face. He tried to look nonchalant.

But she knew him too well, and he had a feeling he hadn't fooled her.

She sat back. "Do you suppose Arnold's planning something?"

"Like what?"

"Revenge." The whispered word seemed to hang on the air, and a shadow crossed her face.

He felt his emotions take a nosedive. After all this, she was still concerned about Warren.

"I don't think you have to worry. Arnold's the kind who might threaten, but I think he's basically too weak to try anything. He'll just talk about it."

"I wonder." She looked away for a moment, then turned back and stared at her salad. After a few seconds more, she said, "I had the strangest feeling when he said what he did…this creepy feeling ran through me."

Brett remembered her shiver at Arnold's menacing "sooner than you think."

"It was the way he said it," he reassured her, then repeated, "I wouldn't worry about it."

"Even weak people, like Arnold, are capable of violence if pushed hard enough," Julie said. "And I'd guess he's been plotting some kind of revenge since he went to jail."

"He can plot all he wants," Brett said. "But from his jail cell, it's doubtful he'll be able to do anything."

"That's true," Julie said. "I guess I'm worrying for nothing." She took a deep breath. "Poor Arnold. I do feel sorry for him. Warren was—well, he was awful to him."

Brett's spirits rebounded as quickly as a basketball on the court.

"I agree," he said firmly.

Julie regarded him, sipping her soda. He wished he could read her mind.

She sat back, brushing aside a lock of dark hair. "It's difficult to…learn these things about…someone you thought you knew." She said the words carefully, as if measuring them.

Was she afraid to reveal to him just how difficult it was? It didn't matter. At least she was seeing Warren in a different light.

An unflattering light.

Julie must have recognized something in Brett's expression that reflected his sudden optimism. She leaned forward, a smile spreading on her beautiful face.

"Let's finish eating so we can go shopping!"

****

The mall was unusually busy for an early Friday afternoon, packed with teenage shoppers who were free from school because of the teachers' convention. Julie pushed her way toward her favorite department store, with Brett close behind. She hadn't missed the pained expression that crossed his face when they entered the mall. But he was being a surprisingly good sport about it, and wasn't complaining—at least not out loud.

Despite the fact that it was early November, Christmas, Hanukkah and Kwanzaa decorations adorned the shops. Julie led Brett through the department store, past a large Christmas tree sparkling with gold tinsel and red ribbons, and around the corner past the shoe section where four teenage girls compared the trendy boots on display.

The petite section was quieter, and Julie moved toward the dressier clothes. She began examining cocktail dresses.

"You just need a dress, right?" Brett asked. He stood awkwardly, and Julie knew he was unused to spending time in the ladies' clothing section. Maybe he hadn't done so since they'd dated, and she'd occasionally dragged him shopping.

"Hmm..." She lifted out one blue dress, checking it over, before deciding it was too revealing. Warren wouldn't approve of the low-cut neckline, since this cocktail party was a political celebration, and he expected her to look elegant but conservative.

What a hypocrite. She'd bet any amount of money Warren appreciated it when Shannon wore sexy clothes.

But she owed Warren this much. He may have been a snake to Arnold and even worse to Shannon, but he had always treated her well. She had promised him she'd see the cocktail party through, stay at his side for appearance's sake, before quietly exiting his life. He'd probably soon have another girlfriend, she thought, pushing aside a flashy black-and-gold pants set.

She paused at a purple dress, then lifted it out and looked it over.

"That's nice."

Julie glanced at Brett. The pained expression was still there. Obviously he was hoping she'd make a quick choice.

"Yes, but I always wanted a little black cocktail dress...and I never got one. You know, there are some things you always wanted to have or to do, and..." She let her voice drift off, a memory piercing her thoughts with the suddenness of a sword.

She had always wanted to go out for dinner and dancing. And yet, in all the time she'd dated Brett, they'd never done that. When she would mention it, he'd say "one of these days we'll go." But it never happened. And she'd never had the opportunity with anyone else.

She hadn't even spoken about the idea to Warren. He took her to enough glamorous places— Broadway shows, horse races with the best seats, posh restaurants—so she hadn't told him of her secret wish.

But she had spoken of her wish to Brett, and the night she'd broken up with him, she'd reminded him of it again.

"*You never did take me for dinner and dancing,*" she'd whispered that night.

"I'll take you," he had said. But she'd thought it was too late.

"…and?" Brett's question now snapped her back to the present.

"Oh! And…and you just want the experience of doing them," she said hastily.

"Like what?" he asked, his brows furrowing.

"Like—" Julie turned to stare at the purple dress. "Like going out for dinner and dancing. Or visiting the Acropolis in Greece and Stonehenge in England. Or owning a sexy little black evening dress. I never had a dress like that," she finished, wanting to emphasize the latter, and not sound like she was complaining.

But her voice came out more wistfully than she'd intended.

Against the backdrop noise of chattering customers, Brett's silence seemed ominous. Julie glanced up at him.

His face was flushed.

It was the first time she could remember ever seeing Brett look embarrassed. Julie looked away, embarrassed herself. She shouldn't have brought it up. Old wishes and dreams—she shouldn't be remembering them. Maybe alone, in the dark—but not now. Not here, with Brett. She should never have mentioned it, she chastised herself.

"I'm sorry." She turned back to him and felt a stinging in her eyes. "I didn't mean to—to—"

To what? Bring up lost dreams? she asked herself harshly.

"—to remind you of an unpleasant experience," she finished.

"There's nothing to apologize for," Brett said, his voice rough around the edges. He reached out and touched the purple dress. "That will look nice on you."

She accepted the change of topic gladly. "I'll try it on, but I really want a sophisticated black dress." She returned to checking the dresses. Silk and velvet brushed her hands, and she let her fingers drift over the varied textures. Feeling instead of thinking.

After a moment of going through black dresses, she pulled out a short one. The style was deceptively simple, but the clingy material felt sensual to the touch. It was sleeveless, and the back had an oval opening where two bands of white satin criss-crossed.

It was exactly what she wanted. Julie sucked in her breath. "This is the kind of dress I was looking for. I have to try it on."

"Try on the purple too," Brett urged.

His face wore a neutral expression, which Julie sensed he had plastered on.

"Okay," she agreed.

She tried the purple dress first. It was flattering, slim fitting with a matching jacket and a side slit. She left the dressing room and went to show Brett.

He was waiting patiently right outside the dressing room, by a triple mirror. "That's nice," he said, sweeping her with a glance.

It would be fine for the cocktail party, Julie decided as she studied her reflection. The dress was simple and understated, except for the vibrant color. She needed a new dress to wear on special occasions and she knew she'd get a lot of use from this one.

But she loved the other dress.

She returned to the dressing room and slipped into the black dress, feeling the fabric swirl sensually around her. She turned and looked at her reflection.

It was perfect.

The dress was sexy and stylish. She felt glamorous and feminine as she twirled one way, then the other.

She exited the dressing room.

"I like this one—"

She stopped. Brett was staring at her as if she was some kind of delicious dessert and he was starving.

No, not a dessert, she thought, swallowing. Her nerves tightened, and she felt suddenly like she was in a runaway elevator, swooping upward at out-of-control speed.

Brett was looking at her with more than simple admiration. He was scrutinizing her the way a man looks at a woman he finds desirable.

She reached out and touched the mirror, searching for something solid to hold onto.

"I really like this dress—" She fought to keep her voice level.

"You look *gorgeous*." The words seemed to tumble from Brett's mouth, which had opened slightly. His tone was hoarse. He stared at her, and Julie felt her cheeks flush.

"Thank you." Her own voice sounded breathless. She looked back at her reflection. Brett stepped behind her. She could feel his warmth, and their eyes met in the mirror. Met and held.

She almost gasped when she saw the expression in Brett's eyes.

Longing.

Julie started to tremble as an answering need flooded her.

For one long moment they gazed at each other in the mirror. The air around them was charged with electricity, practically sizzling.

Never had she felt so conscious of any other

man.

"I'll—I'll get changed." She whirled suddenly and hurried back to the dressing room, her heart hammering.

She had wanted to spend time with Brett. And now, she had gotten more than she'd bargained for. She felt like the legendary Pandora, opening the forbidden box.

Was she ready to see that intense emotion in Brett's face? Was she ready for her own answering sensations?

What exactly had she unleashed?

Exactly what you'd hoped for deep inside, a little voice whispered within her. You unleashed powerful emotions in Brett. Longing. Desire.

She took off the dress carefully, trying to still her shaking fingers. She wanted to buy the dress. She wanted to wear it for Brett.

And see Brett look at her like that again.

She caught her breath. Okay, she told herself. She took one deep breath, then another, and stretched out her hands. Her initial response subsided only slightly.

She could do this. She could spend time with Brett, have him look at her the way a man looks at a woman he's attracted to. She could handle it. Maybe, even, welcome it.

She left the dressing room carrying both garments, and tried to act like her normal self.

Brett was waiting for her. His eyes were still bright. "Why don't you buy both?" he asked.

"Both?" she repeated, startled by his suggestion. She didn't really need both.

"Yes. You can wear the purple to Warren's party, and the black one another time."

"I don't know," she said. The idea was tempting, but she didn't really want to spend the money for both.

"It's my treat." Brett pulled out his wallet.

Julie's mouth dropped. "Oh, no, I couldn't—"

"I insist." He took the hangers from her, holding the dresses carefully. "It's the least I can do, after putting you through what you've gone through the last few days." He turned toward the counter where a saleswoman was handing a charge card back to another customer.

Julie scampered after him. "Brett—"

"We'll take these," he said. Julie started to remove her charge card, still protesting. "My treat," he repeated, and handed over several hundred-dollar bills.

Julie felt a moment of surprise that Brett was carrying so much cash. He had, she realized as she watched him, been paying cash for everything lately.

So he wouldn't leave a paper trail?

"Brett, I can't let you do this. I was going to buy one dress, I have the money—"

"It's done," he said tersely as the register clicked.

His face had become set, and Julie stopped. Was he trying to prove something? Something to do with owing her dinner and dancing? Maybe he was substituting the dress she'd always wanted for the evening she'd always desired?

Perhaps, Julie decided, this was not the time to argue with him. She could bring it up later.

"All right," she said meekly. She took a deep breath, and then gave him a grateful smile. "Thank you, Brett. That's very generous of you."

His expression softened. "You're welcome."

He carried the carefully wrapped dresses on one arm as they left the dress section of the store. "Need anything else?"

"I have shoes, but yes, I do need to do more shopping," Julie said. "Why don't we put these in the car so you don't have to carry them, and I'll just pick up a couple of items I need? It won't take more than half an hour," she coaxed.

"All right. But stay with me," he ordered.

They left the dresses in Brett's car, then returned to the mall. Julie spent the next few minutes in a shop that sold natural cosmetics and bath items, where she picked up more vanilla lotion and a few other things she needed. She paid cash, aware of Brett's hawk-like watch over her.

Back in the crowded mall, they plowed through throngs of shoppers, narrowly avoiding bulging bags and running preteens.

"I want to get pajamas," Julie said, leading the way to the escalator. "And a birthday gift for Jessica."

"Jessica? Are you two still close?" Brett asked as they rode upward, the cheerful noise of chattering people cushioning them.

"Mm-hm. We always have been and always will be," Julie replied.

Jessica had been her best friend since they'd hit it off in first grade. Julie's mother was married to Ted Shaw by then, and they were living in a larger home, still in Stanhope. But by the time Julie was eleven her mom and Ted decided to move to an even larger home in a wealthier area, and chose their brick colonial in Randolph. It was Elise who had pushed the idea, but Ted could easily afford to support his growing family in style. Julie had always liked Ted, but she was unhappy about moving and leaving her friends behind. Most of all, Jessica.

She had managed to stay close with Jessica, though. They'd shared sleepovers and talked on the phone. Julie did make friends in her new town, but she was never as close to any of them as she was to Jessica. They had both attended different colleges, but tried to see each other sometimes on weekends. Even after all these years, Jessica was Julie's closest friend, followed by Kendra and Lindsay, her friend from college.

"I still see Jessica pretty frequently," Julie said as she stepped off the escalator. "She lives outside Reading and teaches French there. She just got engaged to a really nice guy. And we talk and e-mail all the time. In fact, I was hoping to see her Saturday. I'll have to call her or e-mail, to tell her it won't work."

What would Jessica say about Julie's circumstances now? She'd probably be as surprised as Kendra. Jessica knew Julie had been planning to break up with Warren, and Julie had e-mailed her a long letter Tuesday night, telling her about how she'd done it, the week before Warren's election. And how she'd promised to keep it a secret till after Sunday. But she hadn't heard back from Jessica. Of course, she hadn't checked her e-mail in the last forty-eight hours. Julie guessed her friend would be supportive of her decision to spend time with Brett, since Jessica was more daring than Julie. Julie could almost hear Jessica laugh.

"Go for it."

Julie took a determined step and led Brett toward the Victoria's Secret shop.

"I want to get Jessica something from here," she said, stopping. "And I'll buy myself pajamas."

"From here?" Brett's voice held a strange note.

Julie stifled a chuckle. Brett made it sound like she was going shopping on an alien planet.

"Yes. You've been in this store before." She purposely kept her voice light. She could remember one time when they'd shopped there together, and Brett had bought her a revealing red nightgown for Valentine's Day. Just thinking about the night that followed made Julie's cheeks grow hot, and made her acutely conscious of the man beside her.

"I know. Several times, actually." His voice held

a dry note.

Julie turned her head and stared at him for a moment before facing front again.

Several times? *Of course*. She fought the wave of jealousy that swept over her. A handsome man like Brett must have had plenty of girlfriends in the three years since they'd broken up. He must have bought at least one of them something from this store.

Julie realized her nails were digging into her palms.

"Don't worry." She fought to sound unaffected. "I won't buy anything...provocative."

Brett stared at her as she said the word "provocative." She wondered if she should have even mentioned it. She smiled, but was sure it came out stiff.

"All right." His voice was a low rumble. "I'll wait out here. But don't take too long," he added.

Trying to push aside the lingering jealous feelings, Julie left Brett standing awkwardly outside the lingerie shop. Was she crazy to shop here? She could have picked up conservative flannel pajamas at one of the department stores.

But she had already decided to get something pretty from this store for her friend.

And for herself?

The music of stringed instruments wrapped around Julie as she walked into the shop. She could almost feel the melody soothing her jumpy nerves.

She was aware that Brett's patience would wear thin if she took too long. Moving farther into the store, she scanned the beautiful, sensual lingerie before approaching a display of silky nightgowns. She let her fingers glide over the smooth material and selected a dark blue for Jessica. Perfect.

It took her a few minutes longer to find something for herself. Nothing too provocative, she had promised Brett, and she didn't want to give him the wrong idea. She didn't want him to think she was trying to seduce him.

Although for just a moment, she could picture—

She squashed the image.

No.

She looked at one display, then another, conscious that time was running out. She caught a glimpse of satin nightshirts on a rack and hurried over to examine them.

The style was plain. They were simple, long-sleeved nightshirts, but the satin fabric was cool and smooth and seductive as she stroked it.

Julie cocked her head. The nightshirts seemed to be a good compromise between wild lingerie and old-fashioned nightwear. She selected an emerald green one. It was her size, and she proceeded to the counter, pleased that she'd taken less than ten minutes to choose both items. At the last minute, she remembered she needed a bra for the new black dress and scrambled to get the right one.

A glance told her Brett was still waiting outside. He was staring off into space.

Right by the counter was a display of the store's own brand of perfumes. Julie bent forward to try one. The romantic scent engulfed her, and on impulse, she added a box of cologne to her purchases.

"Did you find everything you need?" a slender, stylish blonde woman dressed all in black asked her.

"Yes." Julie smiled.

She dug into her purse and took out her Visa card. She didn't want to use up all her cash, so she charged her purchases.

As the salesgirl handed the charge back to Julie, she saw Brett striding toward her.

"I'll pay for those," he said as he reached her side.

"I already did."

He had his wallet out, and was again sifting through bills. "No, it's all right—"

She'd been right. Brett really didn't want her charging anything. She took the package from the salesgirl.

Was he afraid she'd leave a record of where she'd been? He hadn't minded her paying cash at the bath shop, so that must be it. She tilted her head to look up at him.

"You shouldn't have to pay for Jessica's present," she said. "And you've bought me enough already. It's all right. I took care of it."

"Did you—"

Julie slipped her hand into his. "C'mon, let's go." She wanted to avoid any arguments about who was paying for what. She led the way out of the store and back into the crowded mall.

"Do you need anything while we're shopping?" she asked, raising her voice above the din of talkative shoppers. Loud rock music blared from a nearby store.

Brett hesitated. "Well...I do need a new pair of sneakers. I play basketball in the winter with some guys from the condo association."

"I'll help you," Julie said eagerly. "There's a good sneaker place this way." She pointed toward the end of the corridor.

They started down the wide hallway, brushing past a mother with a double stroller and two wide-eyed babies. Her hand remained in Brett's, and a delicious little thrill rode up her spine.

The aroma of fresh coffee struck Julie as they neared the mall's center and looked down to see a gourmet coffee shop. She glanced longingly at the small store downstairs, chock full of colorful mugs and bags of coffee beans.

Brett must have guessed her thoughts, because

he asked instantly, "Do you want a cup?"

"I'd love some," Julie admitted.

"I know you like your afternoon coffee," Brett said.

They rode the escalator downstairs, then lined up behind four other people, but the store had a number of employees behind the counter and the line advanced quickly. Brett let go of her hand and removed his wallet before Julie could take out her own. "What flavor do you want?"

Julie checked the day's specials that were written on a blackboard. "Hazelnut sounds good."

Brett ordered hazelnut coffee, light, with Sweet and Low for Julie, and regular with milk and sugar for himself.

"You remembered." She met his eyes. Amazing, that Brett still remembered her favorite way to drink coffee.

"Of course." A flash of green light appeared in his hazel eyes. He handed the employee several singles. "Want anything to eat?"

Julie shook her head, accepting the cup eagerly. She'd missed her regular cup of coffee yesterday, and she intended to savor this one.

"Let's see if we can find a place to sit," Brett suggested.

"There's usually room around the fountain."

They held their coffee cups carefully and squeezed in between two groups of teenagers showing off their purchases. The pleasant splashing of the fountain provided backdrop music as they sat.

"Did you see what I found on sale?" one girl was enthusiastically asking another who perched beside Julie.

Julie tried to observe Brett without staring as he drank from his thick paper cup. He was turning out to be as kind and considerate as she remembered, despite the gruff outer appearance he'd often displayed the last three days. She wondered if he was deliberately covering up his softer side.

Julie sipped the coffee. It was delicious, and the sweet brew slid down her throat. Between the rich aroma and the warm feeling inside, Julie found herself truly relaxing for the first time in days. Or was it because Brett himself seemed more at ease?

He turned his head slightly and met her eyes. For just a moment, the noise of the crowded mall receded and Julie felt as if she and Brett were alone on their own island. Just her. And Brett. With the splashing water contributing its music behind them. One man and one woman.

He blinked, and Julie snapped back to reality.

"You still like to go shopping, don't you?" His tone was that of someone perplexed.

"I think shopping's fun," Julie said. "Once I'm in the mall, I usually stay for a while. You don't?"

"Depends what I'm shopping for." He gave her a sudden smile, boyish and endearing, and Julie was reminded again of the guy she'd fallen in love with long ago. "Sports equipment, CDs...those are fun."

"Talking about sports stuff..." Julie took another gulp. "I know you want to get those sneakers." She could have remained here happily for many minutes. But she knew Brett would soon be impatient to complete their shopping.

"Yeah, let's go." In one smooth motion Brett stood up, towering over her.

Julie finished her coffee, and they walked past a junior clothing store and a crowded McDonald's. Julie paused for a few seconds to inhale the spicy scents coming from a candle shop, then continued, walking rapidly to keep up with Brett's long strides.

They took the escalator up to the sneaker store Brett wanted to investigate first.

He found a pair he liked almost at once, though they had to wait for help getting his size. When he had tried on the correct sneakers and pronounced them perfect, Brett paid cash again.

They wandered back through the mall. It was almost as if they were a couple, out for an afternoon's shopping trip. For the first time they were quietly at ease with each other. Bombarded by the sounds of people talking and laughing, the heat from lots of bodies and the atmosphere of hustle and bustle, they walked back toward the center of the mall.

She wished they could stay like this, quietly content.

She glanced at Brett. His profile was relaxed. He almost looked like he was enjoying himself.

She knew she was. Right now, she felt happy. Happier than she had in a long time.

She was with Brett Ryerson, and she was glad!

Aside from the fact that she was with Brett under highly unusual circumstances, there was nothing exciting going on. They were doing a routine shopping trip, on a rather normal day. There was nothing about their location, or their activity, that anyone could call unique or glamorous.

But she was happy anyway.

She tilted her head to study Brett again. *I don't need excitement. I'm happy being with you.* She knew it with a sudden, distinct clarity, a knowledge that went down deep into her bones. And her heart.

She'd told him when they'd broken up that she still cared. But she wasn't ready for a commitment. "I need to spread my wings, have some excitement in my life, maybe some adventures," she'd said.

And she'd found that excitement, at first, with Warren.

But it had quickly worn thin. And she hadn't stayed happy.

Yet here she was, in a mundane place with Brett, and she was suddenly very happy.

She wanted to say something to Brett. Something to indicate her contentment. She opened her mouth. "Brett..." But she was at a loss. How could she tell him how happy she was without revealing that she'd lied about her engagement?

"Yeah?" Brett turned to her.

"I—" she began. "I'm having a good time." She smiled up at him. She'd *have* to tell him, soon.

He looked surprised. "You are?"

"Yes."

He gazed at her, his expression thoughtful.

She wanted to put her hand in his. Before she could give in to temptation, something caught Brett's eye beyond her. His expression changed to one of shock.

They were nearing the lingerie store again. Brett froze, and Julie stopped beside him. His surprised look rapidly changed to one of concern.

"Turn around slowly." His voice was quietly calm but firm. "We're going back the way we came. Don't move too fast. We don't want to attract attention."

"What...?" Julie looked to where Brett's gaze had been fixed seconds before.

With a start, she saw he was looking at a heavyset man with black, curly hair who stood only a few yards away. The man was turned away from the store, looking down the main corridor, and was speaking into a cell phone.

She recognized the man. It was Juan Comacho, a friend of Warren's. Warren had told her he'd hired him as a bodyguard for a couple of political rallies, and they'd become friendly after that. Beside him stood another, shorter man, whom Julie didn't recognize.

Brett grabbed her arm and tugged. "C'mon." His low voice held an urgent note.

He pulled her down the hall.

"What? Brett, I—"

"Hurry." He was pulling her faster now, and she caught a tone in his voice she hadn't heard before. Anxiety?

They passed a large group of teenage girls, went around two mothers standing with strollers face-to-face, and almost collided with a boy with wild orange hair who had his arm around a girl dressed in a black-and-purple goth outfit.

"What's the matter?" She was almost running to keep up with Brett's long strides.

"Let's get out of here." He pulled her toward the escalator.

"Why? Brett, what's wrong?"

"That was one of Warren's henchmen. I'll tell you later. Just stay with me," he commanded. "We're going to try an evasive maneuver."

They rode the smaller escalator. Julie was certain Brett would have run down the moving steps if they weren't blocked by other shoppers. The minute they reached the ground floor, Brett stepped off and pulled Julie with him.

Her shopping bags slapped her thigh. He pulled her along, back past the McDonald's, where the smell of French fries steamed out to hit them. A young girl screeched, "Hey, Mandy!" close behind Julie. They passed the coffee shop, with its rich aromas. Julie could still taste the hazelnut flavor. The sound of water splashing in the fountain reached her, and as they passed, a young boy threw in a handful of change. Spray spattered, touching her face.

"Hurry. He might see us from upstairs. Don't look up," Brett ordered.

"But why?"

Julie was confused. Why would Brett be running from Warren's pal? Why was he so reluctant to have Julie see Juan? How did he know him, anyway?

She heard someone shout, but in the crowded mall she couldn't tell where it was coming from. And then, "*Vamos! Vamos!*" This time, she knew the yells in Spanish came from the second floor.

Brett swore. "C'mon!" He pulled Julie at a run, rushing through the throng of shoppers. The kiosk with Christmas ornaments passed in a blur. Julie's heart pumped as she ran to keep up with Brett's long legs. No time to ask questions now. But a bad feeling swept through her, fueled by Brett's obvious concern.

Julie almost ran into a mother holding a toddler. "Sorry!"

Brett glanced at her as he tugged her along, but said nothing.

She hurried, the bag hitting her again, till they reached the department store—which they practically raced through. She was breathless when they reached the exit.

Brett pushed the outer doors open. Cold air whipped at them, cooling Julie's warm cheeks instantly.

"What—" she began.

"Keep going." It was an order. With Julie in tow, he dashed for his Jeep.

Brett's car was two-thirds down the row, and she scrambled to keep up with him. Once he reached it, he opened the doors and threw their packages in the back. "Get in."

Julie obeyed.

He started the car and backed out faster than usual, while she was still buckling her seatbelt. There was a lot of traffic, but he wove in and out, heading for a side exit from the mall.

Instead of going toward Route 80, Brett took a county road toward Route 46.

Julie was still trying to catch her breath. "Tell me—what that—was all about."

Brett's expression was grim. He signaled and passed a slower car.

"I saw at least two of Warren's henchmen. I think they were looking for us." His words were terse, his mouth set in a tight line.

"Two of—what do you mean, Warren's henchmen? And why would they be—"

"The big guy was Juan Comacho. There was at least one other guy with him."

"So? And what do you mean by Warren's henchmen?" Julie demanded. The fear that Brett had sparked with their flight was being replaced by anger.

"I mean..." Brett steered down a hill. "Guys who work for Warren, doing everything from paying people off to covering up his dirty little secrets—like Shannon. Maybe one of those guys set the fire at Arnold's restaurant. They do all the nasty jobs for him."

"Even if they work for him," Julie said, "why drag me out of the mall like that? So what if they knew we were there? They have a right to go shopping. I've met Juan."

"You have?"

"Yes. And I..." She hesitated. "I admit, I thought Warren hired him as a bodyguard, and then they got friendly. I was even proud of Warren for becoming friends with Juan," she said reflectively.

"Proud?"

"Yes. Because he finally was making friends with someone from a different ethnic group," Julie finished. She had really hoped that Warren was coming out of his sheltered cocoon, getting to know different types of people.

"Ha! Friends. He was paying Juan to do different jobs," Brett stated. "You really are still naïve. People like Warren Wesley don't become friends with Juan. They use them or pay them for their services."

Naïve? Julie bent her head. *Not as naïve as you think.* "I may have been naïve about their relationship," she admitted slowly. "It may be that Juan does Warren's dirty work. But why on earth did you rush me out of there when you saw him? What do you mean, he was looking for us?"

"I mean..." Brett turned the car onto Route 46 and headed east. "I believe Warren sent them to look for us. For you, that is," he amended. "Did you see them looking around, carrying those cell phones? I think Warren is trying to find you. And I don't want that to happen."

"Why would—" Julie stopped.

Brett didn't know she had ended her engagement. Clearly, he was under the impression that Warren was searching for her.

She wanted to tell him then, tell him everything. But he was already upset, and she decided that while he was driving was no time to tell him the truth. She would explain later, when he was calmer and they were sitting down.

And hope he would understand.

In the meantime, she tried to reassure him.

"We weren't going to speak while he was in Boston," she said quietly. That much, at least, was the truth. "He knew I'd be running around here and there, at the convention, and seeing friends. I told him I'd see him at the party Sunday."

"Well, he must have changed his mind. He was worried about you and wanted his buddies to find you. What I don't get," he continued, "was how they knew you were at the mall. Did you—"

"I doubt if he'd change his mind," Julie said. "We—agreed—we'd speak on Sunday," she reiterated.

Brett was silent for a long time. His car slowed as he approached a red light. Julie turned slightly, regarding his profile. His mouth was set. There was no mistaking the worried look on his face.

At the light, he turned to meet her gaze. And looked away immediately.

Something about his expression made Julie's stomach tighten. There was something in his eyes...

"Is there something you're not telling me?" she asked.

"Why do you think that?"

It was the defensive tone of his voice that alerted Julie. He felt guilty about something, and she'd bet it wasn't the fact that he'd "borrowed" her. Something else was eating at him.

"Brett, tell me what's bothering you." She said it quietly, hoping her firm but soothing tone would get him to open up.

He glanced at her again, then sighed.

"I might as well tell you. I e-mailed Warren."

"And...?" Julie asked, tensing.

"I told him you'd be out of touch for a few days. I pretended the note was from you, and signed your name."

Julie went rigid.

"You sent him an e-mail from *me*?"

Chapter 8

"Yes." Brett shifted in his seat.

Julie stared at him, her thoughts racing. "How did—"

"I didn't know his private e-mail, so I sent it to his Web page," Brett said. "In fact, I had a friend send the note from a public library in Essex County, so he couldn't trace it back to me." He glanced at her again, then moved the car forward when the light changed. "He's a computer geek and he logged on with your school e-mail address."

Julie found her fingers were shaking, and she entwined them in her lap. "Warren must have guessed it was a fake. He knows I wouldn't do that. What did the note—say?"

"Dear Warren," he quoted, "I won't have a chance to write for a few days, but I wanted to let you know I'm fine. I'll see you on Sunday. Love, Julie." Brett slanted a look at her. "That's all."

"He'll know that wasn't from me," Julie said firmly.

"How will he know?"

"Because—" She stopped. She couldn't tell him, *because I wouldn't sign it "love."* Not after breaking off with him. She took a deep breath. Aloud she continued, "Because it doesn't—sound like me. I'd write a longer note. And I wouldn't send it to his Web page."

"What if your forgot his e-mail address and only had a few minutes to send the note?"

"I wouldn't. Why did you send it, anyway?" Julie stared at Brett.

117

"I didn't want him to grow suspicious because he hadn't heard anything from you, so I asked my friend to send it yesterday. But Don—my private eye friend—told me that Warren had one of his friends checking your house yesterday. So it looks like my idea backfired. Now he's really trying to find you."

"I don't think so," Julie protested. "I doubt if he's looking for me. He's busy up in Boston, with his grandfather. But you shouldn't have sent that note, Brett, it was a bad idea."

"I'm sure he was worried about you."

"Warren wouldn't worry." She said it decisively.

"Any guy who hadn't heard from his fiancée for a couple of days would be worried," Brett protested. "Especially about someone like you."

"Someone like me?"

"You know what I mean. Sweet and trusting."

"Like I trusted you?" Julie didn't try to hide the tart note in her voice.

"You know me." The look he sent her was indignant. "I'd never harm you. I didn't want to hurt your feelings, except that couldn't be helped, when you learned about Shannon and—Warren's past."

He hadn't wanted to hurt her feelings. She filed that thought away for future examination and took a deep breath. "Warren definitely did not expect to hear from me. That's why I haven't even tried to phone him. And I've kept my phone off. The fact that he did get a note—that probably made him suspicious."

Brett muttered an obscenity under his breath. "Maybe you're right. Maybe I'm the one who caused them to come looking for us, instead of allaying any fears Warren had." His voice rumbled.

The car was approaching Denville now. Julie sighed, looking down at her hands. They felt cold, and she rubbed them together. "I'm going to check my messages." She groped through her purse and found her cell phone. Turning it on, she discovered she had four messages. A text from Jonathan asking if she was okay. Another text from Adam. And two voice mails from Kendra.

As she scrolled through the missed calls, she saw one had come in from Warren's private cell phone this morning, though he hadn't left a message.

"I have to call my brothers and tell them I'm okay," she said hastily. "Warren called but didn't leave a message."

Brett grimaced.

Julie took a few minutes to call her brothers. Neither picked up his cell phone. She left short messages assuring them she was fine, then flipped the phone off. She'd call Kendra later.

"I really don't understand how they knew to look for us there," Brett was saying reflectively when she slid the cell phone back in her purse. He slowed for another light. "Did you—you didn't use one of your charge cards, did you? When you were in the store alone?"

She'd been right. He didn't want to use charge cards, only cash. She met Brett's eyes.

"Yes, I did," she said calmly, but her stomach was twisting. "I charged my purchases. I only have so much cash with me—"

"Damn." Brett hit the steering wheel. "I should have told you not to use a charge. I should have given you cash—"

"But why?" Julie asked. "I noticed you've been paying for everything in cash, but why? What's the difference?"

Brett sighed heavily, steering the car through traffic.

"Because your boyfriend has a couple of police officers from his hometown in his back pocket." He almost spat out the words. "And he employs a couple of computer hackers too. Because they're capable of tracing any charge purchases you make with their computers, and locating you quickly. And me, if they even suspect we're together."

Julie stared at Brett. "You mean, they can find us? That quickly?" Her voice squeaked.

"Yeah."

She struggled to absorb the idea. Warren keeping tabs on her, knowing where and how she spent her money?

"It doesn't seem worth his time to pay someone to do that. And anyway, I thought only the FBI does that sort of thing, when someone's missing."

"If you're paying people, and they can utilize the technology, it's amazing what they can find out. It would be simple enough for Warren to keep informed. Especially if he thought something was going on and was trying to find you. Damn, I was afraid of this." Brett ran a hand through his hair.

"Don't berate yourself." Julie put her hand on Brett's where it rested on the steering wheel, in what she hoped was a reassuring motion. His hand felt hot next to her cold skin. He stopped at a red light and turned to face her.

Realizing her hand still lay on his, she snatched it away, her cheeks warming as she met his eyes.

"I—I shouldn't have used the card." Her words tumbled out. "Especially since I noticed you were paying cash. I thought you didn't want to leave a paper trail. But it didn't occur to me that something like this could happen. How on earth did they get to the mall so quickly? I used the card less than an hour ago."

"They must have been somewhere in the vicinity." The car moved forward slowly. "Maybe watching your home—or even surveying my condo, if they somehow knew I was in the picture. Or maybe there were several guys looking for you, and those two were closest to the mall. From Route 80, my condo isn't that far from the mall."

"I'm about half an hour from the mall," Julie mused. "But why would they suspect I'm with you?"

"I don't know. I'm conjecturing here."

"And why would they be looking for me anyway?"

"Because, as you said, they suspected the e-mail wasn't from you. It looks like I'm the one who made them suspicious." His frown deepened.

"Maybe Warren's always been keeping tabs on me." Julie said the words slowly, with distaste. "And," she added, anger beginning to simmer inside her, "how dare he try to find out what my charge card numbers are!"

She recalled, only a month ago, coming upon Warren looking at her wallet. He'd smiled and said he was looking at the photos there.

Now she guessed that had been a ruse.

Brett's sigh was heavy, briefly interrupting her thoughts.

They fell silent. The car crawled through the late afternoon traffic. Julie stared out the window. Most of the cars were headed west, but there were still plenty of vehicles on their side of the road.

It wasn't until Brett pulled into a gas station that Julie wondered where they were going. Once they were driving again, he went a little farther on the highway, then turned onto a road that wound through Parsippany Township.

"This is the way to your house." Julie said the words quietly.

"Yes." He glanced at her. "I had intended for us to go back to my condo tonight. But it's too risky to go back there now."

"Risky? Really, Brett, don't you think you might be blowing things out of proportion?" Julie tried to keep her voice gentle.

"No. I want you to stay away from Warren till we're done." Another glance at her. "I don't like the fact that those goons were chasing us that way. Something's wrong, and I have a bad feeling about it." He turned onto a smaller road. "I'm going to go to my parents' house and pick up some extra clothes I keep there. We won't stay at the condo tonight. We'll stay somewhere else. I'll have my friend Don check on my place. If the coast is clear, we'll go back tomorrow so I can get more clothes."

"I think you're being overly cautious," Julie said, then turned to look out the window. "Why would Warren suspect I'm with you?"

But was he being too careful? The idea of Warren sending his employees to chase after them was highly disturbing. Why was Warren so concerned about her, even after their break-up? Did he suspect something was amiss? Did he want her back?

Or did he simply want control over her? Want to know exactly what she was doing?

Now that was something Julie could believe. And she didn't like it. Not at all.

They turned into an older development, full of mature trees and houses, mostly bi-levels and splits. Brett made a couple of turns, then pulled up to a neat, large bi-level. The gold shingles and black shutters that Julie remembered were gone, replaced by beige vinyl siding and forest green shutters.

But the inside of the house was still much the same, and Julie recognized the old familiar feeling of coziness she always experienced when she entered Brett's home. It might be smaller and much less pretentious than her family's house, but there was a warm feeling in Brett's childhood home that never failed to embrace her upon entering.

"I'll just be a few minutes," Brett said. "Make yourself at home." He sprinted up the stairs toward his bedroom.

Julie took the short set of stairs downward and went to freshen up in the half bath off the family room. Before leaving the room, she gave Kendra a call, assuring her friend all was well. Then she wandered through the family room and turned toward the fourth, downstairs bedroom.

Brett's parents had used the room as an extra den, with a pullout sofa for guests, a TV and computer. Brett and Julie had spent many hours closeted away there, in each other's arms, kissing and sharing embraces.

Julie could close her eyes and picture the room just as vividly as if she'd been there yesterday. The brown carpet, the worn beige-and-brown sofa, the beige vertical shades...the TV on while they only half watched...

The door stood ajar, and she moved to stand in the doorway.

The old carpet had been replaced with a pale beige one, and a new cream, gold and dark red sofa stood where the old couch used to be. There were pleated shades across the front window.

The most notable change in the room was the addition of an oak computer desk and a new, flat-screened computer. Surrounding the computer and printer were a number of the family photos Mrs. Ryerson had always displayed, ranging from old black-and-whites of previous generations to pictures of Brett and Jodi as children and teenagers. There were even a couple of their Brittany Spaniel, who had passed away several years ago.

The TV had been moved slightly, and automatically Julie walked over, her feet sinking into the plush carpet. She turned on the Weather Channel.

An advertisement was playing, and she made herself at home on the couch. The material was soft, and she ran her hand over the tufted surface.

Memories rushed at her, memories of being held by Brett in this room, his hands moving over her, stroking...

Longing pierced her, sudden and intense. It shook her to her toes. Because she knew that if Brett were next to her now, instead of upstairs, she would end up in his arms.

Which was exactly where she *wanted* to be.

She sprang up.

What would Brett do if he knew what she was thinking? Would he take her into his arms and kiss her soundly?

Or would he laugh and tell her she'd lost her chance for any romantic relationship with him?

Still, he *had* "borrowed" her. And surely he wouldn't have been motivated to open her eyes regarding Warren if he didn't still care. Even if it was only a little bit.

She'd have to hold on to that slight thread of hope. Something within her wanted him to care. Because she cared, too.

She cocked her head, listening to the footsteps as Brett moved around upstairs. He must be almost finished getting whatever it was he needed. She paid only half attention to the weather report.

Then she heard another sound. After a moment, she recognized it as a garage door opening, and seconds later she heard a car pulling into the garage.

The motor turned off, a door slammed, and Julie found herself standing uncomfortably, wondering what on earth she was going to say to whichever of Brett's parents was entering the house. She hastily turned off the TV.

Maybe it would be Jodi? Home for the weekend from law school? It would be easier to face Brett's sister after all these years than his parents.

Julie had always loved Brett's family, but seeing

them again, under these circumstances, would be awkward at best. And she was unsure of what kind of reception they'd give the woman who'd broken Brett's heart.

The door to the hall opened.

"Brett? Is that you?" David Ryerson's cheerful voice boomed. "I saw your car out front—"

He stopped abruptly as Julie moved into the hall.

The range of expressions on his face would have been amusing on another occasion. First came total surprise. Mr. Ryerson's eyes widened as he recognized Julie. Then he smiled, and a look of gladness and welcome enveloped his face. Within seconds, his expression slid into a bland one, and Julie knew he was making a deliberate attempt to look neutral.

But she couldn't contain her own rush of pleasure at seeing him. "Mr. Ryerson!" Without thinking, she stepped forward and gave him a hug.

The older man's arms were as warm and welcoming as his previous expression.

"Julie. It's good to see you." As she stepped back, he surveyed her again. "You look wonderful."

"So do you!" Brett's father hadn't changed at all. His hair had been silver for years, but his youthful face had remained the same. Brett looked almost exactly like his father, and Julie knew this was what Brett would look like when he was older. Both were tall, with the same classic features. Only Brett's eye color was his mother's. David Ryerson's eyes were blue.

Those blue eyes were twinkling now. "How are you, Julie?"

"Fine," Julie replied automatically. "How are you and Mrs. Ryerson? And Jodi? I hear she's in law school."

"We're all fine, just fine." Mr. Ryerson made no

125

attempt to conceal the fact that he was studying her.

Brett's footsteps were moving overhead. "Dad?"

His steps thudded down the stairs, and he rounded the corner.

His expression, too, might have been amusing under different circumstances. He looked chagrinned, almost—embarrassed. Like he'd been caught with a handful of cookies right before dinner.

Or with his old girlfriend in a compromising position.

"Hi, Dad. I—we just stopped in so I could pick up a couple of things." His hand swung a filled bag from Old Navy.

"That's all right. Do you want to stay for dinner? Your mom should be home from Aunt Lucille's soon. We have leftovers."

Julie turned to regard Brett.

"Uh, no, thanks," Brett began, when they heard another garage door opening.

"There she is," David stated.

Brett looked distinctly uncomfortable. And Julie knew it was because she was with him.

There was an awkward pause, and then the sound of more footsteps from the garage. Brett's mother opened the door to the hall.

Anne Ryerson entered the room. A pretty, small-boned woman, her dark hair was streaked with more gray than the last time Julie had seen her. Otherwise, she looked almost the same.

"Hi, dear," she said, as David bent down to kiss her. She turned and got her first look at Julie. "Oh—Julie!" Her astonished expression changed to a more guarded one than her husband's. "How nice to see you."

Julie stepped forward and hugged Brett's mother too. She recognized the familiar scent of her usual Chanel perfume "I'm glad to see you too," she said sincerely.

Anne turned, and Brett gave his mother an affectionate kiss. "Hi, Mom." His face looked a little flushed.

"I was just asking them to stay and have dinner with us," David began. "Or we could send for a pizza instead of leftovers."

"We can't." Brett's words shot out. "We're—uh, running late as it is."

Anne Ryerson was regarding them carefully. Julie wondered what she was thinking. Certainly she must have been surprised to see Brett with his old girlfriend in tow. She was a more reserved person than Brett's father, and it was difficult to gauge her reaction. While she didn't seem resentful at seeing Julie, she didn't exactly look pleased either. Julie detected an air of caution about her.

"Can you stay a bit longer?" David was asking.

"No." Brett's reply was firm. "We have to get going. We just stopped by for a few minutes."

Julie saw that Anne was observing the bag in her son's hand, with a blue sweater sleeve poking out. She must be wondering why he needed a change of clothes—and why he hadn't gone to the condo for them. But she said nothing.

"Where are you off to?" David persisted.

"Julie and I are trying to solve a little problem." Brett shifted his stance.

Anne's eyebrows rose. "I hope everything's all right." She said the words quietly, but Julie heard the note of concern in her voice.

David seemed not to notice anything amiss. "Well, it was nice seeing you again, Julie."

"It was so nice to see you too." Julie gave them both a warm smile, hoping they could tell how much she'd enjoyed seeing them. "I promise, I'll come by and visit with you again soon." She said the words without thinking. But she meant them, she realized. She had always cared deeply for Brett's parents.

"Do that," David urged.

"Yes, please come by," Anne seconded.

"We've got to get going." Brett's words were terse, and the look he gave Julie was a warning one.

"I will," Julie reiterated, smiling at Brett's parents. "I need my coat," she said to Brett. She went into the family room and got her shoulder bag and coat from the ottoman where she'd left them. Turning to the others, she caught both David and Anne giving Brett a long, searching look.

She turned to look at him too.

Without giving her a chance to hug them again, Brett took Julie's elbow and began steering her toward the stairs.

"Bye!" Julie said.

David reached out and put an arm around his wife. "Bye."

"Bye," Anne echoed.

Brett called goodbye to his parents as he led Julie out the door.

A stiff wind had started up while they were inside. As she slid into the Jeep, Julie felt absurdly pleased. The chance meeting with Brett's parents may have been awkward for all of them. But she had been glad to see them, and their reaction to her had been fairly amicable.

Julie settled back with a smile on her lips and buckled her seatbelt.

Brett drove for a few minutes in silence as wind buffeted the car. Then, abruptly, he spoke.

"You look like the Cheshire cat."

The Cheshire Cat? Julie visualized the cartoon character from Disney's *Alice in Wonderland*, all smiles and full of secrets.

"I do?" She turned to study Brett.

"Yes. As if you're real pleased about something."

"Oh." Julie experienced a momentary loss of words. What could she say? She looked down. That she was happy Brett's parents had been so cordial when they'd found her in their home? That they didn't seem to be holding a grudge against her?

She straightened her head and looked back at Brett. He was watching the roadway.

"I was very happy to see your parents," she began hesitantly. "They're such great people! I've always liked them."

When he remained silent, she continued cautiously, "I'd like to see Jodi too."

"You don't have to visit them."

Brett's tone was like cold water dashed at her face.

"But I'd like to—" Julie stopped.

It was apparent that Brett didn't want her getting friendly with them again.

She turned back to look out the window, sudden tears stinging her eyes.

Maybe she deserved that. She had hurt him badly, once. And now he wanted to stay far from her. And keep his family far away.

Then why was he going through with this whole "borrowing" scheme? Educating her about Warren's true nature, which he believed she knew nothing about? Out of the goodness of his heart?

No. There must be something more. Some spark of the affection he'd once had for her. She had to believe it, had to hold onto the hope that there was more than just good intentions in Brett's heart.

She felt as if a battle was going on within her. Did Brett care? Yes? No? She swiped at a tear. It was becoming clear to her that *she* cared about what he thought.

"Julie?" Brett's voice had softened. "Are you all right?"

"Fine." She made a deliberate effort to keep her voice calm and cool. She bent her head and dug through her purse for a tissue, then blew her nose.

"Can we turn the radio on?" There. She sounded almost normal.

"Sure." Brett clicked on the radio. Rock and roll music poured into the car.

Julie busied herself applying lip balm, not glancing at Brett. Eventually she looked up. They were headed back west on Route 46.

"Where are we going?"

"A small bed-and-breakfast I know of. Not far from my condo." When Julie sat in silence, he continued. "They'll be expecting us to go far from the mall, if they saw us running. They probably won't look for us nearby, except my place or yours."

"So you believe they're still searching for us?" Julie knew she sounded skeptical.

"Yes, I do. And I don't trust 'them' anymore than I trust Warren."

"Warren's not going to do anything if he finds us," Julie said flatly. "And I doubt he would even think to look for you."

Brett glanced at her, his expression skeptical. "I don't trust him, or his buddies."

"Well...you're right about one thing. He's not trustworthy," Julie admitted. She settled back in her seat as Brett drove through the quickly falling darkness.

Brett might be overly concerned. But the fact was, Julie didn't like being chased by Juan Comacho and his friends. And she was annoyed that Warren was keeping tabs on her. Despite the fact that they'd broken up, he still wanted some kind of control.

For the first time, she wondered if Warren was going to try to hold on to her in some way.

She hated the thought.

****

Under different circumstances, Julie would have delighted in exploring the entire Victorian mansion that had been turned into a bed-and-breakfast. Gray and stately, with curved turrets and ornate scrollwork, it was an intriguing place. Now that the trees were bare, the view from the large picture window overlooking a part of Lake Hopatcong was a breathtaking one.

Julie wandered through the front and back parlors, decorated in shades of green, containing heavy wooden antique furniture. A grand piano occupied one corner, and a tall bookcase held volumes that looked appropriately old, including several aged Nancy Drew and Hardy Boy books and a collection of mystery novels by Agatha Christie and Mary Roberts Rinehart.

There were several bedrooms available this evening, and Brett chose a suite in the back, made up of a large bedroom, a small sitting room and its own bathroom. He hustled Julie upstairs once he'd checked them in.

"You've stayed here before?" Julie asked, as he carried their suitcases.

"Once."

Once. Of course. He'd probably come here for a romantic getaway weekend. He must have been with some beautiful, sophisticated woman. They'd spent a passionate night together—

Her teeth clenched. She tried to wipe the picture from her mind.

Brett moved down the hall on the second floor, glancing at the numbered doors. Muffled laughter came from behind one.

He paused at the end and fitted the key in the lock.

The suite was charming. The sitting room held a flowered sofa, tables and a TV. The bedroom contained a large bed draped with a floral canopy. Thick green window drapes, a pedestal table and a Victorian-style lamp added to the ambiance.

Julie turned her head, taking in the elegant

room. She'd like to come back here someday, with Brett, under different circumstances. For a split second, she visualized Brett pulling her down beside him on the bed—

Where had that thought come from? She glanced at Brett, who was putting his suitcase in the small sitting room. He looked up, and his eyes met hers.

She looked away. Hopefully he'd have no idea what she was thinking. But her cheeks had grown hot, and she wondered if he noticed.

The attraction she was feeling for Brett was growing stronger by the hour. It was getting harder to suppress feelings and thoughts like these.

She sighed. The one bed would present a problem. She placed her suitcase nearby, regarding it.

"You can have the bed. I'll take the couch," he said. It was as if he'd read her thoughts.

She hoped he hadn't suspected what else she was thinking.

"Oh, no," she said. hastily. "You're bigger than me. You'd be uncomfortable. I'll take the couch."

"No." His tone was firm. "I got you into this. I'm not going to let you be uncomfortable."

"For a captor, you're awfully nice," Julie said and smiled at him.

His eyes flashed. "I'm not your captor."

"Sorry." She didn't want to offend him, especially since he'd been nice enough to take her shopping—and now was worried about Warren's people coming after them.

She busied herself with unpacking, keeping it to a minimum since he'd told her they'd be leaving in the morning.

"Where are we going tomorrow?" she asked, hanging up the two dresses she'd bought. A slight hint of roses hung in the air. She looked around and located a beautiful cut crystal bowl full of potpourri.

"To see Felicia Cohen." Brett was rummaging through the plastic bag he'd brought from his parents' house. "Let's go eat. There's a good pizza place half a mile up the road."

"Okay." Julie shut the closet door. Warren had mentioned Felicia Cohen to her once. Another ex-girlfriend. "Where does Felicia live?"

"In High Bridge."

Julie had heard of the quaint town, located in Hunterdon County, but had never been there. "What—"

"Felicia will answer your questions tomorrow." Brett ran a hand through his dark blond hair, and Julie noticed he looked weary. "I'm starved."

The place Brett took her to was small and homey. They were doing a brisk takeout business this Friday evening, but there were also a few customers in the booths and tables in the back. He had been right about the pizza, Julie reflected after a few bites. It was delicious.

They spent most of their time talking about each other's friends and families, catching up on what they were doing. When they returned to the bed-and-breakfast, Brett hooked up his laptop computer, settled on the floor with a cushion, and got busy with e-mails.

"Mind if I watch TV while I do this?" he asked, indicating the TV in the sitting room. "The Knicks are playing tonight."

"That's okay. There's nothing I want to watch." Julie curled up on the couch.

She picked up the issue of *Cosmo* she'd started yesterday. But she felt uncomfortable sitting near Brett, with articles like "Ten Ways to Seduce a Man" screaming from the cover. She bent back the cover, but the article she turned to at random was a quiz called "How Fast Do You Get Satisfied in Bed?" Hardly appropriate.

She placed the magazine down and picked up the Heather Graham book.

She lost herself in the book for a while, only half aware of the clicking as Brett typed messages, and the background noise of the basketball game on TV.

Brett's sudden victory shout of "yes!" startled her. He was grinning widely at the TV, obviously elated by some play the Knicks had achieved.

For one moment, as she regarded Brett, she felt unbelievably comfortable and warm inside. Like they were a couple, spending a cozy evening together. Each doing their own thing, but in close proximity.

And something tugged at her heart. She felt a yearning, a reaching out for Brett.

She wanted to be with him. She wanted other evenings spent like this.

She swallowed. She was the one who had broken up with Brett. She'd relinquished any right to be his girlfriend. But oh, how appealing the idea was now!

I should never have broken up with him. The thought reverberated through her mind.

Brett must have become aware that she was staring at him, because he turned suddenly and looked at her.

She tried to look casual and glanced at her watch. It was after nine. "I'm going to take a shower." She quickly got up.

When she came out of the shower she grabbed the chenille throw draped over the couch, wrapping herself in it, and curled up on the couch with her book. Brett would be cramped sleeping here, she knew, and decided to simply take it for herself.

"I'll turn the TV down," Brett said. "It's a good game." He regarded Julie. "By the way, Don says that he and one of his friends drove by your home a couple of hours ago. They saw a man in a car across the street, sitting there, watching your place."

Julie shivered. "You mean—waiting for me?"

"I don't know. What do you think?"

"I don't like the idea," she said. "Why would Warren send someone to wait for me to come home?"

"Because he's worried about you?" Brett guessed.

Julie doubted that. But she didn't say so. Instead, she added the other thought that could be equally true: "Maybe he just wants to know what I'm doing. All the time," she finished dryly.

"He seems pretty controlling," Brett pointed out.

"I'm beginning to realize that," Julie said. "And I don't like it. *At all.*"

****

Brett found himself grinning as the exciting game ended and the Knicks celebrated their four-point victory. He listened to the commentators wrap up the game, then switched to a news channel and watched for a while, catching up on the latest in world news and politics.

An ad came on, and he stretched. He glanced around, suddenly becoming sharply aware of his surroundings. He wasn't in his favorite chair at home. He was sitting on the floor in the sitting room of the B&B, comfortably slouched against the couch.

Julie?

He turned and saw Julie lying on the couch. She was wrapped in a blanket, her eyes closed.

He got up carefully, suspecting she had dozed off. A book resting loosely by her hand confirmed his suspicions. Julie had fallen asleep while he was watching TV.

He stood there and stared at her. He couldn't help it.

She looked beautiful, and innocent, lying on the couch. Her almost-black hair curled softly around her shoulders. He caught that sweet vanilla scent again. Dark-tinged smudges were apparent beneath her closed lids. She must be exhausted.

But despite that, she still managed to look beautiful. And almost angelic.

Something tightened in Brett. How could Warren Wesley command the respect and loyalty of someone like Julie?

Would Julie finally see Warren as he really was?

The elation of the basketball game had faded, and Brett was left with a feeling of concern for Julie. Concern for her well-being and her emotional health. The last few days were taking a toll on her.

Yet she'd met these people, bravely, without complaint, and dealt with the anxiety and hurt these encounters were generating.

He swallowed. Julie deserved better than Warren Wesley. Someone like…

Him?

He hesitated. No, Julie wasn't interested in him. Well, maybe as a friend. He'd caught glimpses of the fact that she seemed to care about his well-being, his friendship, even. But that was it.

He'd had her as a girlfriend long ago. He'd loved her but taken her for granted. He'd been young, careless, maybe selfish. He hadn't taken her too many places or done the things she wanted.

Had she ever gone to dinner and dancing with Warren? Had she ever traveled to the places she aspired to visit?

Weariness was enveloping him, and he couldn't stop a yawn. He needed to put aside these thoughts and feelings and go to sleep.

But he couldn't leave Julie on the couch. And looking at it, he realized it was kind of small for his frame.

There was only one thing to do. They'd have to share the king-sized bed.

He reached down and gently, carefully, scooped Julie and the blanket up in his arms.

She was still light, and she fit into his arms as if it hadn't been three years since the last time he'd held her.

He carried her over to the side of the bed. Gently, he placed her on the comforter, then slowly pulled it down until he could get it over her bare feet and pull it back up again.

The small blanket she'd held on the couch was tangled around her, and he pulled it away, replacing it with the heavier comforter. As he did, his hand touched the satiny fabric of her green nightshirt, which rode up her pale thighs.

She was beautiful.

He swallowed again, feeling himself hardening. This was no time to think like this, to feel this kind of heat. Julie was fast asleep, and she was off-limits anyway. He'd better get used to that fact.

He rapidly pulled up the comforter, placing the smaller blanket on top of it, hoping Julie wouldn't be cold.

At least it was a big bed, and he would be separated from her by a large space in the middle.

Yeah, tell that to my libido.

A frown suddenly crossed her face. He paused, his fingers reaching as if he'd wipe it away.

He froze.

Then the frown disappeared, and her face became peaceful and angelic looking again.

He reached out and gently stroked a finger through her silky hair, then down her soft cheek. How could one woman look so cute and so sensual at the same time?

She stirred slightly. She made a sound—a whisper—and he could have sworn she said, "Brett."

Brett backed away slowly. He didn't want her to wake and find him hovering over her.

He'd better get ready for bed and try to get some sleep.

When he crawled underneath the covers, he was still too aware of Julie sleeping peacefully on the other side of the bed. He closed his eyes, forcing himself to relax, to think of the basketball game and not the alluring woman nearby.

But it wasn't easy.

****

The drive to High Bridge on this Saturday morning was a peaceful one. The day was cool but sunny, with wind-chased clouds racing across the sky. Passing by a mountain and state forests, they could appreciate the autumn scenery, with little traffic to impede the view. Julie didn't talk much but seemed relaxed, sitting back and listening to the cool jazz station Brett had turned on. As they drove farther west, the station's signal faded and he switched to a Pennsylvania station that featured rock music from the sixties and seventies.

He had woken up around seven thirty, and she'd woken shortly afterward. He was surprised that his sleep had been so peaceful, and he felt refreshed.

"How did I get here?" she'd asked, her eyes clear as she regarded him. She must have slept well, too, he guessed.

"You fell asleep and I carried you here," he'd answered.

She'd opened her mouth, then closed it.

He'd gotten into the shower, and then they'd had a delicious buffet breakfast at the Victorian mansion. By nine thirty they were on their way.

They'd driven first to his condo. Don's e-mail said it appeared no one was watching it. When Brett was satisfied that Don was correct and it was not being watched—maybe Juan had no idea that he was the man with Julie at the mall yesterday—Brett and Julie had gone inside. He'd left some clothes and taken others, and briefly checked both his land line and his cell phone for messages that had come in recently.

The only new message at home was from his mom, asking him to call when he had a chance. It had come in at eight last night.

She must be very curious as to what on earth he was doing with his former girlfriend.

He wished they hadn't run into his parents. Although he was oddly gratified by how happy Julie was to see them, he was also uncomfortably aware that they might get the wrong impression about his being with Julie.

An impression it would be too easy for him to believe was true.

Worrying that one of Warren's buddies could show up at any time, Brett had kept the trip to his condo short, and they were making the hour-long trip from Mt. Arlington to High Bridge before ten o'clock.

Julie seemed at ease today. She had been surprisingly serene about the incident with Warren's henchmen. Brett suspected she believed that he had blown it out of proportion, and maybe he had. But he was taking no chances where Julie was concerned. Warren's pals would have tried to persuade her to leave him and go straight to Warren, he guessed. And if they hadn't been able to convince her, they might have tried to take her by force.

Just imagining that scenario made Brett's hands clench on the steering wheel and his stomach tighten.

He wasn't going to let anything happen to her.

Brett made the turn onto the main street of High Bridge. The town, full of quaint shops containing crafts and antiques, was a quiet little oasis for people to explore. Both Victorian homes and ones built around the 1920s lined the main street.

He found a parking spot on the street a block from Felicia's art gallery. Julie got out of the car at the same time as he did and glanced appreciatively up and down the street. Her attention was caught by the nearest store, which featured teddy bears made from fabric in the window.

"How charming!" she exclaimed. "It's kind of like the town of Chester here, but on a smaller scale, and quieter."

They walked down the street, passing a pizza place, a small restaurant, and an antiques store. Brett held open the door to the Hunterdon Gallery.

A bell tinkled as they walked into the bright, sunny room.

Felicia's art gallery occupied the first floor of a two-storied building. The large windows let in plenty of sunlight, and the high ceilings, painted white over sculpted designs and scrollwork, made the whole place feel open and spacious. Artwork of all kinds, from black-and-white photographs to ceramic pottery and handcrafted jewelry, occupied the walls, shelves, and antique bookcases. Scattered chunks of crystals glistened on shelves, and flute music flowed through speakers. The whole effect was artistic yet comfortable.

"Good morning," said a sleek, dark-haired woman as Julie gazed around the room.

"We're here to see Felicia," Brett began, when she approached from the back of the store.

Felicia was a tall, very attractive woman, probably in her late twenties or early thirties. Her red hair cascaded over her shoulders in curls. She wore large oval gold and turquoise earrings, and was dressed in a gold silky pants outfit with large carved wooden buttons. She looked like an artist.

"Hello," Felicia greeted them, extending her hand to shake Brett's, then Julie's hands. "I'm Felicia Cohen. C'mon back to the sitting area and we'll talk."

"It's nice to meet you," Julie said, and Brett

sensed from her tone that she liked Felicia at once. "I'm Julie Merritt."

Felicia led the way to an area in the back that was partially screened off. Her smile was warm as they sat on the comfortable flowered cushions of the old-fashioned couch. "How about some tea? I made peach tea today."

Julie accepted while Brett shook his head no. Julie took off her coat and tossed it over a chair, and Brett placed his beside it.

In her black jeans and orange, pink and white trendy sweater, Julie looked as beautiful as always as she sat down. Beautiful and somehow innocent.

And too damned attractive for his peace of mind.

Felicia took a seat in a chair facing them and poured tea from a gold and pink china teapot. Brett suspected it was a real antique. She passed Julie a pink and white cup and saucer. "Here you are."

Felicia took the lead in the conversation. "Well." She paused. "I'll tell you a little about myself. I grew up in Millburn. I went to Mt. Holyoke and studied Art History, much to my parents' disappointment. They wanted me to be a doctor or a lawyer or an accountant or a stockbroker. Something with money and power." She wrinkled her nose. "Not the kind of lifestyle I wanted. You see, my father's a physician— a cardiologist—and my mother spends her time either at the country club or fundraising for the hospital. I have a younger brother and sister. I'm twenty-nine. I'm a painter and I do some pottery work. I started my art gallery two years ago with money my grandfather left me. We're open Thursdays through Sundays. We feature local New Jersey and Pennsylvania artists and craftspeople and their work. I also teach some art classes."

She had left out some details, Brett noticed. Like the fact that she had rebelled against her parents, left her comfortable existence and moved out on her own years ago.

But perhaps Julie could read between the lines and guessed that.

Felicia sipped her tea. "But enough about me. Brett tells me you want to know more about Warren Wesley."

"How do you know Warren?" Julie asked, sipping her own tea.

"Are you a Cancer?" Felicia asked suddenly.

"Yes. What about you?"

"I thought so." Felicia nodded. "Me, too."

The two smiled at each other, as if they shared a secret bond. Brett shifted his position, and a fruit-filled fragrance reached him from the tea's vapors. He hoped this wasn't going to dwindle into a long discussion of astrological signs.

But Felicia returned to the topic of Warren. "I met Warren last year when I hosted the exhibit of Zachary Greave's sculptures. He comes from the same town as Warren, and Zach invited some of the town politicians to attend. Warren came with his mother, and that's when we met. He called me the next day."

"Is that when you started to date him?" Julie asked cautiously.

"Yes. We dated on and off." Felicia waved a hand. The teacup and saucer in her other hand clattered, and she put them down on the dark wood table. "Warren could be fun...well, you must know."

"Yes." Julie nodded her head.

Felicia glanced at Brett. "We both knew it wasn't a serious relationship. A few months ago I met Joe, and frankly, we had a lot more in common than Warren and I. Joe's an award-winning photographer." Her voice glowed with pride. "I had already begun to ease out of the relationship with Warren, and to tell you the truth, I think he was losing interest too. He'd met you"—she looked at

Julie—"and was talking about how sweet you were. He even remarked that he thought you'd make a good politician's wife." When Julie made a sound, Felicia smiled. "You come from a well-to-do family, and you're friendly and people like you."

"Warren mentioned you to me once," Julie said, surprising Brett. He looked from her to Felicia and back. She'd never said a word to him about recognizing Felicia's name. "He said you were exotic and exciting, but the two of you kind of drifted apart."

"That's true," Felicia said, still smiling. "We started to grow apart, and I purposefully ended our relationship. You see, I'd found out something about Warren that really disturbed me."

Julie glanced at Brett.

An uneasy feeling welled up in Brett's middle. When he'd first spoken to Felicia, he'd gotten the impression that Warren was cheating on Julie, and he wanted Julie to know. But Felicia had been evasive to him, indicating that she wanted to speak directly to Julie

Now he wondered what Felicia wanted to say. Was it something darker and even more disturbing than a guy cheating on a girlfriend?

Felicia's face grew serious as she and Julie regarded each other.

"When Brett first came around a few weeks ago, asking about Warren, I told him this much and no more. I hinted that I would only tell the whole story to *you*." She nodded at Julie. "I just felt it was something I didn't want you to hear secondhand."

Brett gripped the arm of the sofa.

"What?" Julie asked.

Felicia leaned forward and lowered her voice. "Warren is connected to the mob."

Chapter 9

"What!?" Brett's exclamation overrode Julie's gasp. His heart seemed to stop, then plunge to the floor.

"Yes. I'm sorry to have to tell you this." Felicia's gaze was steady. "He's involved with the mob. I heard him on the phone once when he thought I was asleep, making some sort of deal. That opened my eyes, and after that, I listened whenever he thought I wasn't paying attention. There were signs, things I'd missed before that became obvious. He had given orders for someone to be followed and frightened into making some kind of payment. And another time he was talking about making sure someone stayed in jail. And there were all those mysterious meetings...I'm sorry, am I shocking you?" Her brows furrowed.

Julie shook her head. "Not really. I can easily believe it."

She sure as hell was shocking *him*. With all their background research, this was something Brett and Don had failed to turn up.

"You should have told me," Brett said, his voice sharp. If he had known...

Felicia regarded Brett for a few seconds. "I felt this was something I had to tell Julie myself." She calmly turned back to Julie. "The thing is, I have no proof, only what I've heard, plus a gut feeling."

"I suspect you're right," Julie stated. She faced Felicia squarely. "I had some questions recently about Warren, and then when Brett appeared, I learned some things that I—that I didn't like about

Warren. I can't say I'm shocked." She took a deep breath. "Although I should have guessed there was something like this going on." She sent Brett a glance.

"You can hardly be blamed for not knowing your fiancé was dealing with the mob," Felicia said, her voice gentle. "It's a well-kept secret. Look, Julie, I've dated a lot of guys, and I've been around. Even *I* didn't suspect at first. That's how well hidden Warren's connections are."

"Hidden even from me, and my PI friend," Brett said, aware of the bitter tone in his voice. He sprang up and began to pace. "Damn! Don and I should have dug deeper. We should have uncovered this!"

His thoughts were tumbling like flood water. Warren connected with the mob...that explained a lot of things, like the fire and implications about Arnold's guilt at the restaurant. And the fact that Warren had been able to trace Julie so quickly after her one credit card purchase, and that he'd had goons available to rush out looking for her.

But it also presented a terrifying possibility: that along with his scheme to expose Warren's dark side to Julie, he'd somehow unleashed Warren's wrath and put her in jeopardy.

What would Warren do if he knew that Julie had learned the truth? His heart hammered with concern.

He paced back to where Julie sat, quietly talking to Felicia.

"I didn't know, and I should have," he began.

"Please don't feel that way," Felicia said reassuringly. "Sit down. Sure you don't want some tea? Look, it was months before I found out myself. It certainly wasn't obvious." She turned back to look at Julie.

"I should have seen it too," Julie said slowly. She reached for her teacup. It clattered against the china saucer in her trembling hand. She sipped the drink. "Now that I think back, there were signs...I should have noticed them, should have questioned some things. Like you said, he had a lot of meetings—I thought it was all politics." She set the cup and saucer down abruptly. "I guess this explains why he was able to trace me so fast yesterday, after I bought something. He's probably paid some crooked investigator or some computer whiz to find out where I'm shopping..." She stopped.

Her whole face darkened, and now Brett heard real anger in her voice. "He has a lot of nerve, keeping tabs on me like that. No one has the right to know all the details of my life. *No one.*"

Felicia was nodding. "Not even your fiancé. A woman has to have her privacy."

Brett couldn't sit. He resumed pacing. He saw Felicia and Julie exchange a glance, but was at a loss to understand its meaning.

"That's right." Julie's sweet face was set in a grim line that Brett had never seen before. "Everyone's entitled to some privacy."

Brett strode beyond the sitting area, barely glancing at a couple of colorful oil paintings of local scenery with Felicia's name written in a bold flourish in the corner. He returned seconds later to where Felicia and Julie sat, speaking calmly, their voices subdued.

No, not so calmly. He could see Julie's hands were both still shaking as they rested on her lap. His own clenched.

Felicia reached over and covered Julie's hands with one of hers. "Please don't be alarmed," she said. "Warren would certainly never harm you. He cares about you."

"He's not capable of caring about anyone but himself." Julie's voice was hard as steel.

Brett stared at her. So, Julie had accepted the

truth about Warren! A rush of gladness engulfed him. But he'd have to contemplate *that* later. At least she sounded more angry than hurt.

"I'm not alarmed," she continued, squeezing Felicia's hand, "at least not for myself."

Her eyes met Brett's, and she looked away, staring at a nearby sculpture.

If she was not alarmed for herself, then who was...?

Brett exhaled and plopped down beside her.

Him? Was she worried about him?

She was. He could see it in her dark eyes as she turned and met his look again.

A feeling of pleasure shot through him, intense and overwhelming. Instantly, he tried to quell it. He shouldn't be feeling so gratified that Julie was worried about him. This wasn't the time or place to examine any feelings that could be awakening in her.

But as they regarded each other, the air around them suddenly still, he could almost hear Julie's thoughts.

I care.

It was as if the words had been whispered in his ears.

And for just one second, he lost track of everything else.

Felicia gave a slight cough, breaking the spell that isolated Julie and him.

Julie started. She hastily picked up her cup and took a sip of her tea. He couldn't see her eyes. She finished and placed the china on the table. When she looked up, her expression was less angry and almost unruffled, revealing nothing. Her hands were steady.

"Are you in any danger?" Julie asked Felicia simply, turning to the other woman.

Felicia laughed, the sound musical and

pleasant. "Hardly. Warren's no longer interested in me. I was an amusing diversion, and I always knew it. If I had been interested in him, I could have played games, maybe played hard-to-get, and he would have thought of me as a challenge. But that's not me." She shook her head and reached for her own teacup. "No, we simply enjoyed each others' company for a while, period. And we went on to other people."

The bell on the front door tinkled, and they heard the saleswoman greeting a customer.

"Is Julie in any danger?" Brett dropped his voice and leaned toward Felicia.

"I don't think so." Felicia shook her head. "He cares for Julie in his own way, and he wants to marry her. I'm sure she'll be fine."

Brett had to ask. "Even if she breaks off the engagement?" His clipped words came out tersely, and he held his breath, waiting for the answer.

Felicia studied him for a moment, considering his question. "If she did break it off, I still don't believe Julie would have anything to worry about." She said the words slowly and thoughtfully. "You don't know Warren. He's the type who wouldn't want someone who rejected him." She turned to Julie. "He'd want to be the one to do the rejecting. If you don't want him, he sure wouldn't let himself pine for you."

Brett let out his breath. "He wouldn't try to get revenge?" he persisted, his heart still hammering away.

"I don't think so," Felicia answered. "I think he would try to make it look like any break-up was his idea, then he'd find someone else immediately. To soothe his ego." She grinned.

"What about Brett?" Julie's question startled him, and he turned to look at her. Her dark eyes were worried.

He was correct. She *was* concerned about his welfare.

This time Felicia didn't answer right away. She looked from Julie to Brett, then back to Julie again.

"I don't know," she said. "That's as honest an answer as I can give you." She hesitated, tapping a dark red polished nail against the table. "I'd like to reassure you that Warren wouldn't be angry if he finds out about you two, but I honestly don't know how he'd react. If he learns that you two are involved..."

"We're not—" Brett protested.

"We're not—" Julie said at the same instant.

They both stopped. Felicia looked at Brett, then Julie. Brett turned to regard Julie too, and saw that her cheeks were flushed.

"We're not involved," Julie said, very carefully and precisely.

For just a moment, a smile touched Felicia's face, then disappeared. Her expression once again neutral, she continued. "If Warren *thinks* you're involved, he may be angry enough to do something. He might take some sort of revenge. Especially if he believes you stole Julie from him." She turned to Brett as she said the words, concern flowing over her features.

From the corner of his eye he saw Julie shudder. Stole? Yes, Warren might believe that, Brett realized. A guy with an ego as big as Warren Wesley's would probably never believe that Julie, after learning the truth about his character, might willingly walk away from her engagement.

"But he didn't—" Julie responded.

"I'm not saying that's what happened. Only that's what Warren could believe," Felicia said. "In the worst-case scenario, Warren would believe that was true and try for some kind of revenge. That's the worst case. It doesn't mean it will happen."

"But it's possible." Julie's whisper was strained. Her face had grown pale. "If Warren thinks it's true, if he even suspects that Brett has influenced me somehow—" She broke off.

She turned to face Brett, and he saw tears in her eyes. "I'm sorry. I'm afraid I've gotten us in over our heads. I only hope we're all wrong."

"You've gotten us in? Don't be ridiculous! This whole plan was *my* idea." Brett spoke more roughly than he'd intended. He stood and resumed his pacing. "Don't apologize! It's not *your* fault if Warren's involved with a crime family."

"He's the kind who would try to get revenge," Julie continued. "You could very well be in danger."

"Don't be ridiculous," Brett repeated. "The only one who could be in danger is *you*. After all, you're engaged to him."

Julie was looking down at her fingers. The large diamond flashed, a reminder to them of Warren's claim on Julie.

"No," she said with conviction, "I'm positive he wouldn't do anything to me."

"And I'm sure he's not going to do anything to me," Brett said firmly. "Warren wouldn't dare. Besides, he doesn't even know who I am." He regarded Julie, then Felicia, as his thoughts raced. If Warren tried to hurt Julie in any way, he'd have him in jail so fast his head would be spinning. After he'd given him a piece of his mind. And broken his nose.

"I'm glad you're so certain," Julie said.

"I'm not letting him hurt you. Either of you," he said grimly, shoving his hands in his pockets.

"I certainly don't believe we should worry about it," Felicia said. "Why send out negative energy? Warren will do what he will do. Frankly, I think that since he's now in the political arena, with the spotlight shining on him, he'll be very, very careful about what he says and does."

"You're probably right," Julie agreed. "Warren does care an awful lot about his image and how things look."

But Brett knew Warren was capable of trying something, and then making it look like something else. Like in Arnold's case. "We'll be on our guard," he declared.

Felicia sat back. "Hmm." She seemed to be pondering something. Then she smiled. "I know." She got up. "I'm going to give you something for protection, just in case."

She walked gracefully over to an antique dresser that held an oval mirror. On top was a basket with multicolored stones and crystals, and Felicia began rummaging through them. She stopped and withdrew one, studying it.

Returning to Julie and Brett, she held out her hand to Julie. "Here. This is for you."

In her hand she held a clear two-inch crystal with white streaks.

Julie took it carefully from Felicia's hand. "Are you sure?" she asked, cradling the crystal in her palm. "It's beautiful."

"It's yours. I could feel it calling to you," Felicia said.

Brett didn't realize he'd made a sound until Felicia looked at him. "You may not believe," she said softly, "but crystals have positive energy that can help you." She turned back to Julie. "This will help protect you from evil, and give you courage when you need it."

"Thank you so much," Julie said. "It's really lovely. I *will* keep it with me." She looked at Brett. "It will help."

Brett kept silent, nodding his head briefly. He wasn't about to scoff when Felicia had been so helpful and kind to them. But he doubted that a little stone would give them any help.

Felicia had guessed his feelings. "You're skeptical," she said, still smiling. "It's all right. It will offer you help anyway."

"Thank you," he said gravely, not contradicting her.

"This is very sweet of you," Julie said. "We'll take good care of it."

"I always keep some crystals with me," Felicia continued. "And you can see I keep them around the gallery." She waved her hand.

Brett noticed again the myriad of small and large crystals placed on furniture and around the room. Of assorted shapes and a rainbow of colors, they blended in with the variety of artwork.

The bell tinkled once more. A moment later a man with jet-black hair strode into the area of the gallery where they sat. He was the same height as Brett but heftier, and wore a leather jacket and jeans. Felicia sprang up.

"Hi, Joe!" Felicia's smile was warm as he reached for her. They hugged and kissed. This must be Felicia's new love.

Joe's arm remained around Felicia as they turned to face Brett and Julie. Joe showed no surprise when Felicia introduced them. She must have told him about their meeting.

"Is there any other information or help I can give you?" Felicia asked.

Brett shook his head. "No, I don't think so. But you've been very helpful."

"Felicia's told me about Warren," Joe said. "He sounds like a character. I'd steer clear of him." He regarded Julie as he said the last.

"Thank you." Julie stood up, her eyes meeting Joe's, then Felicia's. "You've given me a lot to think about."

"Please, call me if you want to talk," Felicia urged. She picked up a business card from a nearby shelf and handed it to Julie.

Julie stepped forward, and the two women hugged. It was amazing, Brett thought as he watched them. People seemed to gravitate to Julie, to feel her warmth and caring and return it. It was as if on some level they recognized her empathetic characteristics. And he supposed Felicia was much the same, although more unconventional than Julie.

"Take care of yourself," Felicia was saying as they put their coats on.

"Thank you for the crystal," Julie replied, stepping back. "And for everything else."

"And keep in touch."

"We will," Julie promised.

Brett shook hands with Joe, then Felicia. "Thank you. For everything."

Felicia was smiling. "Good luck. Don't worry, Brett, everything will be fine." She leaned toward him, her voice dropping to a whisper. "Everything's going to work out between you two. I sense a very deep bond." Before Brett could say another word, she stepped back and focused her smile on Joe.

Brett glanced at Julie. She was watching him.

"Thanks again," he said, and Julie echoed his words. He took Julie's elbow and steered her toward the door.

They passed a series of sculptures on a long table and approached the entrance. Julie glanced back once, smiled, and then followed his lead as Brett pushed the door open.

The day had remained a mix of sun and clouds, but had grown windier. Brown leaves skidded across the sidewalk as they started up the street. Brett could smell spices as they passed the pizza place. Across the street, four children rode by on bikes, laughing loudly.

His hand still placed lightly on Julie's elbow, Brett walked along. "Are you hungry?" he asked as they neared his car.

She shook her head. "No. Not right now. Let's—let's go for a walk." Her face had gone from smiling to a solemn expression.

Warren Wesley was obviously on her mind.

Was she going to tell him she was having second thoughts about her engagement? Or that she was scared of Warren?

****

Thoughts bombarded Julie, coming at her faster and more furiously than the dry leaves whisked in their path by the stiff wind.

She hadn't been shocked to learn about Shannon. Or about Arnold. She'd been saddened.

But Felicia's revelations about Warren's mob connections had been a real surprise. She hadn't known, hadn't suspected. Maybe she'd been too naïve and trusting. Still, she should have realized. There were probably clues she'd overlooked.

But what worried her the most was that, in her innocence, she had put Brett in some kind of danger when she'd gone along with his crazy scheme.

If Warren found out she was staying with Brett, that he was trying to reveal Warren's true nature to her, would Warren get angry? He might jump to the conclusion that she'd been involved with Brett before she'd broken her engagement. Warren had accepted their break-up placidly, with only a small protest. But if he thought Brett was the cause...Warren's macho self-image would be shattered. What if he tried to get revenge?

"Don't worry." Brett's voice broke into her thoughts like a chisel piercing the stones in one of the sculptures Felicia displayed. "I'm not going to let him hurt you."

Julie paused in front of a large Victorian home and turned to face Brett. His eyes sparked gold and green in the sunlight.

Instinctively she grabbed his hands. "I'm not worried about me!"

Brett stared at her.

"It's you," she insisted. "Brett, if he finds out we're together, that we've been learning his secrets, Warren could go after you, not me! I'm worried about *you*!"

"About me?" Brett's expression was one of astonishment. "You're worried about me?"

"Yes!" She recognized the desperation in her voice as she clutched his hands. Her heart hammered in her chest.

For another split second, he stared at her.

And then Brett pulled her into his arms.

His lips came down on hers, hard.

Every cell in Julie's body came alive as a current of electricity shot through her. Within seconds, she felt the tingling from the top of her head to every finger and every toe.

Instinctively, Julie's arms wrapped around Brett's neck as she leaned into him. The sounds of the street faded away. She was conscious only of Brett's warm lips against hers, his arms crushing her to him, his possessive kiss.

And a feeling that she never wanted to move from this position.

She clung to him as the sparks careened wildly through her.

He pulled away slightly. "Julie…" Her name was a caress on his lips. As if he couldn't help himself, his lips returned to hers, kissing, demanding.

Julie lost herself in a galaxy of sensations. Brett's hungry mouth…the scent of his spicy aftershave…the feel of his springy hair as her fingers glided up his neck.

Nearby laughter brought her back to the present. Brett loosened his hold.

She was as unbalanced as if she'd stepped off an

amusement park ride. "Brett," she whispered against his mouth.

He stepped back abruptly. She held on to his arms, trying to regain her composure, as she watched emotions chasing each other across Brett's face. Desire, then concern battled in his eyes.

Concern won. "Julie." His breathing was as rapid as her own, his voice roughened. "If I had known about Warren—if I'd had any idea—"

"I told you, I have nothing to fear." Her voice rasped. Brett's kisses had always stirred her. But this was more overwhelming than any she could remember. More overwhelming than anything she'd ever felt before. "I'm—worried about you." Still dazed from Brett's kiss, she shook her head. She had to think.

And she had to tell him the truth.

Brett grabbed hold of her hand and started to pull her back to the car. "We have to talk. God, Julie, I never meant to put you in any danger—"

"I'm in no danger!" Julie declared. "Brett, I—"

They stared at each other again, and for a moment, Julie thought he was going to pull her back into his arms. And she wanted more than anything to be there.

"Julie. I—I should say I'm sorry I borrowed you. But I'm not."

Her voice came out in wisps. "I'm—not—either." His hand on hers radiated heat.

"Tell me what you're thinking, what you feel about Warren Wesley now, after all these meetings." Bending toward her, his face revealed his concern— and something more. "You've always been scrupulously honest. Tell me."

Scrupulously honest?

Julie swallowed. It hurt to breathe.

She had always been scrupulously honest...until now.

When she had lied to him about her engagement.

Not lied, exactly. But she hadn't told him the full truth, that she'd ended her engagement.

What would Brett say when she told him? When she admitted that this whole thing was unnecessary?

That she'd gone along with Brett's plan because she wanted to spend time with him?

The truth was, she'd never gotten Brett David Ryerson out of her system. And Brett's scheme had been like a gift-wrapped package, perfect for finding out if sparks would still fly between them—or if their love was dead and gone.

Well, she'd gotten her answer.

The sparks were enough to ignite the whole street.

She sucked in her breath, searching for the right words.

She wanted to tell him. She needed to tell him.

But now? Just when she was beginning to realize that sparks were flying, sparks that could fan the flame of their former romance? When she knew deep inside that *something* between them was very much alive?

If she told him now, Brett might be angry, might even turn away from her in disgust.

"Julie?" He was peering at her anxiously. "Are you all right?"

"Not—quite," she managed, breathlessly.

The briefest smile spread across Brett's face.

"I'm not quite myself either," he admitted.

She mentally shook herself. She had to tell him. But perhaps it would be better to break it to Brett gradually. Starting with her change in feelings about Warren.

"Brett, I—"

A strong wind whipped autumn leaves against

their legs, bringing the comforting scent of wood burning in a fireplace from a nearby house. Julie took a deep breath of the cool, dry air.

"C'mon, it's cold. Let's get into the car." Brett tugged her, and they walked rapidly until they reached his Jeep. Once inside, Julie turned to meet Brett's eyes.

"I—I had some misgivings about Warren," Julie said slowly, chafing her hands together. She'd left her gloves in the car. Her hands felt icy, although the rest of her body was still burning from Brett's kiss. "And now—" She paused, searching for words as she slipped on her gloves.

"Now...?" Brett prompted.

"Now..." Julie was conscious of the desire to stop talking, to put her arms around Brett's neck and kiss him fervently. In the enclosed space of the car, she could smell his spicy aftershave, hear his ragged breathing—and her own—and feel his concern like a warm blanket engulfing her. She fought her desires. She had to talk to him.

"Now my misgivings have turned into—into grave worries," she said slowly, picking her words with care. "I have serious doubts about Warren's character. How he could do what he did to Shannon and Arnold is beyond me." She paused, taking a deep breath, as Brett regarded her, a serious expression on his face. "It's just terrible. But the fact that he has underworld connections..." She looked away, staring out the car window at the front of Felicia's store down the street. As she watched, an elegantly dressed woman entered.

"It's just...unbelievable," she finished.

"You don't believe Felicia?" Brett demanded.

Julie turned back to him. Brett's expression was worried.

"It's not that," she reassured him. "It's just...incomprehensible to me why Warren would even need—or want—that kind of association." She heard the edge of anger in her own voice. She gripped the straps of her shoulder bag. "Warren can be charming, and he's bright and influential. He doesn't need that kind of 'help' for his political career!"

"No, he probably doesn't." Brett's tone grew calmer. "He has his own family connections, his own wealth. Unless—"

She knew what he was thinking. "No," she said, shaking her head. "There's never even been a hint that Warren's father had any association like that. No, I think this is something Warren got into on his own. Knowing what I do now about his character, it shouldn't surprise me." Julie heard the world-weary note in her voice, and looked down at her hands. "But even without that—what he did to Shannon alone was enough to make me think twice."

"I'm glad."

Julie's head shot up. Brett was studying her. There was no trace of sarcasm in his voice, only concern written on his face.

"So, I learned things about Warren I didn't know previously. It seems that your plan is working." The words came out before Julie could stop herself. She didn't know why she said it. She knew his plan didn't have to work. She'd had enough doubts before this to end her engagement. This was just the icing on the cake, the knowledge that she'd been absolutely right to break off with Warren.

"Is it?" Brett regarded her, his tone cautious.

She searched for the right answer. "It seems to be—" She broke off as a disturbing thought occurred to her.

She had to face Warren tomorrow, had to spend one more afternoon pretending to be his devoted fiancée. She felt a little sick at the thought. How was she going to pull off the act that she was unchanged?

It would have been only slightly difficult before her journey with Brett. Now, it seemed to be a gargantuan task.

"I don't know how I'm going to look Warren in the eyes tomorrow."

"You don't have to," Brett said firmly. "Just don't go."

"No, that would be cowardly," Julie protested. She had promised Warren she would go through the charade of being his fiancée this last time. "I have to go to the party. I—I made the commitment. Besides," she said, as she saw Brett was about to protest, "I have to speak to Warren face to face. I owe him that." She stopped and looked down at her gloved fingers. She hadn't realized she was twisting the ring around and around under the glove until now.

She looked back up at Brett. "I'm not the kind of girl who avoids something just because it's unpleasant. I'll do what I have to do."

"I know." Brett's voice was quiet. "You've always been one of the best people I've ever met."

The best? When she still hadn't told him the whole truth?

Julie opened her mouth, ready to confess the rest of the story.

Laughter reached their ears, and they both glanced toward Felicia's store again. This time Felicia and Joe, arms wrapped around each other, were leaving. They walked toward a dark sports car.

Julie shut her mouth. Perhaps she'd said enough for now. There would be time later to finish telling Brett the whole truth.

She looked back at Brett, feeling drained. Warren had been on her mind constantly the last few days. She could use a break.

"Can we talk about something else for a change?" she asked.

"Of course." Brett paused, looked out the window, and then turned to Julie again. When he spoke, his voice was quiet and cool and nonjudgmental.

"Will you tell me the real reason you broke up with me?"

Chapter 10

Had she heard him correctly?

The last thing she had expected was a question about their break-up years ago. Julie stared at Brett, acutely aware of their close proximity in the car. Each movement of his hands or shoulders seemed magnified. With every breath she took she could smell his potent masculine aftershave, and the attraction she felt grew infinitely stronger.

"You want me to tell you why we broke up?" She repeated the question in disbelief.

"Yes." He leaned back against the door, facing her. "You were always honest. But that day…" He let his words fade.

Julie sighed. When she'd broken off with him, she'd known Brett hadn't believed her reason. She didn't know if he would now. But it was important that she convince him she'd been telling the truth. Just how important, she didn't want to consider right now.

"I told you the truth then," Julie began, searching Brett's face for his reaction. "We'd dated for the last three years I was in college. I hadn't dated much before I met you, and—I just felt restless, like I needed some space and some other experiences. And…" Recalling her words that day, she continued, "I thought I needed some excitement, adventures. We'd gotten into kind of a comfortable existence, but I wanted something new and different, a change of pace. I think—I think I was too young and immature to realize I was going through some kind of phase."

"I remember your saying all that." Brett's voice sounded strained. "But wasn't there more to it than that? What about your parents—especially your mother? Wasn't she telling you to look for a rich boyfriend?" His mouth settled into a straight line.

He'd accused her of that same thing the day they'd broken up. Julie tried to choose her words carefully. She wanted to make him understand the truth. She *had* to make him understand.

"My parents made it known they would prefer if I married someone wealthy," she said slowly. "Especially, as you said, my mother felt that way. But they never tried to force the idea down my throat. They never twisted my arm or said I *had* to do that. I wouldn't have listened." She shook her head. "And I knew they liked you as a person."

"Then why did they push the idea of a break-up?"

"They didn't—not in the way you believed." A lump formed in her throat, and Julie swallowed. "I know Adam and Jonathan told you once they'd overheard my mother lecturing me about marrying for reasons other than love. I found out much later that you'd asked them, and they'd talked to you. But they were kids then, and didn't understand. And they didn't hear the whole conversation."

Brett looked at her quizzically.

She swallowed again, then continued. "No, my mother pushed the idea that marriage was like a—like a business arrangement."

"*A business arrangement*?" Brett sounded incredulous. His eyes, fastened on Julie, were wide.

She watched him carefully as she spoke. "Yes. A business arrangement." Julie paused, and sighed. "You see, she married my father—my real father—for love, but they were on a tight budget. My father worked for a corporation that didn't pay particularly well. And after he died, I guess things were tough.

163

My dad left insurance, so we weren't starving, and my mother was able to continue to stay home with me. I was three. But my mom was worried about the future. Then my mother met Ted. She respected and liked him. They had the same goals. Ted wanted to get married and he cared for her. They both wanted stability, a home and family." She took a breath. Brett was still staring at her. "There was no great romance there, just a nice relationship with mutual respect and goals.

"So they got married, and somewhere along the way, I believe they *did* come to love each other. They're devoted now in a kind of independent, casual way. Just like business partners who respect each other but allow each other plenty of space."

Julie noted the dubious expression crossing Brett's face. "I'm telling you the truth, Brett," she whispered, her voice gaining in urgency. "My parents—my mom in particular—never said I had to marry someone for money. What she did say was that marriage was like a business arrangement, and I had to be practical. I had to make a logical choice, like any good businessperson." *But a business partner would never be enough for me*, she added silently—the same thought she'd had years ago.

"Is that why you broke up with me?" Brett's voice was subdued. But Julie recognized Brett's own pain, and the old resentments in his expression.

"No. Like I said, I was restless—going through a phase, I realized later. Perhaps I had to see if I was missing something, some excitement. Unlike my mom, I believed there should be excitement in a relationship, not just practicality. Maybe part of me also wanted to test my mother's theory—I'm not sure about that." Julie wanted to reach out and touch Brett, but forced her hands to lay still. "I just know I wasn't quite ready for the commitment you wanted. Probably I was too immature. I just needed a little time, some space. But you took it to mean I wanted to meet someone wealthy, and I couldn't convince you otherwise. Even though I told you I still loved you." Her voice faltered. "And you—walked out." At the memory of Brett's accusation, his anger, tears stung Julie's eyes. She looked down. "You didn't believe me," she whispered raggedly.

"I believe you now."

Her head shot up and her pulse jumped. "You do?"

"Yes." He was regarding her, and—did she dare believe it?—the resentment she had recognized on his face previously faded as they spoke. "I do." He said it firmly. He reached out and touched her face with a gentle finger, tracing the line of her jaw.

"Why?" she asked shakily.

"Because I don't believe you're interested only in money. I saw your reactions with Felicia and Arnold—and especially with Shannon." His finger stopped. "If you'd been interested only in Warren's money, I don't think you would have been so upset when you learned about his true character."

Julie felt a tear edge out and trickle down. "Thank you," she managed.

"Don't cry, Julie." His warm fingers cupped her chin. "Please. I never meant to cause you pain."

"I know. I—I'm glad you believe me now. I'm so sorry I couldn't convince you—before." She hesitated. "Did you—did you know I called you, about six weeks later?"

"You did?"

"Yes. I wanted to tell you—that I was sorry, that I loved you and—wanted you back." Her voice dwindled as she gazed at his golden-brown eyes.

He stared at her. "You didn't leave a message."

"Because a woman answered the phone. When I asked—who it was—she said Lorraine, your—girlfriend."

165

"Lorraine? Lorraine—oh, her." His tone dismissed her as nobody. "That was just a temporary fling—to ease my pain."

"Oh." Julie took a deep, shaken breath. She should have guessed. "I should have called you again. But I...I didn't want to mess things up for you...and I was so confused. Maybe I was a coward too. Like I said, I was immature. I needed to—to grow up."

There was silence for a heartbeat.

"Julie..."

Brett bent closer, and his fingers brushed her cheek tenderly.

Julie caught her breath, feeling the warmth in his touch, and more tears welled up in her eyes. She shut them.

Could he still care?

"Julie. Look at me."

She obeyed the command in his voice, opening her eyes to look at Brett.

Brett inhaled sharply, then reached out and gathered her close.

Their lips met and clung. Julie felt flames ignite deep within her. The kiss burned, consuming her whole body. In that precise instant, she knew what she'd suspected was true.

She loved Brett.

She had never stopped loving him, and her love, though it had been lying dormant for years, was just as powerful now as it had ever been. More so. After spending the last few days with Brett, seeing the man he was, she knew deep down that she'd never love anyone else.

Brett deepened the kiss, his tongue sliding inside her mouth, twining with hers. Her pulse bounced and she wrapped her hands around Brett's warm neck to bring him even closer. She felt his hands surround her waist, pulling her toward him, until she bumped against the car's gear shift. Brett loosened his hold a fraction.

"Brett..." Julie recognized the longing in her voice.

"Julie...Julie..." Brett kissed her cheek, her face, the top of her head, then returned to her lips.

They clung together, and Julie lost track of time as she savored the feel of Brett's lips pressed against hers, the ecstasy of being held close to the man she loved.

Shouting near the car jarred them, and Julie pulled back, suddenly conscious that they were parked on a public street, making out like a couple of teenagers. She felt her face grow hotter.

Brett must have read her mind. "I know." His eyes, alight with passion, met hers. "This is not the time or place—""

A couple of teenage boys passed right by the car, hooting and shoving at each other playfully.

"Yes." Still dazed by the intensity of the kiss, Julie shook her head, trying to clear her clouded mind.

"Let's get out of here," Brett suggested. "We can grab some lunch on the way to the hotel where we'll be staying tonight."

"Where are we going?" Julie asked. Without Brett's arms, she felt cold.

"Not far from the hotel where Warren is going to have his party." Brett reached into his pocket and brought out his keys, which jangled noisily. He hesitated, then put them into the ignition, and turned slowly to face her.

"I have a surprise for you."

"A surprise?" Julie couldn't imagine what it could be.

"Yeah. I thought about this last night, after you went to sleep." Again he hesitated. Then he smiled, and the grin reached from his mouth to his eyes, lighting up his whole face. It was the biggest, most genuine smile Julie had seen on Brett since he'd accosted her on Wednesday.

"How would you like the opportunity to wear that slinky black number you bought yesterday?"

"The black—you mean the black dress?" Julie looked at him, confused. Whatever was Brett talking about? He'd practically ordered her to wear the purple one tomorrow at Warren's party.

"That's right. Let's forget about Warren Wesley. How would you like to go out with me for dinner and dancing? Tonight?"

A burst of sunshine, warm and glowing, erupted in Julie.

"Tonight? With you?" She didn't try to suppress the delight in her voice.

"That's right. I owe you dinner and dancing." His smile became teasing. "And I'm not about to let anyone else take you out—or get near you—when you're in that dress."

The possessive note in his voice ricocheted through her.

Julie answered with her own smile. "I'd *love* to."

****

Julie stood before the large bathroom mirror, applying her makeup with extra care. She felt like her heart was flying through the air.

The fact that she was finally going out for her dream date—a glamorous evening of dinner and dancing at this posh hotel—was exhilarating enough. But since she was going out with Brett, the man of her dreams—well, it was enough to cause tingles of anticipation to skyrocket through her.

After visiting Felicia, they'd headed back from High Bridge, stopping for a quick lunch at a small diner. Then they'd taken Route 80, driving east until they reached Bergen County. Brett had a large, luxurious hotel in mind that catered to corporate and business travelers during the week. It also had a fancy restaurant and nightclub. Though they hosted weddings on weekends, the hotel had plenty of rooms available.

While Brett checked them in, Julie wondered what their room situation would be. There were probably enough vacancies on a weekend so he could get two rooms, but did he trust her now to stay in another room?

Or did he want her in the same room as him?

He selected a suite with a sitting room and large bedroom. Then, while he went to make reservations for dinner, Julie went to the hotel's shop to purchase extra pantyhose.

By the time they got up to the large and elegantly furnished rooms, they were both starting to droop. The events and emotions of the last few days had tired them out, and Julie had caught Brett yawning, as she tried to stifle her own yawn. Announcing she wanted to rest, she'd dropped into the king-sized bed for a nap. Her last conscious thoughts were of her love for Brett.

She had slept surprisingly well, deeply and with only wisps of pleasant dreams, and when she awoke over two hours later she felt happy and refreshed. Sitting up, she saw her watch said just after four thirty. The room was quiet, and she glanced around.

After a moment she saw that Brett, too, had decided to nap. He was stretched out on the opposite side of the huge bed, fast asleep. The king-sized bed was so large that she hadn't even been disturbed.

Julie left the bed quietly and had taken a shower. When she emerged, Brett was no longer sleeping. She poked her head into the sitting room. The shower in the smaller bathroom off that room was going, and she knew that Brett, too, was getting ready for the evening.

As she finished with her makeup, she heard the

TV in the next room. A rap on the door startled her and she dropped her makeup brush. It clattered against the polished counter.

"Julie?" Brett asked. "Do you think you'll be ready for dinner in half an hour?"

"Yes," she called out, wondering if Brett could hear the anticipation in her voice. She didn't think she'd been this excited about any date since the formal fraternity dinner she'd gone to with Brett her sophomore year. But this was even more exciting. Because now she was in love.

"Okay," he said, and she heard him move away from the door.

She removed her dress from the closet and slid it carefully over her head. After smoothing the soft black material into place, she turned to survey herself from all angles.

Next she picked up her hairbrush. When she was satisfied with her hair, she looked through the small travel jewelry case for the earrings she'd packed. Originally she'd planned to wear the clear, glittery, cascading fake gems to Warren's party. He'd always disliked this pair, calling them gaudy, and she'd tucked them away months ago. It had seemed fitting to her to take them out and wear them to his party, their last official appearance together.

Julie held the costume jewelry up to her ears, studying her reflection critically. Next to the elegant, sexy black dress, the earrings weren't gaudy. On the contrary, they looked perfect.

She put the pair on and turned this way and that. The whole effect was nice—sexy without being blatantly so.

She smiled suddenly at her reflection.

Tonight, she would enjoy herself. She would forget all about Warren Wesley, about sneaky affairs and arson and mob connections. She would simply be a woman going out for an evening on the town with a handsome, desirable, wonderful man.

She dropped her engagement ring inside the case and shut it firmly. After tomorrow, she vowed she'd never wear it again.

She picked up the cologne she'd bought at the store and spritzed herself liberally. Then she slid her black-stockinged feet into black patent pumps.

She checked herself one more time. Taking a deep breath, she tried to quiet her thumping heart. She turned toward the door of the adjoining room.

****

Brett was straightening his tie when he heard the bedroom door open, whispering as it brushed against the burgundy carpet.

He turned as Julie entered the room. And froze.

She was a vision.

He felt almost dizzy. He'd never seen her look more beautiful—or alluring. His pulse raced as he gazed at every luscious inch of her.

Julie was wearing the sexy, short black dress she'd selected on Friday. And as good as it had looked on her in the store, it looked even better now. With her dark hair softly curling around her shoulders, and her lips a kissable rosy color, Julie was the epitome of a feminine, desirable woman. Sparkly earrings peeked through the waves of her dark hair. She was absolutely stunning.

The warmth that washed over him was like a hot Caribbean tide. He swallowed.

She was smiling at him. "I'm ready." As she moved forward, her dress swished against her thighs. Though not revealing, the dress accentuated every feminine curve of her lush breasts and small waist. Her legs, clad in sheer black stockings, were slim and curvy and sexy enough to make his mouth water.

"You look *gorgeous*," he declared.

Her smile deepened. For a moment, he couldn't

think of another word to say, and he wondered if she'd caught the note of awe in his voice. He'd seen Julie looking stunning before—but not for three years. And never as desirable as she looked this moment. The impact was like being in the center of an earthquake.

"Thank you," she was saying. "You look fantastic yourself." She regarded him in his dark suit.

Brett had to fight the urge to pull Julie right into his arms and kiss her all over. He had promised her a special evening of dinner and dancing, and he was not going back on his word. Even though he was tempted to pull her down on the bed and make love to her all night long.

"Julie—" His voice was hoarse. He hesitated, cleared his throat, then started again. "I'm glad you're wearing that dress with *me*. Shall we go?"

She slid her hand into the crook of his arm, smiling up at him.

They took the elevator to the top floor. Julie stood close beside him, and he caught the sensual scent of her perfume. It wasn't the cute vanilla scent she usually wore. This cologne was feminine and beguiling.

The elevator paused at the ninth floor, and a heavyset couple squeezed in. Julie moved closer, her shoulder brushing against his dark suit.

The elevator stopped at the top floor, where the hotel had their fanciest restaurant and live music. They followed the large couple at a discreet pace.

Brett gave the name Brett David to the host, and they were escorted past a table with two couples. Both men were about Brett's age. One was with a woman who was so skinny she looked like a poster for a starving nation. The other man's date was definitely chunky. Neither man tried to hide the fact that they were looking Julie over.

Brett placed his arm firmly around Julie's

shoulders and drew her close.

The maître d' indicated a corner table, then held out a chair for Julie. He handed them menus, told them to enjoy the meal, and quietly left them alone.

The tables here were spaced far apart, lending themselves to intimate conversations. A large candle in a glass jar glowed in the middle of the pale blue tablecloth. In a corner, some musicians were tuning up their instruments.

"This is elegant," Julie said, glancing around the room. She opened her menu.

Brett watched her as she studied it.

When she'd made the remark yesterday that he'd never taken her out for dinner and dancing, it was like a punch to his gut. It had been true. All too clearly, he recalled how Julie had always said she wanted to go for a romantic evening of dinner and dancing with him. And he'd always replied, in an offhanded way, that he'd take her. One of these days.

But "one of these days" had never arrived.

Yesterday he'd decided, then and there, that he'd give Julie the kind of evening she'd always dreamed about.

He owed her that much. And he couldn't wait for one of these days. After all, she'd been a good sport and had gone along with his plan. He'd give her the evening right away, before turning her over to Warren.

But the thought kept popping up that maybe he wouldn't be turning her over to Warren.

Because she had expressed serious doubts about Warren Wesley. Enough doubts to raise Brett's hopes that she didn't want to continue with her fiancé.

His plan was working. Except that he hadn't counted on the overwhelming feelings Julie stirred in him.

He didn't want to get jubilant too soon. She still

had to face Warren tomorrow. Who knows what persuasive powers Warren might use in person? Still, Julie was intelligent, and certainly not a pushover. She seemed to realize by now that Warren was a creep, and would be a rotten husband.

He would just have to depend on Julie's common sense, and Warren's poor character, to bring about the right decision. He was confident that Julie would make the correct choice. Warren Wesley would never be good enough for her, not in a million years.

Not that Julie would think of it that way. Brett scanned the appetizers listed on the menu. She was too modest to conclude that Warren wasn't good enough to be her husband. No, she'd probably just feel he wasn't the kind of person she'd want to spend her life with.

She needed someone who would love her and cherish her, someone who wanted her to be happy, who respected her and cared for her feelings, someone like…

Brett stopped, slamming the brakes of his thoughts quicker than he could in the car.

Someone like…him?

"What are you going to order?"

Julie's voice broke into the clouds in his mind. He focused on her.

"I think I'll start with the curried mushroom soup." He picked the first thing listed on the menu. "As for the main course…I still haven't decided."

He had to refocus and stop thinking about Warren Wesley. He had to concentrate on the here and now, on being attentive and giving Julie a night to remember. On being her dream date.

"What about you?" he asked.

"I'm going to have the Veal Cordon Bleu," she said. "And a salad to start."

"That sounds good. Mmm…" Brett studied the menu. "Everything sounds good."

A waiter approached and asked them if they wanted something to drink. Brett requested a bottle of champagne, and Julie's eyes glowed as he did. After studying the menu for another minute, he decided on filet mignon.

When the champagne arrived, he held his glass up.

"A toast," he said, and Julie lifted her flute.

"To what?" she asked.

"To old friends." He was afraid to say more than that.

"To old friends..." she echoed, touching her glass to his. They clinked musically, reverberating. "And to new beginnings," she added, her eyes sparkling more than their drinks.

Warmth spread throughout him at her words.

The waiter brought them a basket of warm rolls, and as they began their meal, Brett steered the conversation to Julie's family and friends.

"Has Jonathan decided where he wants to go to college next year?" he asked.

"I think he's favoring Lafayette or Cornell, although he hasn't ruled out Amherst." Julie buttered her roll. "Ted graduated from Amherst, and you know Adam's going there. But I think Jonathan wants to do something a little different. He's planning to study pre-med. He still wants to be a psychiatrist."

"And Adam's still interested in business?" Brett asked.

"Yes." Julie bit delicately into her roll. "Mmm. This is good."

The homey smell of the rolls was comforting. Brett sampled his. She was right. "What are your parents up to lately?"

"Oh, the usual." Julie waved her hand. "Ted often works long hours with his family's investments and businesses—his father is retired completely now, and my grandparents—Ted's parents—live in Florida during the winter. And Ted's younger sisters have shares in the business, but don't actively participate. But he and my mother have done more traveling in the last few years. This summer, they were in Italy and Switzerland."

"What about your other grandparents?" Brett questioned, curious. Julie had always been close to all her grandparents—her mother's parents, her father's, and Ted's. In fact, she often said she had three sets of grandparents. Ted's parents had always accepted Julie as another of their grandchildren. And Julie's mom had always been careful not to overlook her late husband's parents when it came to family activities.

"They're all doing well, except that Paul—my mother's father—had open heart surgery last year. But he recovered nicely. By the way, my father's mother, Nina, asked about you the last time I visited them. They're still living in Union."

Brett continued to ask Julie about family members, and her friends Jessica and Lindsay. She told him about Kendra, her closest friend from work, and they spoke about the school and other faculty members.

She asked about his friends, family, and his job. He described the excitement of working with a pro basketball team he really liked, and the new minor league baseball team that was his most recent account.

He kept the conversation bright, making some amusing comments that had Julie laughing. With her eyes sparkling and her lips curved into a smile, she appeared to be having a wonderful time, which was just what he wanted.

More than anything, he wanted her to have a special evening.

The food was delicious, and Julie commented

that it was presented with the extra flourishes typical of the best restaurants.

"This is really a wonderful place," she said, lifting a forkful to her mouth. "Have you been here before?"

"Never." Brett shook his head. Did he imagine it, or did a satisfied look skim over Julie's features? "One of my coworkers recommended it."

He switched topics. "So, did you ever get to Stonehenge or the Acropolis?" he asked lightly.

"I finally got to Stonehenge. When I was in England with my mom and Ted during high school, we didn't have time to go, and I was determined to go back. I went with Jessica two years ago, and yes, we made it a priority to visit Stonehenge. It was incredible," she finished.

"And the Acropolis?"

She shook her head, her sparkling earrings swirling seductively. "No. But I'll get to Athens someday."

The band began playing, first a medley of show tunes, then a Duke Ellington jazz number. When their plates were cleared away and the waiter brought them a dessert menu, Brett looked at Julie, who was watching him.

"Do you want to dance?"

"Yes," she answered eagerly.

He stood up and extended his hand. She placed hers inside his and followed him onto the dance floor.

Brett turned and drew Julie into his arms. She moved easily into them and rested her head against his shoulder, swaying to the music.

Brett savored the feel of her in his arms, all softness and femininity. Though she was tiny compared to him, she fit so well in his embrace, as if she belonged there, her body brushing against his, the scent of her perfume swirling around them.

He was piercingly aware that Julie was not just the cute, pretty girl he'd once been in love with. She was an alluring, beautiful woman, one any man would be proud to be seen with.

And for the evening, she was his.

His. Brett tightened his grip, reveling in the feel of holding Julie close. He bent his head so his lips brushed her soft hair. It held the slightest scent of a fruity shampoo. Her head nestled into the niche by his shoulder, and they moved in sync to the music.

The music, a love song, reached out, circled around them, until he felt that they were floating together, away from everyone and everything troubling in the world.

He felt rather than heard Julie's soft sigh, and tightened his fingers through hers.

They danced, moving to the music, just two people locked together, isolated from the cares and dangers of the world.

Holding Julie like this, knowing he was giving her the kind of evening she'd dreamed about, Brett felt pure happiness.

It ran through him like a current, and he felt pretty sure that it was running through Julie too.

The music ended, and he held on to her a few moments longer than was necessary. After several seconds she pulled back, tilting her head up to meet his eyes.

The expression in Julie's dark eyes heated him to the core. Slowly, he lifted her hand to his lips and kissed it.

He felt a tremor go through Julie at his kiss, but her eyes never left his.

The band swung into a hot Latin song, and he led her off the dance floor and back to their table. The dessert menus waited for them.

He pulled out the chair for Julie, and she seated herself gracefully and opened the menu.

178

As Brett sat down, he saw the expression on Julie's face.

It was a smile of sheer happiness.

She glanced up then, meeting his eyes again.

"Are you having a good time?" he asked, hoping he'd hear the answer he wanted.

"Oh, yes," Julie said emphatically. "The best."

Brett smiled back at her. "Good." He looked down at his menu.

And the evening wasn't over yet.

****

It was the most wonderful night of her life.

Julie looked at herself in the mirror in the ladies' room and carefully reapplied her lipstick.

Her cheeks were flushed, and her lips curved in a continual smile. She knew it wasn't just from the champagne they'd shared at dinner. No, this was from total happiness.

She was out for a night on the town, the kind of evening she'd always dreamed about. A night of dinner and dancing and the company of the most wonderful man she could imagine.

Brett had been attentive, seeing to her every need, making sure she enjoyed herself. He had given her exactly the romantic evening she'd always wanted.

And she fell a little more in love with him with every passing minute.

She loved Brett. The knowledge sparkled through her like the fine champagne they were drinking.

She finished combing her hair, still smiling at her reflection, and returned to Brett.

The waiter had brought their desserts. Brett was waiting patiently, and when Julie sat down, he dug into his pecan pie.

She picked up a spoon and sampled her chocolate mousse. "Hmm, this is delicious," she said.

"Brett, you picked a great restaurant. Everything—the food, the music—is just wonderful."

"I'm glad." Brett smiled at her. "I wanted to give you a special evening."

"It is special," Julie repeated. She could see the pleasure in Brett's face.

After dessert, they returned to the dance floor when the band played a popular slow tune. Held in Brett's arms, her head close against his chest, Julie could hear the thudding of his heart. She smiled. She couldn't remember ever feeling so happy. The way Brett held her, the looks he gave her, the tender kiss on her hand—she was positive they were signs that he cared.

Maybe, just maybe, they were signs that he loved her too.

They danced slowly, and Julie clung to Brett, wishing the music would go on and on. If she stayed like this forever, she'd be content.

The song ended, and the band took a break. They went back to their table, finished their coffee, and talked quietly.

"This was wonderful," Julie said again as she polished off her coffee. "I'm full."

"Me too." Brett drained his cup. "I could use a nice long walk."

"That's a good idea," Julie agreed.

"You don't mind?" Brett asked. "I mean, we could dance some more after the band returns."

Julie shook her head. When she'd dated Brett, they'd often gone for long walks after eating out, something they enjoyed doing together. "We've danced and had a great meal. You've given me the kind of evening I've always dreamed of. I don't mind taking a walk around the hotel." She stretched her hand out. "Thank you, Brett."

"You're welcome." Brett paused, then covered her hand firmly with his warm one. He added, "I'm glad you had a good time, Julie," as he gazed at her. She couldn't quite read the expression in his eyes.

"I did," she said. As Brett paid the bill, Julie knew that the memory of this evening would wrap itself around her for a long time.

But she didn't want the evening to be just a memory. And she didn't want the only reminder of the time she spent with Brett to be a fancy dinner and dancing. She wanted to spend time with Brett doing everything, from the exciting to the mundane, from dancing to just taking long walks.

She wanted to spend time in Brett's arms, making passionate love, bringing him the pleasure she used to, leaving him totally sated.

She wanted to keep spending time with him. An eternity.

Julie slipped her hand into Brett's as they left the restaurant and took the elevator to the main floor. Once there, they strolled through the hallways, quietly content, letting the enchantment of the music remain wrapped around them, cushioning them from the rest of the world.

They peeked into the hotel's store windows, walked by the steamy windows overlooking the indoor pool, and past the noisy first floor bar. Julie's hand stayed firmly in Brett's as they walked along, neither talking much.

They walked for over twenty minutes before they found themselves in front of the elevators again. Brett gave Julie a long look, then pushed the button.

It had been a wonderful evening. *The* most wonderful evening. Julie sighed with pleasure.

Brett met her eyes as a jovial group of middle-aged couples came up behind them, and they all crowded into the elevator. Julie found herself nestled against Brett, and he put his arm around her and pulled her closer.

They rode up in silence, and when they arrived at their floor, they had to squeeze by the laughing people who were going up.

The sixth floor corridor was quiet, almost eerie, compared to the noise on the elevator. Brett kept his arm around Julie as they walked to their suite.

They reached their room, and Brett removed his arm and searched for the electronic room key in his pocket. As they stood close, Julie's heart began to thud. After a few seconds, he took out the card and slid it into the opening.

The door clicked, and he opened it.

What next?

Julie took a breath and walked past him into the room, fumbling for the light switch. She found it and turned on the low light in the sitting room. Her heart accelerated.

Brett shut the door behind her, then carefully slid the safety chain into place. Turning, he looked at Julie.

They were silent for a moment.

Julie found her voice. "That was the best evening of my life," she said softly, smiling. "Brett…it was worth waiting for. *Thank you.*"

Brett moved forward, closing the distance between them, until they stood only inches apart. He reached out, sliding his hands around Julie's waist. His palms burned through the thin material of her dress, and Julie's heart jumped.

"The evening doesn't have to end now," he said, his voice hoarse. He bent his head and gently brushed his lips against Julie's. She sensed the tension in his body, as if he was holding back. "I want to give you the kind of night you've always dreamed of, too. The kind we used to share. I want to make love with you, Julie, and make you feel every thrill you've ever desired."

Every atom in her body leaped at Brett's

suggestion. The longing Julie had been feeling for days rushed through her, flared at the desire she saw in Brett's eyes with a fierceness so intense it shook her. She moved her body closer to his.

"Brett..." Her own voice was breathless.

"If you don't want to, I'll understand," Brett said slowly, as if the words were painful. "But...," his voice dropped to a stirring timbre, "I want you, Julie. More than you could ever imagine."

She recognized with his next words that he was giving her time to turn back.

"If that's not what you want, tell me now," he said, "and then go into the bedroom and lock the door. But if it's what you want..." His lips brushed hers again, warm and sensual. "I'll make love to you and fulfill every fantasy you've ever had."

A shiver of sweet anticipation moved up her spine, and she wanted to lose herself in him.

"Brett...I..." She struggled to get the words out. "I'm not on...I don't have..."

He understood immediately.

"I have protection," he said quietly.

Her hands slid around his neck, locking together, and she stood on tiptoe and pressed her body intimately against him.

"Make love with me," she whispered.

Brett looked at her for one more moment, and she recognized both heat and happiness sparking in his eyes. Then he captured her lips, and Julie's temperature instantly shot up.

His tongue probed her mouth, seeking, and hers met his, tangling together, as he pulled her tightly against him. Julie felt herself melting into his embrace, and Brett's hands slowly molded her body to fit against his.

The sparks that Brett ignited in her body caused a torrent of heat. It was as if a hot flood of lava flowed through her, the desire like nothing Julie had ever felt before. She responded to Brett's kiss by moving against him.

Brett groaned softly, pressing her tightly to him. Julie felt the rock-hard proof of his desire through the thin material of her dress. "Julie...sweetheart...I've wanted you from the first moment we were together..." His lips returned to hers in a sizzling kiss.

He tasted like coffee. Julie caressed his neck, the hard muscles covered by smooth skin, and tangled her fingers in his thick, springy hair.

"Julie," Brett murmured and moved his lips to kiss her face, her neck, her shoulder. A trail of fire followed his lips. She let out a soft cry from the sheer pleasure of his kisses.

Brett bent and easily picked her up. Julie slid her arms around his neck, feeling his warm flesh, hearing his ragged breathing close to her ear. Her gaze met his, and the mixture of caring and pure passion she saw reflected there had her gasping with delight.

He carried her into the bedroom and placed her gently on the bed, then shrugged off his jacket and slid down beside her. He pulled her into his arms again.

His mouth came down and hungrily took hers. She kissed him back just as ardently. She heard rather than felt the buzz of the black dress's zipper sliding, felt the cooler air on her back as it was completely exposed. And then Brett's hands, warmly caressing her bare flesh, pushing the fabric away. Within seconds the dress was gone, and Brett's hands encircled her waist, pulling her even closer.

His lips left hers. "Julie...Julie...tell me what you want."

"You. I want you," she whispered back, her voice full of longing.

She opened her eyes and caught the adoring

look he gave her as he pulled off his tie.

"You are...so...beautiful..." he whispered, his look sweeping over her. His hand moved to unhook the lacy blue bra she wore, and she felt his fingers tremble against her. "So beautiful," he repeated as he brushed her nipples with his thumbs.

Her response was instantaneous. Her nipples tightened and she arched toward him, feeling the heat bubbling deep within her. He bent his head and took one taut bud into his mouth to circle it with his warm tongue. Julie gave a soft cry as his mouth savored her breast.

Desire burned through her, and she gripped his head, her fingers burrowing through his hair.

"Brett...oh, Brett..."

He moved to her other breast, repeating his slow, sensuous circling, and her innermost core melted into a pool of need.

Long murmurs escaped Julie's lips. As sensations bombarded her, she continued to tangle her fingers through Brett's hair, inhaling his masculine, spicy scent.

"Did you like that?" he whispered as his lips moved slowly up her chest and neck.

He seemed to remember her most sensitive areas. "Oh...yes," Julie whispered back. She wanted to touch him, too, to taste him, and her fingers fumbled at the buttons on Brett's shirt.

Brett helped, shedding his shirt and undershirt in seconds. Julie spread her hands on his glorious, masculine chest; her fingers smoothed the golden hair there, caressed his taut muscles. As she played with his nipples, Brett pulled her against him, his hands stroking her waist.

"Julie..." he whispered and rubbed against her.

His hard chest pressed against hers, setting off more sparks of desire. Julie moved against Brett and felt the heat escalate inside as he once more captured her mouth.

She heard the metallic click of his belt buckle, felt him fumbling at his pants and socks, and then they too were cast aside. His long, lean legs pressed against hers, rasping sensuously against her sheer pantyhose. The heat from his body seared her.

Her hands wrapped around Brett, pulling him closer, and he paused for only seconds to tear away his briefs.

And then she felt him sliding her pantyhose off. His hand traveled up, skimming her bare skin, leaving heat where he touched. His fingers slipped under the lacy top of her bikini and he tugged. Slowly, tantalizingly, he slid it down, his fingers brushing her curls.

Julie moaned, unable to help herself as Brett stroked her. His every touch was magical, left her tingling, wanting, needing him.

She wanted him to feel the pleasure she was, to experience the same thrills and longing. Boldly, Julie reached out and touched him. Brett gave a strangled gasp as her hand stroked his engorged manhood.

Slowly, she closed her fingers over him. He was huge, and hot, and oh-so-ready.

"Julie..." The words were barely above a whisper. He shifted closer. His mouth hardened, his tongue twisting with hers in a sensual dance as he pulled her tightly against him. His fingers crept between her thighs and slowly parted them. And then he was touching her intimately, stroking her.

An intense need, unlike anything she'd ever experienced before, pierced Julie. She moved against Brett, bringing them closer, gasping as he found her core.

She tore her mouth away. "B-Brett...oh, please..." The air around them shimmered, and she was conscious only of this exquisite, pulsating need, a need only Brett could fill.

"Yes," he whispered. His hand moved, and she was dimly aware of his tearing the packet open, heard rather than saw him sheath himself, before his fingers slipped inside her again. She arched, felt herself on the brink. "Brett..."

His fingers moved away, and with one smooth stroke, he thrust into her.

Julie cried out. The completeness, the joy of Brett in her very center, brought tears to her eyes. And then he began to rock, and her moans mingled with his. She couldn't think, she could only feel the wonder and the glory enveloping her entire being.

Waves of sensation rushed through her, spiraling upward, increasing in intensity with every moment. With one powerful thrust, Brett took her up and over the edge. She cried out, clinging to him as she flew out into the ecstasy of space.

And Brett was right there with her, emitting a cry from deep within his throat as he pounded within her.

Slowly, they floated back down to earth, to the bed where they lay joined among tangled covers, their arms and legs intertwined.

She had reached Heaven, was Julie's only hazy thought.

****

A murmur from Julie brought Brett's mind into focus, and he realized he had his full weight pressing her down. He moved to his side, taking her with him.

"Julie..." He couldn't think of another word to say. He kissed her, again and again.

"Hmm..." Her voice, low and satisfied, was so sexy that he felt a prickling of sensation again deep within him.

He'd wanted to take it slow, to draw out the lovemaking long enough to bring Julie to the peak several times. But once he'd begun to touch and stroke her, he hadn't been able to help himself. He wanted her so badly, he could barely wait until he knew she was ready. The wanting, the needing burning in him had been greater and more intense than anything he'd ever felt before. He *had* to have her.

Being enclosed within her satiny warmth, he'd known pure ecstasy.

As he cradled her in his arms, he knew he wanted to feel that ecstasy again.

And again.

Forever.

He'd fallen in love with Julie all over again.

And he was never, ever going to let her go.

Chapter 11

Julie's heart was still beating hard as she clung to Brett. He was absolutely right—he'd given her the perfect night.

"Brett, that was...you were...spectacular," she murmured.

She felt him smile against her cheek. "You were pretty spectacular yourself." His voice was husky.

"Hmmm..." She shifted slightly, pressed her lips to his neck. "You really did give me the kind of evening I always wanted. And...it's not over yet." She leaned back so her eyes could meet his.

Pure desire flashed in Brett's eyes. "No, it's not."

She pressed against him, seeking his mouth. He covered her mouth with his own and brought his hand up to caress her breast. Within seconds she felt him growing rigid against her leg.

Her entire body sizzled in response.

They made love again, slower this time, but no less satisfying. Brett kissed her and stroked her, and Julie explored his body, touching and marveling at his masculine attributes. Julie could see the excitement on Brett's face in response to her own passion.

Afterward, they drifted into a satisfied slumber, entwined together, holding each other close.

****

Brett awoke suddenly, instantly conscious of the warm body cuddled beside his. Julie. He could get used to holding her like this every night.

She stirred. He thought for a moment she was still sleeping, but then she murmured, "Brett..." in a sleepy-but-sexy, ultra feminine drawl.

"Hmmm?" He pulled her closer, expecting she would go right back to sleep.

But her ideas matched his own desires. She wrapped her arms tighter around him and rained kisses on his chest.

He sought her mouth eagerly, and they made love again.

****

Sudden laughter in the hall and a sliver of light poking its way through the curtains of the hotel room were the first things he was conscious of when he opened his eyes. He teetered on the edge of sleep.

Julie's breathing was deep and her body, tangled with his, was warm and peaceful as she slept. He didn't want to go back to sleep. He wanted to enjoy the quiet moments before she awoke, relish the feeling of Julie in his arms, study her in slumber.

Her face looked peaceful, and absolutely beautiful. And, he thought with a surge of pride, satisfied. She looked exactly like a satisfied woman. Exactly the way she had a right to look.

What he wouldn't give to see that look on her face every morning.

She stirred slightly. For just a second, she frowned. Then the frown was smoothed away, and she sighed.

She was so beautiful—inside and out. So giving, so loving. It wasn't just her body that had excited him yesterday. It was Julie herself, holding her, making love to her, feeling her warmth and caring.

He had been correct last night. He was in love with Julie. Somehow, in the last few days, he'd gone from caring about her welfare to being totally, irrevocably in love with her.

And it felt damned good.

He inched his hand to her soft hair, gently

touching the silky strands. Perhaps he'd never stopped caring for Julie. And spending time together these last few days had merely intensified his feelings.

It didn't matter. He knew he loved her, would always love her. It was very simple. And he wanted her back in his life.

She was the most caring, most wonderful woman he'd ever met. She deserved the best.

Someone far better than Warren Wesley. Someone who would love her and cherish her and treat her well.

Him.

He stared at Julie, the thoughts swirling through him.

He could see that his plan was working perfectly. Julie had been disillusioned with Warren.

More than that. She didn't seem to feel about Warren the way a girl should feel about her fiancé. She must be falling out of love with Warren.

And maybe falling for him, Brett hoped.

Thinking about it, about their passionate lovemaking last night, he was convinced that Julie would never have made love with him if she still considered herself engaged to Warren. So, she must be planning to end her engagement. And she must be feeling more than just mere attraction to him. She must have special feelings for him.

Now, it would be easy to insert himself into Warren's place.

Had he done that already?

With that thought came a creeping sense of guilt.

He'd known Julie would be hurt when she learned about Warren's true character. He'd hoped she would break her engagement to that snake.

And he must have held a shred of hope, deep inside, that she'd turn to him.

And he'd taken advantage of that fact. He'd come on to her when she was feeling low, maybe feeling alone and vulnerable.

He shifted his position. Had he taken advantage of Julie?

The longer he stared at her, sleeping peacefully, a half smile on her face, the longer he was afraid he had. Julie had been disillusioned with Warren, saddened by his selfishness, his callous treatment of others. And maybe scared by what they'd learned from Felicia about Warren's mob connections.

Had she turned to him, looking for some solace, some comfort? And had he taken blatant advantage of that fact?

Uncomfortable, he moved back slightly, loosening his hold. As much as he loved her, as much as he desired her, he didn't have the right to take advantage of Julie when she was feeling low.

He tried telling himself that she'd been eager to make love. That she wanted him as much as he'd wanted her. And maybe she had…or maybe she was just seeking comfort, and it had turned into passionate lovemaking.

He gave himself a mental shake. How would she feel when she woke up?

He knew he wanted to make love again. Just thinking about it made him hard. But in the reality of morning light, would she have regrets?

He guessed they would have to talk about last night.

His thoughts bounced in his head like a pinball game. Hitting, echoing in his mind.

Slowly, so as not to wake Julie, he disentangled himself. But it was difficult to leave her warm body, the coziness of the bed. He needed to clear his head and decide what to do next. Before she awoke and all he could think of was making love to her again.

He eased himself up, then slipped out of bed,

walking quietly to the bathroom. There, he turned on the shower and stepped in.

****

The steady beat of water woke her. Julie reached out, found the space beside her empty, and opened her eyes.

A streak of daylight highlighted the room. Brett was no longer lying beside her, but the splash of water from the shower told her he was nearby.

She sighed, stretching, then curled into the blankets again. What a night! She couldn't help smiling. The most romantic night of her life had ended with the most passionate lovemaking she'd ever experienced. Everything had been perfect.

She loved Brett more than ever. She knew, deep down, that she always would. Perhaps she always had, and yesterday had only crystallized those feeling for her. They'd been there, dormant, long before. And now they'd flamed fiercely to life.

It would be wonderful to wake up every morning like this.

She didn't think she'd ever felt so happy, so satisfied. Brett had been the perfect date, and the perfect lover. More than that. He'd fulfilled all her fantasies—and surpassed them.

She pulled the pillow tightly toward her and burrowed into it. She caught the scent of Brett's aftershave, faint but still lingering. Brett. Her lover.

The shower turned off, and she sat up, waiting for Brett. After a few minutes, he poked his head around the door.

"Did I wake you?" he asked, spotting Julie.

"No." She smiled at him. With his hair damp and a towel wrapped around his lower body, he looked utterly masculine. Drops of water reflected from the bathroom light on his thick, dark blond chest hair, and she could see just how muscular his shoulders were.

He approached her, and she instinctively lifted her head. Leaning down, he brushed her lips tenderly with his. Little thrills cascaded through her body.

"Mmm," she murmured. She was about to wrap her arms around his neck, when he pulled back.

"How about coffee and room service?" he asked.

Julie thought she saw a slight hesitancy in his eyes. Was he feeling awkward this morning, the morning after? She didn't. She felt wonderful.

"That sounds heavenly," she said.

He sat on the bed and reached for the phone.

Julie glanced at the clock. It was just after eight. She noticed the small red button on the phone, on the side away from the bed, was blinking.

"You must have a message," she said.

"A message?" Brett sounded startled. He looked at Julie. "I'll order, then pick up the message."

After calling in an order for pancakes, coffee and orange juice, Brett held the phone.

"Julie..." he began, then paused.

She reached up and laid her hand against his cheek. It was smooth and newly shaved. She recognized confusion in his eyes.

"Last night was wonderful," she said simply.

"For me, too." His voice dropped to a husky timbre, and he leaned forward to kiss her again, longer this time.

Julie melted. She knew in a few more seconds she would end up in his arms; but then he pulled away.

"I better get this message," he said reluctantly.

He hit a button to retrieve the message.

His back grew stiff suddenly, and he muttered an oath. His eyes flew to Julie's.

"What is it?" she asked and tensed at the anxiety she saw flaring in his eyes.

"That was my friend, Don. The guy who helped

me find everyone." He held the phone in a tight grip. "He called last night with news. When we were at dinner. I left my cell phone off." He stopped, then went on. "Arnold escaped from jail."

"Arnold escaped—are you sure?" Julie felt like her insides had been drawn into a knot and tightened.

He nodded, then hit another button, repeating the message. This time he held it to Julie's ear.

"Hey Brett, this is Don," the voice said. "Listen, buddy, I got some bad news a few minutes ago and knew I had to let you know right away. I left you a message on your cell too. Arnold just escaped from jail. Yeah, that's right. He busted out, and the police haven't got a clue as to where he is. Call me." He hung up abruptly.

"Oh, my God." Julie sucked in her breath. "Arnold's out...we were probably the last ones to visit him."

Brett's face was grim. "Yeah." He stared at the phone for a moment before replacing it.

"Do you think—did we somehow inspire him to—" She stopped as guilt washed over her.

"No." Brett shook his head.

She wasn't so sure. "He has a huge grudge against Warren." Julie leaned back. "I hope, for his sake, that he doesn't try anything. Warren's mob friends will kill him." She shivered.

"I'm going to call Don," Brett said, "and see if he has any more info."

Julie went into the bathroom, now totally awake. She stared at her face in the mirror. Arnold escaping from jail? She had to admit she was shocked. Whining, weak Arnold didn't seem capable of escaping from a prison, even a minimum security one. Maybe he'd had help?

Julie turned on the water and stepped into the shower, letting the water pelt her, the warmth soothing to her suddenly tense muscles...and soothing to those muscles she rarely used.

Sometime later, she'd tell Brett about her practically nonexistent physical relationship with Warren. How Warren rarely wanted sex, and how she'd found him to be self-centered in bed. Their infrequent encounters had been unsatisfying. In fact, that had been just one more reason she'd decided against marrying him.

Shannon's recounting of sex with Warren had certainly seemed far removed from any experience she'd ever had with him.

She thought again about the startling news of Arnold's escape.

Now she wondered, would Arnold go after Warren? Today?

The same thing must have occurred to Brett, because as soon as she switched off the shower, he called in to her.

"I don't think you should go to that party today."

"I promised—" She stopped.

Guilt flooded through her, fast and merciless.

Brett didn't know. She hadn't told him yet!

She rubbed her face with the thick towel. She'd meant to tell Brett yesterday that her engagement to Warren was off. Had been off for days. But that she felt compelled to attend the party because of the promise she'd made.

She suspected he'd be angry with the deception. More than angry. Probably furious. Maybe that was why she'd put off telling him.

And then he had taken her into his arms last night, and all coherent thoughts had flown away, like leaves blowing in the autumn wind.

She knew she had to tell him. Now.

She shook scented powder on herself, then pulled the thick towel around her and stepped out of the bathroom.

Breakfast awaited her. Brett handed her a cup of coffee, his eyes sweeping over her. They looked concerned.

Julie inhaled the rich aroma, then took a sip of the hot, bracing liquid. "Brett, I—" She had to start somewhere. "There's something I have to tell you-"

The phone jangled, and both of them jumped.

Brett, his eyes on Julie, reached for the phone. "Hello." He sat on the bed.

Julie saw he had already poured himself a generous cup of coffee, and she handed it to him. He took it automatically, now focused on whoever was on the other end of the line.

"Yeah, uh-huh..." He drank. She sipped her own. Brett had already added milk and sweetener, and it was perfect. Like he was.

"Did they try his mother's house?" Brett asked with a touch of sarcasm, and Julie knew he was discussing Arnold with his friend Don. "Not there? Have they looked—well, he might be going after Warren..."

Brett listened, and Julie wandered to the window, peeking outside. The day was gray, and the bending trees outside signaled a brisk wind. She sipped her coffee. Telling Brett the truth was going to be difficult. She had to get it over with. As soon as he got off the phone.

"Something else...?" Brett was saying.

How was she going to explain everything to him? She watched as a gray-haired couple, arm in arm, walked across the parking lot.

"Okay, so what else did you overhear his bodyguard saying? Get to the point."

Julie turned. Was Warren aware of Arnold's escape? She no longer cared for Warren, but she would hate to see Arnold try to harm him, as much for Arnold's sake as Warren's—

"*What?*"

Her eyes flew to Brett's face. He wore an expression of total shock.

A sense of dread crept through her.

And then he turned to stare at Julie.

"*They aren't?* She—" His voice came to a choking halt.

Her blood turned to ice.

Chapter 12

Why? *Why?*

Julie had broken her engagement to Warren Wesley! Over a week ago.

Then why the hell had she pretended she was still engaged?

Don was talking. "Sorry, pal, but I wanted to let you know as soon as I found out—"

"Uh—yeah. Thanks." Somehow, he found the words, though his stomach felt like it had fallen as fast as a runaway elevator.

Julie was watching him, her face pale. She stumbled over to the bed and sat down abruptly, as if her legs could barely hold her.

"I'll call you." Brett replaced the phone, then stared at it for a moment.

Why had Julie lied to him? And why on earth had she gone along with his plan, letting him show her Warren's evil side, if she had already decided to call it quits with that bastard?

Slowly, deliberately, he raised his head to look at her.

She looked disturbed now.

"Brett," she began.

"Would you like to explain," he said, enunciating each word carefully, "why you neglected to tell me you had broken your engagement to Warren Wesley?"

He saw her flinch at his clipped words.

She opened her mouth, and hesitated. "If you remember," she said, her voice hoarse, "I started to say there was something I had to tell you—when the phone rang."

"That may be so." He could hear the chill in his voice, colder than the ice of a hockey rink. "But you waited a long time to tell me. You could have told me when I first—borrowed—you."

For a moment she said nothing.

He desperately tried to ignore how defenseless she looked. How beautiful and upset. He steeled himself against the appealing picture she made.

His hands balled tightly. "All this time, you knew you weren't going to marry the bastard. But you went along with me, let me introduce you to people and spend time trying to convince you Warren's no good—" He stopped. "Why, Julie, *why*? Why this charade?"

He saw her swallow; then she lifted her chin and stared him in the eyes.

"Because"—her voice remained scratchy—"I wanted to—learn the whole truth about Warren. And, more importantly, I wanted to spend time— with you." Her voice dropped so swiftly he wasn't sure he'd heard her correctly.

"Spend time? With me?"

"Yes." She tilted her face further up. "I don't expect you to believe this, but you were—have been—on my mind for a *long* time."

He stared at her.

She took a long, shaky breath, then continued, her fingers playing with a corner of the towel.

"A few weeks ago, I realized that I just didn't have the strong feelings a woman in love should have for her fiancé. It was more like—more like I enjoyed Warren's company, and going out with him and having a good time. Plus, I began to suspect that Warren wasn't quite what he seemed to be. And slowly, by listening and observing carefully, I got a very different picture of him than the one he presented to the public. And to me." She looked down.

"I decided," she continued, looking back up, "that I just couldn't marry him. *No way*."

"I can understand that," Brett broke in, his tone sharp. "But why didn't you tell me?"

She sighed heavily. "I told Warren last weekend we were through, as nicely as possible. Though I didn't know," she added emphatically, "about his mob connections. He took it well, I must say. I thought he'd be angry and hurt. It came out that, apparently, he thought I would be the perfect wife. But he had no deep, abiding love for *me*." Her eyes flashed dark sparks of anger. "But he did ask me for one favor, for his sake."

She stopped.

"What was the favor?" Brett felt some of the tension drain from his hands and heard his voice grow calmer. He sat on the bed, opposite Julie.

"He asked me to pretend to be engaged for one more week. Till after the election. To attend his party today—it's going to be an important function, with lots of politicians there—as his fiancée. After that, we'd just quietly split and go our separate ways." Her fingers twisted the towel.

"All right. Let's suppose you felt compelled to keep the secret." He leaned back, fighting the urge to pull her into his arms, kiss her until they both couldn't think a coherent thought. After all this, he still wanted to hold her close, to kiss her thoroughly. Was he crazy? "But why, *why* did you come along with me and pretend you wanted to find out about Warren? Why did you lie?"

She stood up abruptly and went to the window. "I didn't lie." Her voice was low. "I only said what was necessary to make you think I was still engaged. And I did want to find out the rest of the stuff about Warren."

"The whole thing was a lie!" Brett exploded. He

stood up too, strode over and grabbed her by the elbows, spinning her to face him. "You went along with my plan, pretended to be engaged, let me think I had to convince you Warren was no good—and all along you knew it! You knew you weren't going to marry him! You're a fake, Julie."

"I am not!" Anger leaped into her eyes, and her beautiful face scowled back at him. "I admit I played along with your scheme, crazy as it seemed to me. But I did want to learn about Warren, just in case—in case there were other things I should know. And it turns out there were!" She shook her arms free. "And I promised him that I wouldn't tell anyone. That includes even those I care about. My family doesn't know either!"

"Still, you could have trusted me, and told me," Brett argued. How could he believe her? "And what about last night, Julie? Was that a fake, too?"

She gasped, as if the words had struck her. "No!" She stopped, then suddenly reached for a chair near the window and dropped into it. "No, Brett," she said, and her voice sounded weary. "That was no fake. Everything—the way you made me feel—was real. Wonderfully real." She looked up, and tears glistened in her eyes. "Last night was—unbelievable. Everything I had dreamed of."

"How do I know I can believe that?"

"Because it's *true*." Her breathing sounded ragged as he stepped closer, but she met his look head on.

She looked so honest, so open and sweet. He wanted to believe her. But could he? She'd lied all along.

"I—I went along with your plan," she said, her voice tremulous, "because I wanted to—be with you. To see—" She stopped.

"To see…?" he questioned.

She hesitated, biting her lip. "To see if…we

could have a...second chance." Her voice dropped to a whisper.

Had he heard her correctly? He frowned at her, unable to believe the words.

The phone rang.

Brett jumped. Before he could tell Julie to ignore it, she sprang up and ran across to the nightstand, picking it up like someone grasping for a lifesaver.

"Yes?" she asked, and listened.

She looked up at Brett. "It's for you. It's Don."

Handing the phone over, she stepped back.

****

Julie listened as Brett spoke to his friend. Her throat was hot and tight and unshed tears pricked her.

Brett thought she had lied, had used him. How could she explain that she'd realized she'd made a mistake when she'd broken up with him three years ago? That she was thinking about him constantly, still feeling *something* for Brett? That when he'd presented her with the opportunity to spend time with him, get to know him again, it had been like a gift-wrapped package with her name on it that had been left for her to tear open? Was she so terrible for taking advantage of the opportunity to check the present?

Should she have even mentioned a second chance?

Now was definitely not the time to reveal that she was in love with him. As angry and confused as he sounded, he'd never believe her.

Maybe after the party—

The party. She had to get ready for the party.

She went to her suitcase, scrounging around for her pantyhose and shoes. Going to the closet, she removed the dress. Maybe afterward—

Brett's voice was low as he spoke to his friend. But she heard him clearly discussing the fact that

Arnold had not yet been located by the authorities, and that Warren's henchmen had left to meet Warren when he arrived from Boston. He'd be landing at the airport very soon, and then going directly to the hotel nearby where the party was being held.

Brett hung up and turned to Julie. "Forget it," he said, spotting her with the dress hanging over her arm. "You're not going to the party."

"Oh yes I am." She faced him. "I made a promise, and I'm going to keep it."

"There's no reason for you to," he snapped.

"There's no reason not to," she snapped back.

"Your safety—"

"Don't be silly," Julie interrupted. "I'm in no danger. Maybe Warren is—if Arnold is stupid enough to try something in public—but I'm certainly not. If you don't want to take me there, I'll go myself. I'll call Kendra and have her pick me up. She's going too."

Julie caught the gleam in Brett's eyes. "And don't think," she added, guessing where his thoughts were going, "that you can forcibly detain me. I managed to meet Kendra at the teachers' convention, and told her everything that was going on." She saw the surprise in his face.

"She knows I'm with you," she continued. "If I don't show up to that party, she'll call the police or tell Warren or do something, I don't know what, but she'll definitely raise an alarm. She didn't like this whole idea, and was worried about me. I assured her I'd meet her at the party, safe and sound."

Brett's expression had grown grimmer.

"So I'd better be there," Julie concluded, her heart pounding.

She had to be there. Aside from her promise to Warren, aside from reassuring Kendra that she was all right, she felt she had to see this through. Seeing

Warren for the last time was necessary. Perhaps for her own psyche, she realized. Perhaps to finally finish this chapter of her life and close the door on it. Slam the door, actually.

And open a new one? With Brett?

She ached to. The whole time they were talking so furiously, she'd wanted nothing more than for him to reach out, gather her into his arms and hold her close.

His handsome face was dark, unreadable.

"All right," he said abruptly. "But I'm going with you."

****

Julie walked down the brightly lit corridor of the posh hotel, her heels sinking into the thick wine-colored carpeting. She kept her steps determined and pasted a smile on her face. Risking a sideways glance at Brett, she noted that his expression was still as stiff and unreadable as it had been for the past hour.

The sound of her purple dress swishing against her knees made her wonder what Brett thought about the way she looked. Did he still think she looked sexy and desirable? Or had the revelation of her concealment of her broken engagement wiped all those thoughts from his brain?

They had barely spoken as they got ready for the party and checked out of their hotel. The short drive had passed in uncomfortable silence, and Julie felt almost powerless. She wanted desperately to finish their conversation, to convince Brett that although she hadn't been totally honest, she hadn't wanted to deceive him. She had simply taken advantage of a situation that presented itself, and gambled on finding out whether the feelings they'd once had for each other could be revived.

Would he ever understand?

Had she been totally wrong?

Her thoughts twirled through her brain. If only she had told Brett sooner. If only—

But she had to live with what had happened. And first she had to deal with Warren, and the cocktail reception.

She'd tucked the crystal from Felicia in her purse. She thought about it now, hoping the crystal would bring her some luck. She was going to need it to get through this ordeal.

Rounding a corner in the hall, Julie spotted Kendra, looking attractive and sophisticated and frankly worried, standing right by the door to a banquet room. Light, bright music spilled from the room as she approached her friend.

"Julie. Thank goodness." Kendra stepped forward to hug her, and then pulled back, scanning Julie's face. "Are you all right?"

"Yes, fine," Julie said automatically. She smiled in an attempt to ease the slight frown she saw on Kendra's face. "Really, Kendra." She dropped her voice. "But—a lot has been going on. I'll fill you in later." She took a step back and glanced at Brett, who towered behind her. His expression had gone from stormy to carefully neutral. His professional face, she suspected.

"Kendra, this is Brett," she began.

"I'm glad to meet you." Brett extended his hand.

Kendra shook it. Her friend appeared to be sizing Brett up, and as Julie watched, she gave him a smile. "Nice to meet you." Julie knew Kendra was being her charming self, but was reserving judgment.

"Ah, ladies, there you are!" Julie turned toward the jovial voice of Warren's campaign manager, Tony. He strode toward them, holding two flutes of champagne. "Please, take some," he said. "Come in, come in. We have a lot to celebrate."

"Is Warren here yet?" Julie asked, surveying the

206

banquet room. She tried to sound like an eager girlfriend. Elegantly clad women and men moved about, talking, laughing, chiming glasses together. Black-and-white clothed waiters and waitresses moved among the crowd, holding trays of hors d'œuvres and glasses of champagne.

"No, but he called from the limo. I expect him here any minute," Tony answered. He raised an eyebrow toward Brett.

"This is an old friend of mine, Brett Ryerson," Julie said quickly. "He's become very interested in politics recently."

The two men shook hands, Tony smiling widely, Brett more reserved. Julie knew Tony was speculating as to whether they could count on Brett for future contributions. Julie also wondered how much Tony suspected about Warren's mob connections. She didn't want to know.

"Well, please, come in and meet everybody," Tony invited.

They all stepped farther into the room. Soft music slid around Julie. She searched for familiar faces, spotting a few political friends of Warren's in one corner, and some of his neighbors straight ahead.

"Julie, my dear." The coolly formal voice of her almost-future-mother-in-law touched Julie's ears. Julie turned again to face Claudia Wesley, who looked elegant in a simple but expensive-looking navy blue dress.

Claudia Wesley had always been correct and seemingly cordial, but Julie had never cared for her. There was something cold and calculating in her eyes, something that occasionally surfaced in her well-modulated voice, that made Julie think that when it came down to it, Mrs. Wesley would always look out for her own interests first, and the rest be damned.

"Hello," Julie said. She had learned early on that Claudia reserved outward affection for those closest to her—her son and daughter and her father. Julie made no move to hug or kiss Warren's mother. She smiled, hoping it didn't look as stiff as it felt. "How are you?"

Did Warren's mother know about his mob connections? Had her late husband been connected too? She'd never heard even the slightest rumor of it, so she doubted the possibility.

She would have to work hard not to reveal her own knowledge, to pretend everything was fine. She hadn't thought it would be difficult to act the part of Warren's loving fiancée one more time. She'd been hiding her true feelings for several weeks. Suddenly she wasn't so sure of her acting abilities. And to act like she had no knowledge of his underworld connections—

"Hi, Julie." An uncle of Warren's stepped forward as Mrs. Wesley gave a perfunctory "fine."

Within seconds, Julie found herself surrounded by several of Warren's cousins. She saw Brett and Kendra standing to one side, drinking champagne. She tried to focus on Warren's cousin Madeline as she sipped from her own flute. The smooth liquid went down like silk.

As soon as she could, Julie excused herself and headed for the ladies' room. She met Kendra's eyes as she walked and knew her friend would follow.

Once inside, Julie tried to collect herself, breathing slowly. She had to see this through. She *would* see this through.

"What's going on?" Kendra asked as soon as she entered the luxurious room.

Julie had already ascertained that no one else was occupying the ladies' room. But she kept her voice to a whisper as she quickly told Kendra the highlights of the last two days. When she revealed that Warren had mob connections, Kendra's eyes grew wide, and she groaned.

Julie gave her friend the bare minimum of details as to what was happening between her and Brett.

"So we argued after he found out," she finished, "and now he doesn't trust me. I'll give you more details later."

Kendra nodded. "I know. This isn't the time or place to really talk. We'll have to speak tonight."

The door opened, and an elderly woman wearing lots of heavy gold jewelry came in. Julie recognized her as a supporter of Warren's and a big contributor to his campaign.

"Hello," she greeted the woman and assumed a wide smile. "How are you, Mrs. Carstairs?"

"Hello, my dear," Mrs. Carstairs said. "Warren's just arrived. I believe he's looking for you."

"Oh, good!" She made her voice excited. "I'd better get back to the party." She tried to look the part of an eager fiancée as she fluffed her hair. "I haven't seen him for several days."

She left the ladies' room, accompanied by Kendra. As she walked past a smaller reception room on the way to the larger one where the party was being held, she heard a movement behind her. And then she felt a hand on her shoulder.

"Hello, Julie."

Her back instantly went rigid. Warren's voice was more subdued than usual. Julie whirled around, the stiff smile once more plastered on her face.

"Hello!" She pretended she was a normal girl greeting her normal boyfriend. She was proud that her voice sounded the part. For the benefit of Warren's two friends standing only a few yards away, she wrapped her hands around Warren's neck and gave him a kiss. Or were those men friends? Were they bodyguards? Or something else?

She could smell the sophisticated, expensive cologne Warren favored. He held her for a few seconds, and Julie had to fight the urge to pull back immediately. She didn't want to be in Warren's arms.

She managed another smile when she stepped back. "How was your flight?"

"All right, although we left Boston late." His hand moved down her arm, and Julie had to steel herself not to flinch from the possessive touch. "We have to talk."

A frisson of fear moved up Julie's spine. What could he possibly want to talk about now?

"All right," she agreed, as though nothing had happened in the last few days, and congratulated herself silently for still sounding normal. "But don't you want to join all your guests?" She forced herself to sound innocent.

"In a minute or two." Had she really thought she was in love with this man? For all his handsome features, his expression was just too self-absorbed. It had taken her long enough to realize, and now it hit home doubly.

"Excuse us." He nodded at Kendra with a smile. "I need a moment with my fiancée."

Julie saw concern flash in Kendra's eyes, then disappear as Kendra smiled. "Of course." She sounded natural.

His hand clamped on her arm, Warren steered Julie toward the smaller, empty room, where tables were clothed in heavy white linen but no places were set.

Warren pulled her into a corner of the room. The faint music from his reception next door and the whisper of their feet digging into the thick carpet were the only sounds. Julie swallowed, still able to taste the expensive champagne, and suddenly longed for some more.

Warren paused and turned her around.

He stared at her for a moment. Julie tilted her head up, unable to read his expression. His blue eyes looked harder than she remembered.

"I hate those earrings," he said abruptly, frowning.

Julie had to fight a desire to laugh at his petty comment. She responded, her tone tinged with sarcasm, "That's why I'm wearing them, dear."

His frown deepened. "Did you have to wear them today, of all days? You know how important this reception is to me."

"I doubt a small pair of earrings will have much impact." She strove to make her voice milder. She didn't want him to know what she suspected about his dark connections. But she wasn't about to hide her spirit while they were alone. "Your constituents have better things to do than spending time studying my accessories. And you're fortunate. I didn't have to show up," she concluded.

Anger flashed across his features, and Julie wondered if Warren had ever considered that maybe she wouldn't do as he asked.

"How is your grandfather?" she asked, trying not to sound too annoyed.

He folded his arms and ignored her inquiry. Standing there in his expensive suit, looking polished and wealthy, his eyes were cold, and Julie saw for the first time the resemblance between him and his mother.

"Well, well, well," he drawled.

Annoyance mixed with fear as Julie met his look. Or was it the champagne causing these emotions? After her argument with Brett, she had eaten little. The champagne might be going straight to her brain.

"Well, well, well, what?" she echoed, her voice edgy. She shifted under Warren's gaze.

"It didn't take the busy little girl long to find a new man, did it?" The words were lined with steel. "Or were you seeing your new beau even when we were engaged?"

"No, of course I wasn't seeing anyone!" Julie protested. "And for your information, I think it was generous of me to show up here. I didn't have to," she reminded him again.

"With your boyfriend in tow, I hear." His mouth was set into a frown.

Julie attempted a laugh, but it sounded artificial to her own ears. "I brought a friend. Period." She folded her own arms. "You hardly have to worry, Warren. I'm sure you'll have women chasing you the moment word is out that we've broken up. In fact, from what I heard, you're *already* busy working on that."

He jerked back suddenly, blinking, and she knew her educated guess had been right on the money. He was already dating. He'd probably dated someone during the few days he'd spent in Boston.

It was on the tip of her tongue to say something about Shannon, but she stopped herself. The last thing she wanted was for him to get angry at poor Shannon. Which he would definitely do if he knew his secret had been discovered.

Instead, Julie smoothed her fingers over the fabric of her dress and cleared her throat. "Not that I mind." She lowered her voice to a gentle tone. "You have the right to date others. We're not engaged anymore. This afternoon is just for show—at your request."

"Yes, it is, isn't it?" Warren agreed, but he continued to scrutinize Julie. How much, she wondered, had his buddies learned about her weekend activities?

His hand moved, and suddenly his expression softened. He looked almost entreating. "Don't be too hasty. We could stay engaged, Julie. We're good together." He placed his hand on her shoulder.

"Not good enough," she said, but not as harshly as she wanted to. If Warren knew she was firm in her decision, and if she was kind, maybe she could get out of the party with a minimum of hassles—and soon.

Footsteps broke through the faint music, coming closer. As she glanced at the room's doorway, Brett entered.

He towered above Warren. Although he was some four or five inches taller, his muscular shoulders, plus his air of quiet command and strength, made Brett seem to hover yards above Warren. And psychologically, his concern and caring for others put him years ahead emotionally.

"Kendra said you were in here," Brett said quietly.

"We're having a discussion," Warren snapped, tightening his hand on Julie. "We'd like to be left alone."

"No, we're finished," Julie retorted. She shook off Warren's hand. Warren must have recognized Brett from his friends' descriptions. He certainly wouldn't talk that way to the voters of his town.

Brett approached them. "Julie?" he began.

"Let's rejoin the party." Julie slipped her hand under Warren's elbow and gently attempted to turn him toward the door the way he had steered her only minutes before.

Warren turned and glared at her. A door at the side of the room swished open near Julie. She tugged at him, and he moved, then froze as he caught sight of something behind Julie.

A cold sensation crawled up Julie's spine. Slowly she turned and looked back to see what had grabbed Warren's attention.

Arnold stood in the doorway, holding a gun.

Chapter 13

Julie's heart stopped.

And then it began to thud, sickeningly hard.

For a moment no one spoke.

Arnold's hair stood almost straight up, making him look like he was blown in by the November wind. He wore the black-and-white uniform of a waiter, although his outfit was rumpled and too big. His eyes shone brightly as he held a small handgun. His breathing was rapid, but he held the gun steadily, pointed at Warren.

"Y'didn't think I could do it, did ya?" he demanded. "Thought you had me put away for a long time? Well, I've got friends too, buddy-boy. Once I saw these jokers"—he inclined his head and waved the gun slightly—"I knew I had to get out right away. A couple of my friends helped me. I knew it was time for you to get yours."

Guilt washed over Julie. Their visit had precipitated Arnold's jailbreak.

She glanced at Brett, who stood very still. Her eyes moved to Warren, who had turned a sickly white.

She turned back. "Please, Arnold," she said quietly, in her most soothing teacher's voice, "you don't want to do this. Warren's not worth it. If you do anything, you'll be the one in trouble. I'd hate to see that."

Arnold's eyes blazed. "What makes you think I'll be caught this time?"

"I've got guards all around the place, Arnold." Warren's voice was hoarse. "You won't make it out of here alive."

"Maybe I don't care." Arnold took a step closer.

"She's right," Brett said. "Warren's not worth it, Arnold, not worth your life. Come on, I'll get you out of here. I'll give you money so you can get far away." He inched closer to Arnold. "You can start a new life today."

Julie knew at once that Brett was trying to get rid of Arnold for her sake, so that pointing gun was nowhere near her. Not that she was in danger. It was clear that Warren was the object of Arnold's wrath.

"No thanks." Arnold spat out the words. "Do you think I busted out and got to this point just to walk away from this snake? First I'll have my revenge." He aimed the gun.

"Don't, Arnold," Julie implored.

"Don't be a fool." Warren's voice now held a thread of contempt. "Do you think I'd come here without a bulletproof vest, once I knew you were out?" Despite his voice, Julie felt a tremor go through Warren as he stood beside her. And, in the few seconds that followed, Warren began to shake.

Julie suspected that Warren was close to snapping. What if he became hysterical with fear? Just what they needed! Julie's fingers tensed. She thought about the crystal nestled in the purse she gripped, hoping again that it would give them luck.

Arnold's expression was growing even wilder. For a moment, Julie questioned his sanity. Was he about to lose it?

Arnold laughed then, the sound strident. "What makes you think I'd simply kill you, Warren? There could be a better way. I'll kill something you care about, and you'll have to suffer for the rest of your life, knowing it was all your fault."

The words fell like bricks on the soft carpet of the elegant room. Arnold moved the gun.

Icy awareness burst inside Julie. Her. He was going to kill her.

Because he thought that would make Warren suffer—

She hadn't even told Brett she loved him!

"They're not engaged anymore!" Brett's voice cracked through the room like lightning. "Don't do it, Arnold, it won't hurt Warren!"

He took a step toward Arnold.

Oh God, no! Brett was going to get in the way to save her!

In that split second, Julie knew what true fear was. It whipped her like a frozen winter wind.

"That's not true." Warren spoke rapidly. He obviously had no compunctions about sacrificing her in his place. "We're en-en-engaged."

"You jerk!" Julie cried out, turning to glare at Warren. "Don't lie! Tell him the truth!" She turned back to Arnold. "I broke up with Warren—"

"They broke up!" Brett exclaimed at the same moment, taking another step.

Arnold's hand began to shake. "I don't believe you! Any of you!" And he swung toward Brett, who was drawing closer to him, aiming his gun as he turned.

"NO!" Julie screamed.

She launched herself at Arnold.

****

Brett knew what Julie was going to do a split second before she acted.

Fear for her erupted like a volcano in his gut.

"NO!" she screamed.

"NO!" His shout flew from his throat.

Julie flung herself at Arnold, knocking him sideways. He staggered, and they both toppled to the ground.

Arnold shot the gun.

The noise was ear-splitting. Julie cried out, and

Brett knew true terror.

Julie was hurt!

Brett sprinted toward Arnold as a second shot rang out.

Someone was yelling. There was the sound of running footsteps—

Away. Warren was running away!

Julie was clutching her arm. Arnold had struggled up and he shot again, wildly, this time aiming for Warren's retreating back. Warren dove to the floor. Julie was trying to stand when Arnold shoved her, hard, knocking her aside.

Brett tackled Arnold.

They crashed to the floor as Julie struck her head on a table and crumpled.

Instantly, Arnold thrashed and screeched. Brett pinned Arnold's upper body with his own weight as fury burst inside him. His arms bore down on the struggling Arnold. The gun went off again, but this time it was aimed at the ceiling.

And Julie lay still nearby.

"Julie!" Brett shouted, afraid to turn his head too much. Arnold was fighting fiercely and he had to grip him tightly. "Julie!"

"Help! Call 911!" Kendra's voice, shrieking to someone else.

More footsteps, exclamations. He heard Kendra screaming, "Julie! Julie!"

A hefty man dropped beside Brett, grabbing hold of Arnold too, and together they held Arnold as he fought and swore viciously. Brett recognized the man as one of Warren's troupe.

And all the time, his only coherent thoughts were for Julie. "Julie!"

A third man—a tall waiter—had come to their aid and was practically sitting on Arnold's feet. Someone else knelt by Arnold—Juan Comacho—and wrestled the gun from his hand as Arnold screamed.

Arnold continued to buck and roll, but the three held him securely now as Juan stood up, holding the gun, and pointed it at Arnold.

Dimly, above Arnold's frustrated cries, Brett was aware of more people, exclamations, someone shouting for a doctor.

"Julie!" he called out again, desperately. She didn't respond.

"I'm a nurse!" An unfamiliar woman's voice.

Brett held on to Arnold tightly with the others. "Julie, are you all right?"

No answer.

He tried to turn, to see if Julie was okay. Arnold attempted to roll away, and he had to concentrate with the others to hold him down. It was as if anger and hatred had given Arnold the strength of a maniac.

Someone was calling to them that the police were on their way. Juan continued to point the gun at Arnold but made no move to shoot him. "I can't get a clear shot!" he yelled to someone. Brett heard Warren's voice, but his words were muffled by the other sounds in the room.

It seemed an eternity until two uniformed officers ran into the room.

They grabbed Arnold. "We've got him."

Brett's hands were stiff as he finally released his hold.

They managed to handcuff Arnold. He kicked and swore as Juan handed his gun to one of the policemen.

Brett jumped up, looking desperately for Julie.

She lay on the carpet, her face white. Kendra and a middle-aged woman were leaning over her. The woman was wrapping a tablecloth around Julie's arm, and a red stain was spreading through the fabric of Julie's dress.

Brett's heart fell to the floor.

****

Pain. In her arm. In her head.

She could feel herself floating. She was moving horizontally. Someone near her was crying. A male voice was speaking close by. The words seemed disjointed.

"Hang on—Julie. Please—hang on—sweetheart."

"J—Julie…" She recognized the crying voice now as Kendra's.

She struggled to open her eyes. She was floating through a crowd of people. No, she was lying on something. Through a dizzying blur, she saw Kendra.

"Julie, Julie, you're going to be all right."

She moved her head. It hurt. She tried to look at her other side.

"Hold still." A voice she didn't recognize.

"Julie…sweetheart…"

Brett's voice? She had time to recognize it before thick gray clouds pressed down on her, obliterating everything.

****

She looked so helpless, so defenseless.

Brett swallowed as he stared at Julie. Monitors beeped steadily as she lay unconscious in the hospital bed, her arm bandaged neatly. Her face was pale. Occasionally she murmured, but he couldn't make out any clear words.

For the umpteenth time, his stomach twisted.

The doctors said the bullet wound to her arm wasn't terrible. They'd removed it, stopped the bleeding and were giving her an antibiotic through an IV to prevent infections.

She had a mild concussion too. She'd woken only briefly on the way to the hospital, and a couple of times when they were here. She appeared to be resting now, but not peacefully. He wondered again if she was in much pain. They'd given her something, they'd told him, but how strong was it? He'd neglected to ask. He'd been too overwhelmed with relief when they told him she was going to be all right.

But she had been hurt, and it was his fault.

Brett stared at her. He wanted to cradle Julie, hold her and never let her go. But the IV and hospital paraphernalia prevented that. He wasn't about to do anything to disrupt her treatment.

"Oh, God, Julie," he whispered.

He plopped down on the chair near the bed and leaned his head into his hands. If he hadn't gotten her mixed up in this mess, if they hadn't visited Arnold, if they hadn't attended Warren's party...

He grimaced as he remembered shoving Warren aside to climb into the ambulance with Julie. There was no way he was letting that creep go anywhere near her.

But it was his fault that Julie was injured and lay there so still.

Again and again, he wondered, why? Why had Julie gone along with his plan, when she wasn't going to marry Warren?

Kendra had sat with him for a while, crying a little until they found out Julie was going to be okay. Brett had alternately paced and sat. Warren had appeared briefly, but Brett avoided him, and he left after hearing Julie was going to be okay. Now Kendra was getting coffee before they tried to call Julie's parents again.

So far, they'd been unable to reach the Shaws. They'd left a short message on their answering machine at home, but Brett had no idea where they were or what time they'd be back. He didn't know their cell numbers and neither did Kendra. He'd tried Jonathan on his cell phone, too, but got only voice mail. He'd tried Adam next, but got voice mail there as well.

He lifted his head and glanced out the window. The sky was dark, and his stomach rumbled. He ignored it. He'd been running on the one cup of coffee he'd had a while ago. He'd get himself another cup later. Although he didn't think he'd need it to stay awake tonight. His thoughts would keep him alert.

Footsteps slapped against the tile floor nearby, and Brett looked up.

His father entered the room.

"Hello, son. How is she?"

For a moment Brett could only gape at his father. Then he sat up straighter. "Dad—how did you find out?"

David Ryerson went to stand beside the bed, and stood gazing at Julie's still form for a minute. Brett could see the affection and concern on his father's face. Then the older man moved to the other chair and sat down, his gaze fastening on Brett.

"It was all over the news," he said in a hushed tone. "There was a cameraman and reporter there for the party. They even got some of it on tape. You're quite a hero." He spoke solemnly, but with obvious pride.

"It was on the news—" Brett stopped. Had he heard his father correctly? "A hero?"

"Yes. Is she all right?"

"She has a concussion. And a wound from where the bullet hit her arm." Remembering Julie's cry, the red spreading through the sleeve, he shuddered.

David looked at Julie for another long moment. "All the local TV and radio stations have been covering it. I came as soon as I heard which hospital they took her to." His father smiled briefly. "They're saying that you and Julie are heroes, that you helped prevent this character from killing Warren Wesley. Apparently, the guy has a grudge against

221

him. Warren's campaign manager said on TV that Warren helped you to subdue the guy after the assassination attempt—"

"Helped?" Brett exclaimed, then dropped his voice, not wishing to disturb Julie. "That bastard ran away! He—" He checked himself as he heard Julie stir. He turned to watch her. She moved her head slightly, moaned, and then lay still.

Brett stood and gestured for his father to follow him out of the room. Taking up a position right by the door, where he could observe Julie, he continued. "Warren Wesley is a total coward," he hissed.

"Hmm. That's not how his campaign manager put it. Well, you know these politicians."

"Yeah." Brett's voice seethed with disgust.

"Are you all right?" David studied him.

"I'm okay."

"You're sure?" his father persisted. "Your mother's out shopping, but I got her on her cell phone and told her I was going to check on both of you."

"Yeah, nothing but a scratch." Brett focused on Julie. "Poor Julie. She got the brunt of it. If only—if only I could have convinced her not to go to this party! If only I hadn't persuaded her to visit Arnold—"

"Visit Arnold?" his father questioned. "What were you doing visiting that guy?"

Brett sighed. In a low voice, he told his father the whole story; how he'd decided to "borrow" Julie, convince her Warren was no good; how they'd visited the different people Warren knew well, including Arnold. He skipped over the intimate details, but he had a pretty good feeling his father had filled in the blanks and realized what had motivated him—and exactly how he felt about Julie.

"What I can't understand," he finished, "was why she agreed to come with me in the first place. I mean, if she wasn't really engaged anymore..." His words trailed off. He slumped against the wall and stared into the room at Julie, lying so still in the bed. "It's all my fault," he added brokenly.

David placed a hand on Brett's shoulder, and Brett looked into his father's eyes. He saw understanding and compassion there. *What would Julie's parents think?* he wondered suddenly. Would they be understanding too?

"Don't blame yourself," his dad said firmly. "You didn't bring a gun to the party, this maniac did. You went along to protect her! In fact, you may have saved Julie. After all, you were the one who brought Arnold down."

"I think she was trying to save me." Brett shook his head. "Why, Dad? I don't understand why she went along with this whole plan..."

"You don't?" Something in his father's voice made him look at the older man, hard. There was a look in his dad's eyes, a look of...he almost looked amused, Brett concluded.

"No. Why would she..."

"Because she loves you."

The words echoed in the quiet hum of the hospital corridor, standing out from the sounds of wheeling carts, ringing phones and low conversations.

Brett's heart leaped into his throat. "She...?" He stood up straight.

"As your generation says, *duh*. I think it's obvious," his father said quietly. "Why else would she have gone with you? She loves you and wanted to spend time with you. You presented her with a golden opportunity to do just that! Probably she was hoping to see if you still loved her too. If she didn't care, she would have told you her engagement was over and gone on her merry way."

Brett stared at his father. Now his heart began

a slow, rhythmic slamming against his ribcage.

Could she? Could Julie really love him? "I—I don't know..." He heard the whisper of hope threaded through his voice.

"Even if you hadn't told me this whole story," David said, sweeping his hand, "I could have told you she was crazy about you."

"What?"

"When you came to our house the other day, I saw her expression when she was watching you. There was this certain look on her face—it was the look of a woman who's in love with a man."

Brett sucked in his breath.

"After you left," his father continued, smiling, "I turned to your mother and told her, *Julie's still in love with Brett. And Brett's in love with her. I expect we'll be hearing about wedding plans one of these days*." His smile deepened as Brett stared. "Give me credit for recognizing some things at my age."

Had it been so obvious? To everyone but him? Brett regarded his father, hope wrestling with doubt in his mind. *Could it be true?*

Did he dare to hope...?

But in a second, his heart crashed again.

He had argued with Julie. He had practically called her a liar for not telling him her engagement was broken. He'd been tough on her—way too tough.

And she'd given no real excuse for not telling him about the broken engagement—which might mean his dad was right about her motives. She'd said nothing except that she'd wanted to spend time with him.

And have a second chance, he recalled.

"Oh God, Julie," he whispered and turned to stare at her again.

After the way he'd treated her, so angry and cold—

Oh, no. *No.* He'd blown it.

"What's the matter?" his father was asking, his smile fading.

Brett grimaced. "Maybe that was true—maybe. But I may have wrecked my chances with the only woman I've ever loved."

"You'll find a way to work things out," his father responded confidently.

Brett watched Julie. He loved her. More than anything. All he wanted was to hold her and never let her go. If there was a chance she loved him too—

"If she loves me—I'll never let her go again," he vowed.

****

Slowly Julie surfaced. Her head throbbed, and so did her arm.

Opening her eyes, she peered around the darkened room. A hospital. She was in the hospital.

With a rush, the memories flooded through her. Arnold aiming the gun at Brett. She'd flung herself at him. Pain in her arm, Arnold pushing her, Brett tackling Arnold...then the ride to the hospital. She'd passed out, awoken and slept again, and the memories were jumbled after that. Doctors and nurses, Brett and Kendra close by.

She seemed to be alone at the moment. Trying to sit up, she heard a familiar voice. Brett. He was just outside the room, talking to someone. But she felt so sleepy...

Julie abandoned the attempt to sit up and closed her eyes again.

The next thing that woke her was her mother's voice, and the sound of rustling nearby. Julie opened her eyes to find her parents standing by her bedside, looking anxiously at her.

"Hi..." she murmured; the word came out slurred.

She must be on some medication. Her arm and head didn't hurt as badly as they had before. She felt groggy.

"She's awake!" Kendra's voice came from farther away.

"Oh, Julie!" her mother cried and began asking questions. "How do you feel? Why did you—"

Ted put out a hand to stop his wife. "Shh, Elise. I think Julie needs to rest." He smiled at her with affection. "We're glad you're okay. That's what's important."

"Yes, of course she should rest." Elise turned, said something to someone behind her that Julie couldn't catch. She heard Brett's voice again.

Rest. That's what she needed.

Julie moved in and out of consciousness several times during the next few hours. Different nurses woke and checked her. She heard Brett again.

Once, she thought she was back at the hotel, with Arnold screaming at Warren. She tried to move, but it hurt too much. She called out.

"It's all right, Julie." Brett's hushed words came soothingly out of the dark. When she opened her eyes, she saw Brett bending over her.

"Everything's fine, sweetheart," he whispered and gently touched her cheek. "Go back to sleep. If you need anything, I'm right here."

He'd called her sweetheart. She closed her eyes.

When Julie awoke in the early morning, a nurse was holding her wrist and checking her pulse.

"Well, how are we today?" the middle-aged woman said in a chipper voice.

Julie moved her head. It ached, but it was a dull ache now.

"Better," she said. "Can I have some water?"

The nurse helped her sit up and gave her some ice water. Julie looked around the room.

"Brett?" Had she dreamed Brett was with her last night? She dimly remembered him calling her sweetheart. Was that real or a dream? She ached to

226

see him again.

"Your young man?" The nurse beamed at her. "He stayed here all night. He just went down to get something to eat."

"Oh." Despite her head, Julie felt a sense of comfort. Brett had stayed with her. Maybe it wasn't a dream.

When a breakfast tray was wheeled in, Julie managed to nibble some toast and drink orange juice. She turned her head and saw it was early—not even seven thirty. Before she was finished, her mother appeared. Instead of her usually perfectly put-together look, today Elise Shaw wore no makeup or jewelry, except for her rings.

Julie's mom walked briskly about the room, opening the curtains and pulling the tray out of the way. She'd brought a small suitcase, packed with a few things that Julie kept in her old room at her parents' house. Julie was glad to see the old but decent flannel pajamas, a worn pair of slippers, and even some vanilla shower gel.

"I'll bring some more clothes later," her mother was saying. "After I've spoken to the doctor. You know these hospitals never keep anyone long."

Her mother helped her change into the PJs, which was awkward because of the bandage on her left arm. Elise told her that Adam, who'd been studying at the university library, had gotten a message from Brett when he left the building. He'd called them and Jonathan on their cells. Jon had been practicing basketball with friends. Elise and Ted had been with friends in New York, but they'd rushed over to the hospital as soon as they got Adam's message. They had stayed for a while, but Brett had announced he was staying all night so Elise and Ted had gone home to get some sleep, and Kendra had, too.

"Brett sat with you all night. He just went home

to get some rest," Elise told Julie, sipping from a cup of coffee she'd brought. "He had a friend pick him up so he could get his car when he knew I was on my way. He insisted he's coming back in a few hours." Elise sat down in the chair closest to her bed. "Julie, Kendra gave me a rather sketchy description of what's been going on." She gazed anxiously at her daughter. "If you feel all right enough to talk, then please tell me exactly what's been happening, and why you've been with Brett the last few days. And what happened with Warren? Kendra said you ended your engagement over a week ago." Her mother sounded perplexed, but not critical.

"Well…" Julie switched to a more comfortable position. Something inside her warmed at the thought of Brett watching over her during the night. Maybe, maybe…there was hope that he did care; that he was no longer upset she hadn't told him the truth sooner. "It's a long story…"

"As long as you're not too tired to tell it." Elise studied her daughter, an expression of motherly concern lining her face.

Julie began with her feelings for Warren, and how they'd changed entirely. How she'd realized she didn't love him, and that he was not who he'd appeared to be when she'd first met him.

Her mom listened and nodded. "Ted and I had a discussion about Warren just a couple of days ago," she said when Julie paused. "We were both beginning to wonder about, well, his character," she confessed. "We were thinking he wasn't quite the charming man he'd seemed at first. But then we thought, of course, Julie knows him better than we do."

Julie described how she'd broken her engagement, but for Warren's sake had agreed to keep it a secret for another week.

"You could have told me," her mother said with

a sigh.

"I only told Kendra and Jessica, because they knew that I intended to break it off," Julie said. "I didn't think a week would make much difference."

Her mother listened as Julie described Brett's plan, and how it seemed to be the perfect opportunity to get to know Brett again, to see if the thoughts and feelings she'd been having lately about Brett were still substantial. And to have her suspicions about Warren confirmed.

Her mother gasped and clucked in sympathy when she told her about Shannon. She was startled about Arnold. But when Julie told her about Warren's mob connections, her mother got visibly upset.

"Oh, my God," Elise gasped. "I never suspected! And I'm sure Ted didn't either! Oh, my poor daughter. What a thing to learn. How awful!"

"I was shocked," Julie admitted. "And so was Brett. But I should have guessed—there were little things—anyway, I realized soon afterward that I still loved Brett. And..." she hesitated. She wasn't going to discuss the intimate details of the passionate night she'd shared with Brett, or their argument the following day. "And I was going to tell him I'd broken off with Warren, but I pushed it aside when we went out to dinner. Then Brett found out about it, and was angry that I hadn't told him..."

Julie's mother listened as she described the party for Warren, and exactly what had transpired there.

"Hmph," Elise said when Julie finished. "I knew Warren was no hero, despite what they said on the news last night! Well, I'm certainly glad that selfish man isn't going to be my son-in-law."

"Really?" Julie questioned.

"Really." Her mother leaned over and hugged her, taking care not to disturb her arm. "I'm just sorry you had to go through all this pain!"

When Elise pulled back, something in Julie's expression must have reflected her puzzlement, because Elise gave her a smile. "I know what you're thinking," she said.

"I'm thinking about the advice you used to give me," Julie said. "You know, about marriage being a business arrangement."

"Well. Yes." Elise looked down at her well-manicured hands. Her dark red fingernails and slender fingers were adorned with a large, round diamond and an ornate wedding band.

When she looked back up at Julie, her face wore a pensive expression. "You know I cared for your father, but we struggled financially, and we often fought about money, and other things—like the fact that he thought we should do everything together."

Julie made a small noise of surprise, but didn't ask any questions as her mother continued.

"After he died, and time went by, I began to date. And I felt that the next time I married, it would be to someone who was financially comfortable, who had many of the same goals I did, with whom I could share a mutual respect.

"Ted was all of those things. He treated me well, and wanted the same things I did—a family, a nice comfortable life, a certain amount of independence. Not to cheat, mind you, just to have times when we weren't tied at the hip to each other. We cared about each other, and it was a beneficial arrangement for us both." She smiled suddenly. "And, after a while, I realized I had come to love Ted. It kind of sneaked up on me."

"So why did you…?" Julie began.

Her mother shook her head. "I still believe that a marriage based on mutual respect and liking, like a business partnership, is the best thing. But"—she leaned forward—"I realized something last night. It was right for me—perfect, as a matter of fact. But it's not right for you."

"Ah…" Julie murmured. She'd known it, but it was nice to hear her mother admit it.

Elise smiled, wistfully. "You're different from me in many ways. This is one of them. A business relationship was good for me, but you—you need a more romantic relationship."

"I know that," Julie said steadily. "Warren was, I think, my attempt at a business relationship—with the plus that he took me places and provided me with the excitement I thought I craved. But even if he hadn't turned out to be the kind of person he is, our relationship wasn't what I wanted. Or needed." She gazed out the hospital window. It was another gray, cloudy morning. "What I've always wanted was true love," she concluded.

"And have you found it?" her mother asked softly.

"Yes. I have." Julie refocused on her mother. "But I don't know how he feels."

"I can guess. You should have seen him last night, Julie. He absolutely insisted on staying with you. I wanted to, too, but he and Ted persuaded me I should go home, get some rest, and take care of you when they let you out." She smiled suddenly. "Ted was as worried about you as I was. I don't think I've ever loved him more than when I saw how much he loves you. You are his daughter, too."

"I know," whispered Julie. "And I love Ted. He's wonderful." She meant it, too. Her real father was only a vague memory, and loving him didn't mean she couldn't love her stepfather as well.

"What do you want to do?" Elise asked directly.

Julie had been asking herself the same question. "I think…" she started. She closed her eyes. The ache in her head was fading now, and she was able to picture Brett the night they'd gone out for dinner, and made love. Brett. Her love.

A feeling of determination welled up inside of her. She loved Brett. She wanted him in her life. It was that simple.

And that complicated.

She had to make him understand. It would mean telling him the truth—that she loved him. But it was a chance she had to take.

She opened her eyes.

"I'm going to tell Brett how I feel." She lifted her chin. She would sit Brett down and explain exactly what she felt. And hope he would understand.

He *had* to understand.

She *would* make him understand.

****

Julie dozed off a little during the morning, but by afternoon she had a steady stream of visitors. Plus a private nurse her parents had arranged for.

Ted arrived, and she got a call from her brother Adam. Then Warren arrived, accompanied by two bodyguards and his campaign manager, Tony.

Warren brought a huge, ostentatious bouquet of flowers. For the first time since she had known him, he actually looked embarrassed.

Elise and Ted tactfully went downstairs to get coffee, and with Tony and the bodyguards standing outside the door to her room, Julie finally got to speak to Warren alone.

"How are you?" he asked again, awkwardly, not quite meeting her eyes.

"Fine. You and Tony put a nice spin on this whole incident." She didn't bother to keep the asperity out of her voice.

Warren flushed. "Well…you know how it is. You have to take the facts, turn them to your advantage when you can."

"I'm sure," she replied dryly.

"And I did state publicly that you and—ugh,

what's his name, Brett?—were instrumental in bringing down Arnold, with help from Juan and Sam and a waiter."

"You just didn't happen to mention that you ran away," she stated. Her arm was starting to hurt again.

"Well, I wasn't really wearing a bullet-proof vest," Warren said, as if that explained everything.

"Oh." Her one word said volumes as she regarded him steadily. How could she have ever thought she felt love for this man? "Well, Warren, I have something for you."

"For me?" He looked surprised.

"Yes." She reached into the drawer of the nightstand and withdrew the ring she'd put there earlier. "Here." She handed it to him.

"Are you sure?" She could have sworn he looked disappointed and relieved at the same time.

"Yes," she answered firmly.

He pocketed the ring. "Well…okay." He paused and seemed uncertain of what to say next.

"Take care of yourself," Julie said, her voice mild. Inside she was feeling the beginnings of relief. This was almost done.

"Okay. You too." He turned and left the room without a hug or a backward look. After a moment outside the room, his entourage followed him.

Julie sagged against the pillows. There. It was finished. She'd never have to see Warren again. Or his cohorts.

She relaxed, and felt, for the first time since her discussion with Warren more than a week ago, that she was finally free. *Free.* She was no longer tied in any way to Warren.

It felt wonderful. Relief mixed with a surge of gladness. She was free!

She sighed. One problem was solved.

Now if only she could speak to Brett—

But minutes after Warren's departure, she was surrounded by more visitors. Her mom and Ted returned, along with Jonathan. Then Kendra showed up with two other teacher friends from school, who brought cookies. Brett, looking a little haggard, came in shortly afterward with a beautiful bouquet of fall flowers. He bent down to give her a quick kiss on the cheek and regarded her anxiously.

But they had no time to speak alone.

To Julie's surprise, Felicia arrived as Kendra and the other teachers were leaving. She'd seen the news and had guessed a lot of what wasn't covered by the media.

When Brett left, he told her, "I'll see you soon."

How soon? She tried not to read too much into his statement.

But with everyone else there, she didn't voice the question. He left with her parents and Jonathan, leaving Felicia alone with Julie.

"Don't worry," Felicia said when she got up to leave a few minutes later. She winked. "Everything's going to be fine for you—and Brett."

"Thanks for the crystal," Julie said. "I think it helped. I thought about it during—well, when we were all being threatened by Arnold."

"I'm sure it did help." Felicia smiled broadly. "And I just left another one, by your bedside, to help you heal." She waved at the crystal. "I'll come visit you again, and I'll bring Joe next time."

"I'd like that," Julie said. She was growing tired. "Thank you, for everything."

She closed her eyes to sleep after Felicia left, hearing the nurse draw the blinds. Images of Brett danced in her mind. She considered different ways to tell him how she felt...

She longed for him to come back and hold her. When she dreamt, the dreams were of Brett.

****

Julie folded her PJs, placing them in the suitcase with her toothbrush, shower gel, and one of the crystals from Felicia. The other she was still keeping in her purse.

She wore the worn, comfortable pair of jeans and older turquoise sweater her mother had brought her yesterday. She had showered and the nurse had helped her dress just minutes ago. The doctor had said she could be released this morning, and she was glad. A full day in the hospital had been enough. She could survive the discomfort of her arm and the dull, on-again-off-again headaches in the comfort of her parents' house. The doctor had advised taking the rest of the week off from work.

Her mother and Ted were due to pick her up in a few minutes. Elise had declared that she wanted Julie to recuperate for a few days in her old home, where she could be looked after.

But Julie had already decided that she was going to seek out Brett later. Since her car was still at her apartment, she would persuade her parents to lend her one so she could see Brett when he got home from work. She knew the condo development he lived in, and she was confident she could find his place. She didn't care if her parents thought she wasn't well enough to leave the house yet. She'd call a cab if she had to.

Last night and this morning, almost every waking thought she'd had was about Brett. She wanted—she needed—to speak with him. Alone.

A last glance showed her the only things left that weren't in the suitcase or her purse were the dozen or so flower arrangements on the windowsill. When her mother got here, they'd get an orderly or volunteer to help bring the flowers down.

Julie zipped the case shut. She was straightening slowly, still feeling a little weak, when she heard heavy male footsteps on the linoleum floor outside of her room.

She looked up, fully expecting it to be Ted or another doctor.

Brett came striding into the room.

Chapter 14

For a moment, Julie's heart took a flying leap and she could do nothing but stare at Brett. Then her heart started to beat so hard she wondered if he could hear it.

"Hi, Julie." His expression was serious as he regarded her. "I'm here to pick you up."

She found her voice. "I thought my parents were picking me up."

He shook his head. "I spoke to them last night and told them I wanted to. They agreed. I hope you don't mind. I really want to speak to you, if you're up to it."

The drumming rhythm of her heart vibrated in her ears.

"No, I don't mind." Her voice sounded more fragile than she wished.

Brett's sudden smile unnerved her. "Good." His voice was firm, and he, at least, sounded normal.

He took her suitcase, and an aide brought a cart for all the flower arrangements she'd received. Another aide brought a wheelchair for Julie.

"I can walk," she objected.

"Hospital policy," the dark-skinned young woman told her. "All patients get dismissed from a wheelchair."

Once downstairs, Julie waited with the aide while Brett brought his car around and loaded the flowers. Impulsively, she handed the large arrangement that Warren had brought her to the young woman.

"Here, take these," she said.

The young woman furrowed her brow. "Are you sure?"

"Yes." Julie smiled. "Please."

The girl thanked her profusely. Brett brought the last of the flowers outside, then returned.

"Do you have a coat?" he asked.

The day was sunny, but clouds were scooting across the sky, and she could hear the wind whistling. She'd forgotten to ask her mom to bring her a coat.

"No."

"I left the one you were wearing at home. C'mon, we'll make this quick."

He helped her into the car. The heater was already on and the car was nice and toasty. Julie got comfortable, though she wished her heart wasn't beating so hard.

What was she going to say to Brett? He climbed in without a word and began the drive to the interstate highway.

The radio was on, jazz music playing softly. Julie tried to focus on what she wanted to say. Last night she had considered different things to say to Brett, and different ways to approach him. Her thoughts had kept her up late.

Now she reflected back to all the varied scenarios that had run through her mind. Should she fling herself into his arms and declare her love? Sit down facing him and talk? Write him a love letter? But her mind was like a big, blank chalkboard in a new classroom. She couldn't seem to decide which approach was best.

There was a vague ache around the edges of her mind, and she knew it was the concussion. She breathed slowly, trying to relax her body and not think about it.

For a moment, she let her mind wander away from considering what to say to Brett. Instead, she focused on the night they'd gone to dinner and dancing. She remembered the wonderful feeling of being held in his arms...

Should she throw her arms around him and kiss him when they reached her home? Beg him to listen? Or speak quietly and logically?

Julie let her eyes drift closed as she thought. After a little while she opened them, and realized they had missed the exit they should have taken to get to her parents' house. Instead, they were exiting at Mt. Arlington.

Her heart accelerated. "Which way are we going?" she asked.

"The right way." Brett shot her a sideways look.

She opened her mouth to protest, then shut it. She wanted to talk to Brett. Alone. If they were going to stop at his place, this might be the best chance she'd get.

They took the road that led toward his condo. When they pulled into his garage a few minutes later, Brett turned the car off, then walked around to open the car door for her. "Come in, Julie...please."

She let him help her out, and she preceded him into his condo. Once they were in the living room, she dropped onto the comfortable couch. She was feeling a little lightheaded. Was it the concussion, her wound...or being in Brett's presence? She couldn't be sure.

"Could I have a glass of water?" she asked.

"Would you prefer diet Pepsi?"

"Yes, please." Did Brett still have soda left from when she'd been here on Wednesday? It seemed incredible that not quite a week had gone by since he'd first approached her.

He returned with her soda, and Julie sipped it, wondering where she should begin. When she placed the soda down on a coaster, the sound echoed in the silent room. She raised her eyes to regard Brett.

He sat down at the opposite end of the couch. And suddenly smiled.

Her heart fluttered.

"I thought," he declared, leaning back, "we should come back to where this all started. Or almost started. I didn't think you'd want to stand in the cold outside that bridal shop."

"Are you borrowing me again?" Julie asked. She tried to keep her voice light.

"No."

Her heart plummeted downward.

"Not exactly," he added, leaning forward.

She waited for him to elaborate. For a moment he seemed to hesitate, searching for words.

Like she was. She swallowed. "Brett—"

"Julie—" he started at the same instant.

They both paused. Julie's heart hammered against her ribs.

"No, wait," she said hastily as Brett opened his mouth. "Let me speak. I've been wanting to since Sunday. I owe you an explanation."

"No you don't—"

"Yes, I do. *Please*."

Brett nodded. "Okay."

He was so handsome, so masculine, and his nearness was so compelling. Julie had to battle the desire to throw herself into his arms. She had to speak to him first.

She began, choosing her words with care. "I admit I should have told you earlier I broke my engagement to Warren," she said. What were the phrases she'd rehearsed last night in the hospital? She couldn't remember them anymore. "But I—I had promised I wouldn't tell anyone. Only Kendra and Jessica knew—because I'd told them before breaking it off what I was going to do."

Her arm hurt, and she shifted her position

slightly.

"You see, I had realized weeks ago that Warren was not what he seemed to be. At the core of his friendly front was a hard, self-centered person. I couldn't spend my life with him. There was no way. And I realized I didn't really love him. The only one I had ever truly loved was"—she stopped, then finished softly—"you."

Brett's eyes widened, and he leaned infinitesimally closer.

"Because I made that promise to Warren, I felt I shouldn't tell anyone—and it was only for a week. And Brett—you had been on my mind lately. An awful lot."

"I'd been on your mind?" he asked.

"Yes." She started to nod, then winced from the twinge of pain. "So, when you came up to me and presented me with this golden chance to spend a few days in your company—how could I resist? It was exactly what I wanted the most." She felt tears spring to her eyes. "It was a weird situation—but it was the perfect opportunity to get to know you again—to let you know me again—and to see what would happen."

"But—" Brett began.

"Wait." Julie held up her hand. "Please. I know I should have told you after the first day, but we were getting along so well, and I...I hoped...well, the truth is I was beginning to care for you all over again." The words seemed to rush out of her mouth now. "I kept putting off telling you. And I meant to tell you after we visited Felicia, I really did. But then we went out on my dream date, and when we came back to the room..." She felt herself flushing. Memories of making passionate love, of being tangled with Brett, bombarded her. "Warren was the last thing on my mind," she said emphatically, her voice clear.

"Tell me," Brett interrupted, "why were you carrying your bridal veil when I *borrowed* you?"

His question surprised Julie. "Oh, that." She waved her hand. "One of my students, who doesn't have much money, has an older sister who's getting married soon. I knew the family was trying to save money wherever they could. I had already paid for the veil, and I offered it to her sister. I went to the shop, cancelled the order on my gown, and picked up the veil to give to her."

"Ah ha..." Brett took a long breath. "I thought maybe you had it because—well, you might still have some feelings for Warren."

"Hmph. I have feelings for Warren—not the kind he'd like. Disdain, and anger. Maybe even pity, because I think he'll end up in a lot of trouble some day. Big trouble. Though it's his own fault," she finished. Julie took a deep breath. She looked away for a moment, then back at Brett. The next part was the hardest.

"I told him again yesterday that it's over. I'm going to be totally honest from now on," she said quietly. "I told you I was beginning to care for you. The truth is..." She paused.

"The truth is..." Brett prodded.

She took another deep breath. She had to admit it.

She looked straight into Brett's hazel eyes. He was studying her intently. And the words came easily after all. "The truth is...I never stopped loving you. I realized it when you kissed me. I love you, Brett. I always will."

For one moment, Brett just stared at her, and her heart beat wildly as she held her breath and waited for his reaction.

Then he jumped up. He strode over to the wall unit, and picked up what appeared to be magazines. He turned back to Julie, his eyes glowing. Returning to her, he dropped back down on the couch, close beside her, and spread the magazines on the coffee table before them.

No, not magazines. Julie caught her breath.

They were travel brochures, from a popular agency, for Athens, Greece and the Greek Isles.

Waves of hope swept through her. She turned to look into Brett's eyes.

"You said," he began, "that there were some things you always dreamed of doing…like dinner and dancing, the black dress, and visiting Stonehenge in England and the Acropolis in Greece."

"Yes," she whispered, her heart hammering.

"Well, you've done three out of four." He leaned closer. "How'd you like to see the Acropolis—and Greece—with me?"

"With you—oh, Brett!" she exclaimed and threw her arms around him

Their lips met. His kiss was hard and possessive and made her head spin. When he finally let her get her breath, his mouth was stretched in a great, big, fantastic smile.

"Julie." His hand came up to cup her chin, and she felt it tremble. "I couldn't understand why you went along with me on this whole deal. All I could think those first few days was that Warren didn't deserve you. I started to picture myself replacing him."

Julie's heart was beating so hard she was sure Brett must hear it. His touch was gentle and tender as he continued. "I overreacted when I learned you weren't engaged to Warren anymore. I think it was because I realized I loved you. I know I shouldn't have acted that way—"

"What?" Julie exclaimed. She couldn't help the jump her body gave, the joy that lifted her heart. "What did you say?"

"—and I just didn't know how to handle the

situation," Brett continued. "And I was afraid you didn't feel the same way about me. But then, at the party, when you tried to stop Arnold, and you were injured—suddenly everything was really simple. I don't ever want to lose you." He tilted her face and bent his closer. "I was terrified that you were hurt. That I might lose you for good." His voice shook. "All I could think of was that I loved you, Julie, and this was all my fault. And nothing, not Warren or anything else, will ever get in the way again, if you love me too. I brought you here to tell you the truth. I love you, Julie."

He was saying the words she'd wanted so much to hear, words she'd feared she might never hear from his lips again. She lifted her hand, trembling too, and placed it on his cheek. "I love you, Brett," she whispered. "I always will."

His lips came down on hers, hard and hungry, and Julie responded with all the love welling up in her heart, reveling in his kiss, returning it with passion. They clung together, and the throbbing in her head was instantly replaced by sheer, soaring happiness.

"Julie, Julie," he murmured when his lips left hers. He kissed her again and again all over her face. "I love you."

"I love you," she responded breathlessly, the words tumbling out as she smiled up at him.

Brett pulled back after another minute, and his look was so adoring that Julie caught her breath.

"Did the doctor say when you could—"

Julie laughed. "I asked him when I could make love," she said, "and he told me whenever I felt up to it. As long as I'm careful with my arm."

"I want to make love to you," Brett said. "For hours. Days. But first—" He grinned, his eyes twinkling. "This trip to Greece—there's a catch."

"Oh?" Julie asked archly, raising her eyebrows.

"Yeah. I'm taking you to Greece—but only if it's our honeymoon. Will you marry me, Julie?"

"Brett!" Happiness and delight surged through her. "Oh yes!"

He pulled her into his arms and kissed her soundly.

When they came up for air, they were both smiling at each other, and Julie had never felt so happy.

"You asked me if I was borrowing you before," he continued. "I'm not, you know. Not this time."

"Really?" she asked with a laugh.

"This time, I'm *keeping* you," he said. "Forever."

"Forever," Julie whispered, as he pulled her into his arms for another kiss.

A word about the author...

Roni Denholtz is an award-winning author of romance novels, children's books and magazine stories and articles. She lives in northwest New Jersey with her family, which includes a large dog and a goldfish. She and her husband own an independent real estate brokerage.

Roni enjoys reading, cooking, listening to music and volunteer work. She also collects old girls' series books like Nancy Drew and Judy Bolton.

You can visit her website at
www.ronidenholtz.com.

Thank you for purchasing
this Wild Rose Press publication.
For other wonderful stories of romance,
please visit our on-line bookstore at
www.thewildrosepress.com

For questions or more information,
contact us at
info@thewildrosepress.com

The Wild Rose Press
www.TheWildRosePress.com

To visit with authors of The Wild Rose Press
join our yahoo loop at
http://groups.yahoo.com/group/thewildrosepress/